Glass Promises

by

Janet Franks Little

TELEMACHUS PRESS

Cover designed by Telemachus Press, LLC

Cover art:
Copyright © iStockphoto_175419408_TommL
Copyright © iStockphoto_639409678_ChronowskiPiotr

Published by Telemachus Press, LLC
http://www.telemachuspress.com

Visit the author website:
http://www.janetfrankslittle.com

Library of Congress Control Number: 2018959155

ISBN: 978-1-948046-29-9 (eBook)
ISBN: 978-1-948046-30-5 (Paperback)

Fiction/Romance/Contemporary
Fiction/Women

Telemachus Press, LLC
7652 Sawmill Road, Suite 304
Dublin OH 43016

Version 2021.01.03

Table of Content

A relationship is like glass. Sometimes it's better to leave it broken than try to hurt yourself by putting it back together.

Unknown

Family isn't always blood. It's the people in your life who want you in theirs; the ones who accept you for who you are. The ones who would do anything to see you smile and who love you no matter what.

Unknown

Glass Promises

Chapter 1

GRACE STOPPED AT the traffic light then studied Alice in the passenger seat of the BMW. Her friend's upper body was hunched forward, and she clutched her purse like it contained a weapon which might need to be drawn at any moment.

Grace laughed. "Relax. You look like a bounty hunter after a slippery bond jumper."

Alice inhaled. The tension in her body seemed to deflate as her shoulders dropped. "You may not take this as seriously as I do, but tonight might just change the rest of our lives."

The light turned green as Grace suppressed a *you've-got-to-be-kidding* snort. "C'mon. It's not like we're meeting with heads of state to discuss world peace."

"Maybe not, but don't you want to try everything possible to make Lily happy?"

The question sobered Grace as she pictured her daughter, tears welling up in her crystal-blue eyes. In the last several months, Lily had become concerned with her lack of a father and peppered Grace daily with questions and demands about getting a new one. She refused to accept that it wasn't as easy as ordering home delivery pizza, even though a man always came to the house with one.

With reluctance, Grace had agreed to Alice's repeated suggestion to give speed dating a chance. Her friend tried *RaceDate.Com* three times in the past year. The website promised attendees would meet a minimum of ten local single men who were professionals between the ages of twenty-six and thirty-four. When she registered, Grace filled out the online form with the name Gigi Black, as recommended by her friend who had signed in as Ali Crist.

Alice said, "It's best we keep our professional identities private at this point. You can never be sure who you'll meet. It might be someone who has taken classes at the university. And if they ask what you do, tell them you're a teacher, not a professor. A lot of men are put off by women with PhD's."

"Should I let them know I'm a single mother, or would that scare them away too?"

"Of course, tell them. If the guy doesn't appreciate that you pay your own bills and take care of your kid while working full-time, then you don't want someone who just fell off the stupid truck."

Ahead of them was the neon-lit sign for the Mardi Gras-themed casino located next to a greyhound racetrack. Grace laughed to herself. If gamblers didn't blow money on the dogs, they could walk next door and lose it at slots.

After leaving the car with a valet, she and Alice entered through a re-volving door. They were greeted by a man dressed as a court jester. He held out his arm. A line of plastic beads dangled from his elbow to his wrist like clothes on the line. "Beads, ladies? Do you need directions?"

Alice brushed past. "I know where we're going."

They hustled along carpeted walkways with bad lighting and the stale smell of mildewed carpet and cigarette smoke. Grace shivered in the chilly air conditioning and pulled her white denim jacket tighter. Only in south Florida was it colder inside than outside the weekend before Thanksgiving. Old folks milled around the garish purple and gold setting forcing her and Alice to walk in wide berths around them. Several hustled down the same hallway; their bodies hunched forward, intent on a destination that likely involved something important, like Bingo or a buffet. She and Alice picked up their pace so as not to be outdone by octogenarians.

When they reached the bar, a perky blonde at a table with a *RaceDate* check-in sign marked their names off a list. She handed them adhesive name tags. "Please put these where they're easy to read." Next, she gave them a rectangle of printed card stock. "Here's your Race Card. There are some helpful hints on the back. Gigi, you're at table six. Ali, you're at ten. We'll be starting in a few minutes. You were the last to check in. Have fun, and I hope you both find Mr. Right tonight."

Grace did a quick head count of the people in the roped off area. Including her and Alice, there were twelve women and ten men. "They're two guys short. I thought there would be the same number."

"The hosts try to get even numbers, but some may have cancelled or not shown up." She clasped Grace's elbow and steered her to the right. "Let's get a drink before we take our seats."

The bartender wiped the counter. "What can I get you ladies?"

Grace reached into her purse. "I'll have a Diet Coke with lime." She was determined to keep her wits about her tonight and not just because she was the driver.

Her friend ordered a dirty martini. As they waited, Alice leaned in close, as if she was about to impart state secrets. "Now remember. Don't hold your hands in your lap, especially with crossed wrists. It says you're closed off to meeting new people. Mirror his body. It means you're in sync with him. If he puts his ankle on his knee, he's interested because his package is on display." Alice scanned a group of women huddled together. "The competition doesn't look too fierce tonight."

"I'm not sure about this, Alice. None of these men have been truly vetted. All they did was pay a registration fee like we did. What if one of them is …" What? A serial killer? A pedophile? "… married?"

Her friend's face tightened. "You know that in real life there are no guarantees. If one of these guys doesn't feel right, reject him. You can vet them all you want after you agree to a date. Besides, it's been four years since Michael died. You need to get back into the world of man-woman relationships. Speed dating is a no pressure way of doing that. It'll give you the practice to get involved with men again."

"But I *am* involved with men. I have a close relationship with two of them."

"Your gay neighbors don't count. You need one who doesn't have a pride parade."

"Does that mean veterans are out?"

The bartender slid their drinks toward them across the resin-coated counter. They paid and headed to their assigned tables. Grace was at a two-person pub set which sat in the middle of the room. Alice's place was on a padded bench along the wall with a chair and low table. The grating tap-tap on a microphone quieted the conversations.

"Welcome, everyone." The blonde from the check-in read her clipboard to the attendees. "Please be respectful and write each date's name down on your Race Card, even if you're not interested. I'll collect the cards at the end of the evening. On Tuesday, you can check our website and communicate with your matches through the free online email. Gentlemen, please proceed to the first table on your Race Card."

The men shuffled around the room, checking the posted numbers. Grace smiled at the dark-haired man who sat down across from her. A bell rang to begin her first five-minute date.

"*Hola*, ah, hello. My name is Armando." He smiled with white Chiclet teeth and pointed to her left breast. "Heehee*?*"

Grace touched her name tag. "Yes, my name is Gigi. Where are you from originally, Armando?"

"I am from Peru."

"How long have you been in the United States?"

"Two year."

"Your English is much better than my Spanish after two years. Could you speak it before you came?"

"*Un poquito*. A leetle." He glanced down at the writing on the back of his Race Card and read aloud from *Good Questions to Ask*. "What is your yob, I mean, job, Gi-gi?"

"I'm an English teacher."

Armando's face lit up. "You are tee-sure for peoples to espeak English?"

"No. I teach literature, you know, books."

"Ah, yes, *literatura.*"

"That's right. What is your job?"

"In my country, I was *el farmacéutico*."

"You were a farmer?"

He regarded her with a look of indignation. "I was pharmacist in Lima."

"I'm sorry. Please forgive my poor translation."

"Ees okay. I study here to get license. Now I am pharmacy tech at CVS."

She and Armando chatted about the differences between living in Peru and the United States until the facilitator rang the bell. He thanked her and moved to the next table.

One down, nine to go. She smiled at the man who eased his right buttock onto the high seat across from her and glanced at his name tag. "Hi, Jesse." This date was a thirty-something guy with a round face, square body, and no neck.

"Hi, Gigi." He studied her with narrowed eyes. "You got any kids?"

"I have a daughter."

"When you gave birth did you have a C-section?" Before she could answer, Jesse placed his palms flat on the table. "Let me explain. It's been my experience that after women have given birth the natural way they're just not as tight as they used to be."

"Is that a problem for you?"

It was. Jesse began a monologue on the quality versus quantity argument of penis size. After a two-minute lecture about sex being more than P in V intercourse, Grace conceded proportion wasn't important. But as far as she was concerned, even glorious equipment wouldn't give this guy an edge.

Her eyes shifted to the facilitator. The woman's finger was poised over the bell as she counted down the seconds on her watch. "Sorry, Jesse, but my daughter weighed ten pounds at birth. She was dragged through me like a marble through a straw."

After Grace's sixth dating session, there was a twenty-minute break. She sat down at Alice's table. "Al-lee, how's it going?"

"It's an interesting mix tonight. Anyone you're considering, Gi-gi?"

"Not yet." And not ever.

Alice stood and scanned the room like a meerkat on guard duty. "Has Scott been to your table?"

"I haven't met anyone yet with that name."

"Well, he might be the one to change your mind." Alice fluffed her shoulder-length, curly, dark hair, hiked up the elastic bodice of the strapless dress which almost covered her generous bosom, and sucked in her stomach. "I'm going to get another drink. Do you want anything?"

"I'm good."

Alice let the silky scarf around her shoulders slip down her arms and glided toward the men at the bar as if a mating call had sounded.

Chapter 2

DUE TO THE unequal distribution of men to women, Grace was free for rounds six and seven. She stepped into a side hall to call her neighbors and regular babysitters.

Tariq answered on the first ring. "Hi, Grace. Maxi and Lily are asleep. I think Erin is just pretending. Hold on, Robert wants to talk to you."

Tariq's partner came on the phone. "Have you met anyone good yet?"

"Not so far."

"Don't be too picky. After all, your clock is ticking. Remember your mother said, 'The shortest time of your life is as a desirable young woman.'"

"I know." Grace checked her watch. "I better go back inside. The break is about to end."

She made a quick stop in the ladies' room. Bending at the waist, she flipped her blond hair forward and ran a brush through its length several times then reapplied her lipstick. She hurried down the hall to the bar when the bell rang for the next round. A handsome, tawny-haired man sat at her table. The cashmere V-necked sweater he wore looked as soft as baby hair and matched his blue eyes. His name tag read: *Scott.*

This was the guy Alice mentioned. Grace boosted herself onto the hard, wooden seat of the pub chair with a weak smile. "Sorry I'm late." She sipped at her now fizz-less and warm Coke.

"No problem. You're worth waiting for, Gigi."

"I needed to phone my babysitter and check on my daughter."

Scott's slim, broad-shouldered body didn't tense or lean away from her as if he had just fortified his position on birth control. Instead he smiled. "How old is she?"

"Four. Do you have kids?"

"No kids. No ex-wife. Someday I hope to have both. I mean, I hope to have a wife, not an ex."

She placed her elbows on the table and inclined toward him. "What kind of work do you do?"

"I'm a contracts attorney. I deal mostly with construction and real estate."

While she listened to Scott describe some of his recent projects, the air seemed to crackle with invisible currents. When the bell rang, Grace flashed a frown of regret. He was her only speed date so far she'd like to converse with more.

By the twelfth and final round, Grace was tired and ready to go home. The tall man who sat down across from her wore pressed jeans and a white dress shirt with the tail hanging out. His name tag read: *Beau*. She plastered on a fake smile.

He gave her an infectious grin in return. "I've been waiting all night to get to your table."

Grace opened her palms wide. "And here you are."

Beau nodded. "Here I am." Several seconds of silence descended. He rubbed the back of his neck as if he had used up all his lines and didn't know what to say next.

Grace opened her mouth. "How did—"

"Are you—"

Their words collided, and both fell silent.

She tried again. "What were you going to ask?"

"Are you a native Floridian?"

"Born and raised. You?"

"We moved here when I was seven." He crossed his thick arms on the tabletop. "Have you done speed dating before?"

"This is my first time. A friend insisted I come."

"Yeah, my brother kinda forced me to give it a try too."

She licked her dry lips. Beau's eyes followed her tongue. Heat rose in her cheeks. In a slightly breathless voice, she said, "So, what was the worst question you were asked tonight?"

"She wanted to know my annual income last year."

Grace laughed. "What did you say?"

"Only my accountant and the IRS know for sure. What was your worst question?"

"He asked if I knew he could pick up any woman in this room tonight including me. I said he could but only if it meant lifting me off the ground."

Beau chuckled. "Good comeback."

"Thank you. What's the worst pickup line you've ever used on a woman?"

"You mean other than saying I've been waiting all night to get to your table?"

She laughed. "Yes, other than that one."

By the time the bell rang to signal the end of the dating rounds, Grace had enjoyed talking with Beau. Like Scott and Armando, he was a nice man, but halfway through her ten speed dates, the realization hit her. This was not the way to find a father for Lily and a husband for herself. There were just too many unknowns about these guys to feel comfortable inviting one of them into her and her daughter's life.

Chapter 3

ON THE DRIVE home, Alice twisted in her seat. "What did you think of Scott?"

Grace's eyes shifted to her friend then back to the road. "He was okay."

"Come on. You have to admit he's perfect boyfriend material. Blond, buff, and straight. He's got a good job with a respected law firm. Never been married, although he was engaged two years ago. He broke it off when he found his values and hers didn't mesh. He owns his own condo and has a Lexus with less than forty thousand miles on it."

"Did you ask him how much money he made last year?"

"No, but it's not a bad question." Alice leaned back and stared out the windshield. "Scott is like an urban legend. He'd be perfect with confirmation that he's good in bed. There was only one possible negative."

Grace chanced another quick glance at Alice. "What was that?"

"I asked if he had ever voted Republican, and if he had, what were the extenuating circumstances? The bell rang before I got his answer."

Grace smiled. "Now we'll never know."

"We might if he matched one of us. Did you mark him on your Race Card?"

"I didn't match anyone." Grace sighed. "Speed dating's not for me. I need to develop a deeper connection with someone, especially since I have Lily to consider. What about you? How many men did you pick?"

"Two."

"Which ones?"

"Well, Scott, of course. I'll take my chances he's a liberal and not a conservative. And I matched Armando, the guy from Peru. I loved his smile."

The one other man who piqued Grace's interest was her final date. She turned the car into her friend's driveway and put it in park. "What did you think of the guy named Beau?"

Alice rummaged on the floor for her purse, stopped, and shifted her eyes upward. "Was he the one with his shirttail hanging out?"

"That's him."

She winced and dragged her large bag onto her lap. "Yeah, that was a deal breaker for me."

"You passed on a guy because of the way he was dressed?"

"And he's a registered Republican. He did vote for Obama's re-election and claimed he never votes a straight ticket, but it wasn't enough to compensate for the shirt."

Chapter 4

"WHOA, DR. B!" A male student raced toward the English Department just as Grace headed to the exit. "Your Beemer's been beamed."

She came to an abrupt halt. "What are you talking about?"

He panted and pointed outside. "You gotta check it out." The student brushed his long hair out of his eyes and raced up the nearby staircase two steps at a time.

Grace hustled to the double doors which led to the faculty parking lot and swatted one open. The chaotic scene across the street halted her. Campus security cruisers blocked the street. The blue strobes from their emergency lights flashed like the frenetic lighting on a dance club floor. Several fire trucks rumbled in the faculty parking lot. The intoxicating stink of gasoline wafted on the breeze. Clots of people stood talking, pointing, and holding up their cell phones. The obelisk of an I-beam rose into the air, attached by a chain to the long arm of a tower crane. A second shorter chain, which had obviously broken, dangled in the wind.

Below this, the opposite end of the girder was embedded into the middle of her black BMW, which now looked like a taco.

She choked down a snort of hysteria. Her dead husband's babe-mobile was impaled with the biggest phallic weapon of destruction she'd ever seen. She skirted milling spectators as she dragged her wheeled briefcase behind her and headed to the curb.

The girder swayed in a strong gust of wind. A fireman, spraying a foamy chemical around the car, shouted and backed away. From a cluster of hard-hatted workers one man sprang forward and climbed with nimble grace into the crane's cab. He lowered the beam toward the car's upturned front bumper. Metal screeched and caused some people to cover their ears as the vehicle collapsed under the weight.

Another worker in a hard hat intercepted Grace when she crossed the street. "You have to stay back, Miss." With his hand on her elbow, he turned her around. "Do you know the name of the professor who owns the BMW?"

"Black-Stone."

"Is he in there?" He nodded to the Arts and Humanities building.

"I'm Dr. Black-Stone."

His eyes widened. Without a word, he spun and propelled her toward the scene of the accident. She struggled to keep up with his long strides in her pencil skirt and high-heeled boots.

Meanwhile, the quick-thinking hero who had lowered the beam descended from the cab. He stomped toward the men like he had to extinguish lit cigarettes along the way. "Where the hell is Joe?"

"He's getting the professor who owns the car."

"Goddamn it!" The man jerked the hard hat off his head and thrust it into the midsection of one of the workers. "Why couldn't the four-eyed, pencil-necked nerd have a Kia or Escort? This is a fucking disaster."

"Uh, Boss." The man named Joe halted with Grace behind the group. "This is Dr. Black-Stone, the car's owner."

The boss spun around and cocked his head. He stood over six feet tall, tanned, and muscled. Thick dark brows arched above golden eyes. Short brown hair furred his head, and stubble darkened his cheeks and chin.

He frowned as he peered at her. "Gigi?"

She forced a smile at her tenth rejected speed date. "Hello, Beau."

Chapter 5

HE RAISED HIS eyebrows. "Dr. Black-Stone, huh?"

Grace tilted her blond head back. Beau seemed larger and more im-posing in work clothes. Unlike the somewhat awkward fellow from speed dating, he appeared more confident and in control. After all, the workman called him Boss.

"What happened?" Her voice was croaky.

"Don't worry. We'll find out and make sure you're compensated for the loss of your car." He glanced at the mangled wreck. "What do you need me to do right now?"

Kiss me. The words raced unbidden through her brain. A pulse deep inside throbbed with the involuntary clenching in her belly. She cleared her throat and checked her watch. "I have to pick up my daughter by three. So, I'll need to get a ride home. Will I be able to get my belongings out of the car?"

Beau gave her a bug-eyed look. He spoke in measured tones like he had to explain a vague concept to a dull-witted individual. "It's too dangerous right now. We can't get close. The gas line ruptured."

Joe stood beside Beau and smirked. The other workmen had tuned in like curious children eavesdropping on an adult conversation. Several snick-ered. Beau ignored them and flashed a patronizing smile.

Grace frowned. "I understand, but it appears the hazmat team has contained the fuel leak, and it was only a few gallons."

"That's true, but it would take some heavy equipment to open up what's left of the car to get anything inside. What's so important in there?" Beau swept his arm in a wide gesture that signaled his impatience.

Grace placed her index finger on her chin and narrowed her eyes. "Well, let's see. Because Christmas is in a couple weeks, I was storing presents in the trunk until I could get them wrapped. There was a Coach handbag for my sister and two iPads for my niece and nephew."

Beau gave her a sharp look.

"For my father, I bought a Surface Pro laptop and an iPhone for my brother." The faintest hint of belligerence crept into her voice. "My daughter will be disappointed if I can't get replacements for her Dragon Touch tablet and Barbie's Dream House."

All the men faced her with expressions of stunned amazement. The only one who looked skeptical was Beau.

She inhaled a deep breath. "In the trunk was a box of my grandmother's fifty-year collection of Precious Moments figurines."

Beau cocked his head. "Any more?"

Grace gave him a baleful look as a stab of regret for her lack of relatives pierced her chest. "No, that's it. But I wonder if the transponder for the entry gate at my development and my SunPass device are salvageable. They were on the left side of the windshield. Oh, and I'll need to buy my daughter a new car seat before I pick her up."

"If you give me some time to get things in order here, I can take you to get a car seat and pick up your daughter. Afterward, I'll make sure you get home. How does that sound?"

She checked her watch again. "We have less than two hours to get to her preschool."

"If you want, you can wait in my car to save time." He pointed to the street then looked a little sheepish. "It's the black BMW."

They walked to his car, a newer model than hers. Grace flashed him a wry smile. "Nice wheels."

He opened the passenger door. "I'll need a list of your car's contents for the insurance claim."

Grace settled in the front seat. "Don't worry. There were no Christmas presents inside."

After watching the crew's efforts to reattach the beam to the crane and nothing much happening, she graded exams. At one-thirty, she beeped the horn and pointed to her watch when she had Beau's attention. He nodded and held up his finger. Grace returned to her work and lost track of time. When she looked at the dashboard clock, it was two-fifteen. This time she held the horn down until Beau came on the run.

He flung himself behind the wheel and started the car. "Sorry. Where to?"

She was angry with him for the wait and herself for not paying attention to the time. "We'll have to pick up Lily first."

"What about the car seat?"

"Her preschool is not far from the store. You better drive as carefully as you can. I may be reasonable about my car, but I will go psycho on you if anything happens to my daughter."

She directed him to the Montessori Early Childhood Education Center. Beau waited in the car while she went inside. In a few minutes, she returned with a blond pixie in white tights, a pink corduroy skirt, and a white, long-sleeved shirt.

Grace knelt to face Lily. "I need to talk to you. There was an accident with my car. A big metal bar fell on it."

"No, Mommy. Your car's there." She pointed to the black BMW which idled at the curb.

"That belongs to the man who's taking us home. But first, we need to buy you a new car seat."

Grace walked Lily to the rear passenger door and deposited her Dora the Explorer backpack on the floor. The little girl crawled inside. Beau turned with his arm stretched across the center console. Grace reached over the small body to fasten the center seatbelt.

Beau smiled at the little girl. "Hi."

Lily stared at him. "What's your name?"

Before he could answer, Grace said, "Mr. Charvet." The lettering on his hard hat had spelled out *Charvet Crane*. Grace sat next to her daughter and shut the door. "I'm going to sit with her until we get to the store."

The little girl leaned forward. "My name is Lily Anne Stone."

Beau twisted to face her. "Isn't your name Black-Stone like your mother's?"

"Mommy's name is Stone. Like mine."

Grace patted her daughter's knee but spoke to Beau. "Black-Stone is my hyphenated professional name. In my personal life, I go by Grace Stone."

He blinked. "I thought your name was Gigi."

"Mommy's name isn't Gigi!" Lily squealed.

Grace sighed and directed her explanation to Lily. "Gigi was my nickname when I was little like you."

Beau stared at her with raised eyebrows. She returned his look with one that was deliberately blank, as if to say: *I can use any name I want when I speed date.* He turned in his seat, put the car in gear, and headed out the parking lot.

Lily studied the back of Beau's head. "What's the man's name, Mommy?"

"I told you. Mr. Charvet."

"What's his other name?"

He spoke over his shoulder. "Beau."

"Mommy, can I call him Mr. Beau?"

"Yes, you can call him *Mister* Beau."

They rode for several minutes in silence until Lily spoke. "Mr. Beau, my daddy's in heaven. Maxi and Erin have two daddies. I only have mommy. Do you have any little girls?"

He stopped at a traffic light and craned his neck around. "Not yet."

"Why not?"

"Because I haven't found a mommy for my little girl or boy."

Lily crossed her arms on her chest and spoke with a sour note in her voice. "You want a *boy?*"

"What's wrong with boys?"

"They only want one thing."

Beau's shoulders shook in silent laughter. "What's that?"

"Video games. They won't play house. They don't like dolls. They—"

The light had changed to green, and a car behind them gave the two-second Palm Beach honk. Beau faced forward and accelerated through the intersection.

Grace glanced sideways at her daughter. "Remember what I said about letting a driver concentrate on the road."

Lily lapsed into silence. Her eyes were drawn to Beau like they were magnetized. After a minute, she turned to Grace. "Does Mr. Beau know who broke our car?"

"Yes. It's a man who works for him."

"Did Mr. Beau put him in timeout?"

"No."

"Brandon was in timeout. He ran into Tyler two times with the Big Wheel. He said it was a accident."

"Well, this was *an* accident. A chain broke and a heavy bar dropped on the car."

Beau pulled into a space in the parking lot for *buybuy Baby*. "We're here."

Grace unfastened Lily's seatbelt then the little girl stood and tapped Beau's shoulder. "You coming?"

"I sure am." He opened the driver's door and walked around the rear of the car to meet up with them.

Lily released her mother's hand and wrapped her palm around Beau's pinkie and ring finger. She pulled him inside. The bright florescent lights caused Grace to squint as she was assailed by the tangy smell of plastic and tinny music from loudspeakers. She scanned the overhead signs and led them to the correct aisle. This was the perfect time to get Lily a booster seat. The harnesses in her old car seat were extended to the maximum and barely fastened around her. Beau asked questions and read the product information about construction and safety.

At the checkout line, he retrieved his wallet from a back pocket. "I'll pay for it. My secretary will take care of filing receipts for the claim. It'll be one less thing you have to do."

At the car, he followed Grace's directions for getting the base secured. At one point, his hand brushed against her breast. They both froze. She backed away from the open door like he had touched her with a hot iron. Once Lily was buckled in, Grace sat up front to give Beau directions. At the entrance to her gated community, a truck with *Charvet Crane* painted on the door idled at the curb.

Beau pulled in behind the pickup. "That's my ride. You can drive my car until you get a new one. Let me check with Joe and see if they got your transponders out."

"Wait." She placed her palm on Beau's warm, muscled arm. "I can't take your car. What if something happens to it?"

He shot a quick look at her hand then smiled. "It's insured. Besides, you're used to driving a BMW." He slid out and shut the door.

Grace turned to face Lily. "I'll be right back." She exited the car and approached the men.

"Here's your SunPass and gate device." Beau handed her the items. "If they don't work, let me know."

Joe handed Grace the envelope she kept in the glovebox. "We have photos of this paperwork for our insurance and the tow."

Beau pulled out his phone. "Can I get a contact number for you?" Grace rattled off her mobile number, and he entered the information. "I'll be in touch. Is it okay if I say goodbye to Lily?"

She nodded. Beau walked to the rear door and opened it. He bent down and had a quick conversation with her daughter. Lily wrapped her arms around his neck and kissed his cheek.

He returned with a wide grin. "She's a great little girl. If you need anything, call me." Without warning, he laid a lightning kiss on Grace's cheek, walked to the truck, and waved goodbye.

Inside the BMW, Lily giggled from the back seat. "Mr. Beau kissed you, Mommy."

Chapter 6

THE NEXT MORNING Lily ran next door. Robert waved when the little girl entered his house, and Grace headed to her advanced yoga class. Her devotion to the regimen had enabled her to sail through natural childbirth. She started the program as a teenager when her mother claimed it was the only exercise that kept her lithe and limber. For Juliette, yoga was probably a job requirement, like firefighters who lift weights.

Upon her return, Grace entered the neighbors' screened pool enclosure and crossed the patio to their kitchen's French doors. Robert Chan read the newspaper at the breakfast room table while his partner, Dr. Tariq Mahmoud, stood at his state-of-the-art coffee maker.

As soon as she stepped inside, Robert stood and pushed his glasses up his nose. "You do not have the right to remain silent. Anything you say can and will be repeated. You do not have the right to consult your daughter. Do you understand your rights as I've explained them to you?"

Grace laughed. "Should I also assume the position?"

"Yes." Tariq set a mug of foamy cappuccino redolent of cinnamon and vanilla in front of her. "Put your bottom down and talk." He sat next to her and tucked his long legs under the table.

Grace wrapped her palms around the warm mug. "Lily must have told you about what happened yesterday."

Robert nodded. "Yes, but she waited until I was carrying three glasses of milk. Then she said, 'Mr. Beau broke our car and kissed Mommy.'"

Tariq put his arm around his partner's shoulders. "I was so proud of Robert. He never spilled a drop, despite screaming like a girl."

Robert's eyes softened as he gazed at his partner. "So, tell us about this Mr. Beau. Lily says he's like Tariq but with more *muskles*."

"She's right. He's tall like you." Grace tilted her head to gaze at her doctor neighbor. "But what she doesn't know is that I met him before yesterday."

Her two friends frowned. Robert spoke first. "Where?"

Grace sipped her coffee. "He was one of my speed dates." She told about meeting Beau two weeks ago and how different he seemed yesterday on the job. She did not share that he set off bewildering triggers of attraction within her but related in detail the adult version of yesterday's accident and the ride home. "I wasn't expecting him to kiss my cheek before he left."

Both men gave each other a secret smile while Robert made a clearing throat sound to suppress a laugh.

She eyed them with suspicion. "What do you know that I don't?"

Robert smirked at her over the rim of his coffee cup. "Lily told Mr. Beau he should kiss her mommy because she *really, really* needed it."

"Oh, my God." Grace clapped a hand over her open mouth.

Tariq patted her leg. "Your daughter is more determined than your friend, Alice, to find you a man."

Grace shook her head. "No, Lily is more determined to find herself a daddy. The fact that I would have to marry the guy is inconsequential."

Robert brushed his straight black hair off his forehead. "Now that you've had a second encounter, are you going to see him again for a date?"

She tamped down a feeling of regret. "I'm just not ready yet. I know almost nothing about him and, although Lily likes him, I need to be very sure of a man before I let him get close to her … and me. Besides, with his company damaging my car and any possible legal ramifications in the future, I think we should only have a business relationship at this point."

Robert gave a world-weary sigh. "I suppose you're right. No sense getting involved with a man you might need to sue."

"I hope that doesn't happen. He's been accommodating so far and insisted I use his vehicle until I get a replacement. I'm not very comfortable with that arrangement, so I'm going to start looking for a new car this weekend."

"Do you want any help?" Tariq asked.

Grace's high school graduation present had been her mother's two-year-old Lexus. At the time, Juliette's current lover had gifted her with a new Mercedes. Grace sold the RX sedan after her husband's death and drove his newer BMW, which Michael had chosen and purchased without her knowledge or input.

"Thanks for your offer. Although I've never bought a car before, I'm sure I can handle it. I'm a whiz at research and I'll know what I want, and what I'm willing to pay, before I ever talk with a salesperson."

Chapter 7

TEN DAYS AFTER the accident, Grace entered the kitchen from the laundry room and found Lily with her cell phone. "Who are you talking to?"

"Mr. Beau." Lily turned back to the phone. "Mommy's here." She thrust the device at her mother.

Grace put the dryer-warmed towels on the tabletop and lifted the phone from Lily's outstretched hand. "Hello."

"Hi." His voice was deep, warm, and comforting. "I'm afraid I'm calling with some bad news."

"What now?"

"I've spoken with the insurance company. They're willing to reimburse you the maximum blue book value for your car."

"So, what's the bad news?"

"The total falls way short for a new BMW. You could get a used one though."

"I don't want another one. I'm interested in an SUV or a minivan. How much will I be reimbursed?"

He told her, but she didn't respond. "Grace? Are you still there?"

"I'm here. That's less than I thought it would be."

"Listen, I could—"

"Don't worry. I'll work this out on my own." Unlike her mother, she would not allow a man to buy her a new car in exchange for favors.

"I was going to offer to take you to my brother-in-law's dealership for a family and friends discount."

Grace hesitated for a moment, tempted to accept. "Thank you, but no. I'm not sure what make or model I want yet. Besides I'm neither family nor friend."

"We could be friends." There was a hopeful lilt to his voice.

"I don't think that's a good idea. The issues related to the accident have not been legally resolved yet."

"Okay. I understand." Beau sounded a bit disappointed. "If there's anything I can do, let me know."

"I will." Grace ended the call as her daughter sat at the table and colored with markers.

Lily did not look up from her artwork. "Is Mr. Beau gonna help us get a new car?"

"No."

The little girl's head dropped. "But, Mommy, he's a man."

"So?"

"A man needs to buy a car, not a girl."

The time was perfect for Feminist Lesson Number One. "That's not true. Women buy cars all the time. It's not something only men do. Since I'm going to pay for it, I'm the one who decides what it will be and how much money I want to spend."

Lily spoke in a tone of childish disbelief like she had just learned Santa did not exist. "But girls buy clothes and house stuff, not cars."

"Not any more. Girls can do anything guys can do." Grace ran her hand over her daughter's baby-blond, silky hair. "I want to buy my own car without anybody's help."

Several days later, Beau called again. "I was checking to see if you had decided on a replacement vehicle."

"Not yet. I'll let you know as soon as I have. Any word on when I'll get my reimbursement check?" They talked for several minutes about the insurance process before Grace introduced what had been on her mind. "I think I should rent a car and return your BMW. I worry about something happening while I have it."

"Don't. Like I said, it's insured, and the rental would be another cost for my company. Please drive my car until you get your new one."

She sighed. "Okay."

To speed up her decision process, Grace made the mistake of inquiring online about new cars. She was inundated with emails and calls from salespeople. On the phone, one persistent salesman said, "Since next year's models have come in, we're discounting the 2017's left in stock. They're going fast. We only have a few of them left."

Three days later, after her yoga class, she stopped at a Honda dealership and asked for Javier. A good-looking, twenty-something with a bodybuilder body swaggered toward her. His liberal application of sandalwood cologne reached her before he did. He eyed her slim-fitting yoga leggings and midriff-baring sports bra. "Glad to see you took my advice and got in here today." He hustled her into an office and opened a folder which held several sheets of printed paper. "Here's the contract."

Grace halted. "Excuse me? What contract?"

Javier spoke in measured tones like English was her second language. "The … sales contract … for the Odyssey … you're ready to buy."

She stood tall, her shoulders squared. "Buy? I haven't even looked at the vehicle yet."

"But you reviewed it online. I said we had one in stock with all the features you wanted." Javier leaned back in his office chair and crossed one ankle over a knee as his muscular thighs strained the seams of the khaki pants. "Let's get things straight, Grace."

His expression was one she recognized. It was same look she had seen on her husband's face when she had said or done something to defy him. Before he could continue, she fixed him with a hard stare. "I didn't give you permission to call me by my first name."

He didn't respond for several seconds then arched one eyebrow. "Sorry about that, *Ms.* Black-Stone."

"It's *Dr.* Black-Stone."

"I assumed you weren't coming in here to waste my time, *Dr.* Black-Stone. That's why I had the paperwork printed up for you."

This guy dared to treat her like an idiot, rather than a woman who had more assets and education than him. Grace snatched her purse off the chair. "I never said I was ready to sign a contract. And now, I choose not to do so."

Instead of offering an apology, he smirked. "You're loss. It's a great deal."

Rather than get into a verbal confrontation with this immature chauvinist, Grace walked across the shiny showroom floor to an exit door. She spotted two other salesmen speaking with their heads together as their gazes darted between her and the office she vacated. Then it hit her. The salesman's last name on his shirt and the name of the dealership were the same. How long will Daddy allow his arrogant son to keep driving customers away?

Her next forays into the world of car shopping were more successful as she narrowed her choices to one vehicle. Now it was a matter of getting the best deal.

Several days later while bringing empty trashcans from the curb, Lily ran down the driveway with Grace's cell phone held aloft. "Mommy, it's Mr. Beau. I told him I'm seeing Santa on Saturday." She handed over the device then ran into the house.

"Hello, Beau." No matter how she prepared herself, every time Grace heard his low husky voice she imagined him whispering endearments that would tickle her ear. She shook her head to dispel the fevered image.

"I'm calling to let you know your reimbursement check will be here Wednesday. Do you have a vehicle picked out yet?"

"I've decided on the Toyota Highlander."

Beau paused. "Really? Have you signed a contract yet?"

"No. Why?"

"Remember me telling you my brother-in-law has a dealership. He sells Toyotas. I can find out what kind of deal he'd be willing to give you."

Despite Grace's desire to negotiate and buy this car on her own, she would be foolish to not hear the offer. "I would be interested in a quote from him."

Beau called the following day when she was at work in her office. "I spoke with Tom. He'll accept the insurance settlement if you're okay with last year's model."

She spun her desk chair around to view out her window. "He will? Why?"

"It's a favor for all the work I've done at his house and dealership. Since the accident has been a hassle for both of us, I told him I don't want you to have any out-of-pocket expenses for a new car."

Grace slam-dunked an errant piece of wadded-up paper into her wastebasket. "When and where can I look at his Highlander?"

"I can take you there on Saturday. Would you be available in the afternoon?"

Grace didn't question why he needed to go with her. Obviously not just anybody can walk into a dealership and claim they were entitled to a specific price. "I did promise to take someone to see Santa that day."

"I wouldn't mind seeing him myself."

Grace laughed. "Are you going to tell him what you want for Christmas?"

Beau's voice became soft and velvety. "If I thought he could make it happen, I'd even sit on his lap."

Neither of them spoke for a moment. Grace broke the silence first. "What time on Saturday?"

They agreed on a plan. When the call ended, she hugged the phone to her chest.

Chapter 8

GRACE DIDN'T TELL Lily about the excursion until that morning. "We have something to do before going to see Santa. Mr. Beau is taking us to look at a new car."

Lily looked up from her bowl of cereal. Her self-satisfied look seemed to say: *I told you a man would help.*

At one o'clock when the doorbell rang, Lily ran to the foyer. "It's him."

Grace's heart hammered. She wiped damp palms on her thighs before she opened the door. Beau was dressed in jeans and a red cotton Henley shirt with the sleeves pushed up his thick arms.

"Come in." She took a step back and moved Lily to stand beside her.

Beau filled the doorway and looked around the front hall which opened into a formal dining room and living room. A bank of sliding glass doors stretched across the far wall. The pool and patio were on the other side. "I've never been in this development before. You have a nice place."

Grace locked the door and stepped around him. "Thank you. Let me get my purse."

Lily led him by the hand to the living room. "Come and see our tree, Mr. Beau. Last year it had red lights and bows. Robert said it was Christmas hell."

Grace scowled at her daughter. "Lily."

The little girl ignored her. "I like white lights more better." She cupped the bottom of a shiny, azure ornament in the palm of her hand. "We got this color. The store didn't have pink. I love blue balls. Do you, Mr. Beau?"

His eyes bulged. "They look nice."

Grace took her daughter by the hand and headed toward the garage. "Let's go."

At the dealership, Beau spoke with people in the office. His brother-in-law, Tom, was not there but left information about the discussion he had with Beau. A dapper, older salesman, named Harry, led them outside to where the Highlander was parked.

Harry asked, "Is the white exterior okay with you?"

"Color isn't important." Grace fiddled with the power seat adjustments. Despite being last year's model, the SUV still had that pleasant new-car smell. She inhaled the plastic and vinyl VOCs and ran her palms over the smooth leather steering wheel. "I see it doesn't have a tow bar on the back."

"If you want to pay extra, we can install one."

"Can that be done later, if I need it?"

"No problem."

While Grace checked out the vehicle and questioned Harry, Lily interrogated Beau. "Do you like brock-li? Mommy says I just have to taste it."

"I didn't like it when I was a kid, but I like it now."

"Would you make a little girl eat brock-li if I didn't want to?"

"Like your mom, I'd say just taste it."

"Does falling in love hurt?"

Beau coughed in that fake way to simulate throat clearing. "No. It feels pretty good."

"Do you like milk or beer better?"

"I like them both."

"I'm 'lergic to cats. Do you have one?"

"No cats. I would like to get a dog someday."

"Who's smarter? Siri or Alexa?"

"I guess, Siri. I don't have an Alexa."

Lily's countenance shifted from animated to serious. The little girl fiddled with the straps of her backpack. "Are you gonna die soon?"

"I hope not."

At last, Grace shut the hatchback after examining the spare. "I'd like a test drive to see how it handles."

"Sure," Harry said. "I'll need to make a copy of your driver's license."

When they returned to the air-conditioned showroom, Grace faced Beau. "We'll need Lily's booster seat."

"I can stay here with her while you do the test drive."

The little girl's face fell. "I don't wanna do a test."

Harry looked at the three of them. "It should only take us about twenty minutes." When no one spoke, he fingered the smooth laminated license he held. "I'll be right back."

Grace took her daughter by the hand and sat her in a nearby upholstered chair. "You stay here while I talk to Mr. Beau." She motioned to him, and they moved a few feet away with their backs to the child. "Don't take this the wrong way, but I'm not comfortable leaving you alone with her."

"I understand. It's just that getting the seat transferred would probably take longer than the test drive. How about we sit right here and wait for you?"

Lily hugged her backpack to her chest and pleaded with her eyes. Grace held out her hand. "Give me the car key." Beau gave her the BMW fob. "Give me your wallet." He emptied his pockets into her palm. "Promise me you won't move from this spot."

He placed his hand over his heart. "I promise."

She walked back to her daughter. "While I'm gone, I want you to stay in this chair next to Mr. Beau."

Harry returned with her license and a dealer's plate. "I told the gals in the cashier's office to keep an eye on her." Two women behind a glass window waved.

Upon their return, Beau sat twisted in his seat while Lily knelt on the chair next to him. She combed his hair with a pink toy brush. Her other little hand smoothed the top of his head. His eyes were closed, and he appeared to be asleep.

Lily put her lips close to his ear. "Mommy's back."

Beau's lids snapped open. He twisted around to face his pint-sized stylist. "That felt good."

"'Cause you don't have skin like him." Lily pointed to the bald salesman. "Why's he called Hairy?"

With a straight face, Grace faced Hairy/Harry. "If the bottom line purchase price matches my insurance settlement, I'm willing to buy the Highlander."

"It does. Have a seat while I prepare the paperwork for your approval."

Two hours later, Beau, Grace, and Lily waited in the center of the mall. Santa's red and gold throne was on a platform surrounded by poinsettia plants and large fake presents. The bearded St. Nick was dwarfed by a mammoth artificial Christmas tree decorated with basketball-sized ornaments which rose thirty feet toward a glass ceiling. Christmas carols were piped from a loud speaker system that necessitated speaking in louder than normal conversational levels.

When it was Lily's turn, she marched up the white wooden stairs. After being lifted onto Santa's lap, her monologue began. Beau and Grace waited by the exit gate. Lily's arm shot toward them. Santa nodded.

Beau waved back. "Did you see her point us out?"

"Uh-huh."

Lily chattered more. The red-suited man swiped a bead of sweat from his brow with the back of his white-gloved hand then looked at Grace and Beau again. At last, the little girl finished and climbed down. She flapped a goodbye to Santa who laughed and waved in return.

After a helper elf escorted her out, Beau knelt in front of Lily. "Is Santa going to bring you what you want for Christmas?"

"He's gonna try. You wanna come to our house for a weenie roast? I can teach you." Lily tugged on Grace's hand. "Mommy, can Mr. Beau come?"

What was her daughter up to? "He might have other plans for dinner tonight."

Beau shook his head. "No plans. I'd like to learn how to roast weenies."

Lily jumped in place. "It's fun."

Chapter 9

UPON THEIR ARRIVAL at Grace's house, Beau carried in a bundle of wood from the garage and started a fire in a metal bowl on the patio. When the smoky flames died down, the adults sat in cushioned aluminum chairs pulled close.

Lily stood between her mother's knees and held a grill fork with one hot dog over the red embers. "Don't let it touch the fire, Mr. Beau. The weenie gets black. That's yucky. Turn it when it bubbles."

Beau's fork had two dogs skewered on it. "I haven't done this since I was a kid. Lately, I've just barbecued them on a grill."

"This is way better. Mommy can do good things with a weenie."

Grace stared into the fire.

Beau chuckled. "Does she? Like what?"

Lily flipped the grill fork. "She can make a ockapus."

"A what?"

Grace lifted her gaze to meet his. "I cut slices part way up before I put the hotdog on the grill. The ends curl to look like an octopus."

Following a dinner of slightly charred hot dogs, salty potato chips, and store-bought coleslaw and baked beans, Lily taught Beau how to play Uno while Grace put the food away and cleaned up the kitchen.

After the little girl won the game, Grace announced, "Okay, it's your bedtime."

Lily stood where she had knelt at the coffee table and walked to Beau who remained seated on the couch. She climbed up next to him. "Thank you for our new car."

"You're welcome."

"And for seeing Santa."

"I enjoyed it too."

She threw her arms around his neck, squeezed tight, scrambled to the floor, and ran to her bedroom.

Grace faced Beau. "You don't have to wait around while I get her ready for bed."

"If you don't mind, I'd like to stay and talk with you about something."

When she returned, Beau was in the kitchen, putting his empty glass in the sink. Grace leaned a hip against the edge of the counter. "What did you want to talk about?"

"I was hoping you would consider having dinner with me."

While she had readied Lily for bed, she speculated this was what he wanted to discuss. "Well, I just did."

"Yeah, but I'm talking about just you and me at a restaurant."

She flashed him a smile halfway between rueful and amiable. "I don't think that's a good idea at this time. The insurance matter hasn't been settled."

He raised his eyebrows. "What about afterwards?"

Grace rubbed her fingers along the ogee edge of the granite. Beau's expression was so hopeful. "Please understand that I'm all Lily has, and she's all I have. I've not dated anyone since my husband's death. I need to be cautious with new people, like today at the dealership. I have to know more about someone before I can allow a relationship to proceed to a more personal level."

"I understand. What can I do to convince you I'm a good guy?" Beau didn't appear angry or upset. Instead he looked amused which flustered Grace. It seemed they were playing a game of truth or dare. "You know, if we went on a date, you would learn more about me. That's the usual way a man and woman get to know each other."

He was right, of course. It was just that at odd moments an overwhelming miasma of betrayal followed by the sting of stupidity washed over her. She had been sucker-punched once by infidelity and risking another go-around was tough. Her heart was still stretched thin by Michael's lies and deceit. "I'll think about it, but let's leave things as they are until the insurance claim is resolved. Can I pick up the settlement check on Wednesday and return your car?"

"How will you get home? Or to the dealership?"

"I'll have my neighbor follow me to your office then drop me off at Tri-City Toyota." Grace licked her lips. "I do want to thank you for your help today. And please tell your brother-in-law how much I appreciate the very generous discount."

"I will, and you're welcome."

"It's getting late. Let me walk you out."

At the front door, Beau turned around after he stepped outside. "You know, as soon as you sign the paperwork and get your check, our business arrangement is over." He flashed a seductive grin followed by a lilting whistle and headed to his truck.

The backs of Grace's knees became damp and prickly.

Chapter 10

ON WEDNESDAY MORNING, Grace parked Beau's BMW in front of Charvet Crane at eleven o'clock. Tariq pulled into a nearby empty space. The office building was a small, one-story structure. In the back was an immense lot ringed with tall, razor-wired fencing where trucks, trailers, cranes, and other equipment sat. A sporty, red convertible and a minivan were the only other vehicles in the front. Grace walked over to Tariq's Lexus.

He powered down the window. "Do you want me to come in with you?"

"No. It shouldn't take long."

Inside the entrance, there was a small reception area paneled with faux wood and several molded plastic chairs. A sliding window was closed. An older woman sat behind the glass. Her head was enlarged by a poufy helmet of orange-hued hair. Reading glasses on a beaded lanyard dangled from her neck. She pressed a phone to her ear and held up an index finger with an acrylic nail embellished with crystals. At last, the call ended, and the window slid open. "Sorry 'bout that, hon. Kin I help you?"

Grace held up the BMW fob. "I'm returning Beau's car. It's parked out front."

"And you are?"

"Grace Stone. I was told you have my insurance check and some papers to sign."

The woman's smile brightened with the most crooked teeth Grace had ever seen. "They came this morning. By the way, I'm Cathy, the office manager. I'm so sorry 'bout what happened. Beau said you were sweet as pie though."

"Is there any chance I can take the paperwork with me and mail it back? I have a friend waiting outside to drive me to the dealership."

Cathy's mouth puckered in a moue of regret. "Bless your heart, but you need to read and sign everything 'fore I kin give you the check." The woman glanced over her shoulder into the part of the office Grace couldn't see. "Have a seat. I'll get everything ready for you."

After the receptionist slid the window closed, Grace texted Tariq to inform him it would be a while longer. Seven minutes later, she was ushered into the office.

Cathy shut the door behind her. "Sorry it took so long. We put a sticky tab everywhere you need to initial or sign. By the way, this is Beau's sister, Gen Lundquist. She's our part-time bookkeeper."

Gen was seated behind a desk, partly obscured by a computer monitor. Her long, brown hair was straight and limp. She wore the sour look of an unhappy woman.

Grace mustered a friendly smile. "Hello. It's nice to meet you."

Gen's flat eyes glanced away from the screen to do a quick up-down scan. "Yeah. You too."

"I really appreciate your husband's help in getting me a replacement vehicle."

"Tom's real helpful when it suits him." She began to type as a curt dismissal.

Grace followed Cathy to an office set up as a conference room with mismatched office chairs where the paperwork was laid out on a badly scratched, dark wood table. At the bottom of the last page, she was instructed to check one of two boxes and sign her name. The box on the top absolved Charvet Crane and its insurer of any additional liability. The box underneath did not.

Cathy stood in the doorway. "Just so you know, if you mark the second box, I can't give you the check today. Bring everything out to the office when you're done."

Grace had just read the last page when her cell phone rang.

It was Tariq. "A white truck just drove into the lot. A tall guy with brown hair is heading inside. Would that be Beau?"

"Probably. I'm almost done here and should be out in a minute." She signed the last form. When the door of the conference room opened, she looked up. "Hello, Beau."

"Are you finished with the paperwork?"

She put the pen down and nodded.

Without a word, he walked around the end of the table and slid her wheeled chair out. He dropped into a will-you-marry-me kneel and grasped her hand. "Will you go out with me now?"

He had such a vulnerable look about him, one that her agreement could erase, but that would mean opening a door she wasn't ready to walk through yet. "I need to think about it."

"Take your time." He waited for a beat. "So, what did you decide?"

Grace laughed.

"I've told everyone about this beautiful professor who was a class act when she found her car destroyed and her great little girl. The two days I spent with you and Lily were the best I've had in a long time. I'd like to take you out so we can get to know each other better." Before she could answer, his gaze shifted to his office walls taped with blueprints, the cheap furniture, and banged-up file cabinets. He rose to his feet with a somber expression. "I'm just a construction guy who runs a small business and can't tell you the last time I read a book. So, if you don't want to see me anymore, I guess I can understand why."

Alice was right. Men are threatened by a doctoral degree. Grace angled her neck to view the tall figure in front of her. "The work you do isn't important to me. What matters is that you're the first man I've been attracted to in years. And my daughter likes you too."

"You're attracted to me?" A tiny smile lifted one corner of his mouth. "Good. I feel the same about you. I'm crazy about Lily too." He sat down in the chair next to hers and checked his watch. "When can we go out?"

She laughed again at his dogged persistence. "Well, right now, I need to get to the dealership. I have someone waiting to drive me there."

"Your neighbor?"

"Yes. He's waiting outside."

Beau gave her a sharp look, stood, and held out his hand. "I'd like to meet this guy."

When they exited the building, Tariq opened the driver's door and stood at the front of his car.

Grace touched his arm. "This is my good friend, Dr. Tariq Mahmoud."

"Nice to meet you, Doc." Beau held out his large, tanned hand.

Tariq gripped it with long, slender fingers. He studied Beau's face as if to ascertain any falseness in his countenance. Without looking away, he slipped a proprietary arm around Grace's shoulder. "Likewise."

Beau's eyes shifted to Tariq's hand which cupped her upper arm. "I was hoping Grace would have lunch with me today. Afterwards, I can take her to my brother-in-law's dealership to get the Highlander."

Grace's breath hitched. When had she agreed to lunch?

"I'm here to take her wherever she wants to go." Tariq spoke in a firm, I'm-in-charge voice.

"I appreciate you bringing her to my office, but I can take it from here."

"That's not necessary. I already offered to drive her."

Beau stepped closer. She was now sandwiched between them as their testosterone-fueled conversation continued. "You don't have to, Doc. I'm sure you're a busy guy with lots to do."

Tariq's chin lifted and jutted forward. "I'm never too busy to help a friend."

Grace wiggled free and took a half-step back. "Maybe I should run inside and get a ruler so you two can see whose equipment is bigger."

The men chuckled. The tense male hostility dissolved like an electric current shut off.

She turned to Tariq. "I'll grab a bite to eat with Beau. Then he can take me to get the car. I know you have plans this afternoon with the girls." Having lunch with Beau would provide her with an opportunity to evaluate him as a potential dinner date.

As her friend's Lexus exited the parking lot, Beau touched her elbow. "I know a good place to eat on the way to the dealership. Do you like Mexican food?"

"Love it."

"Let's get your check and head out." Inside the office, Beau halted in front of Gen's desk. "You met my sister, right?"

Gen rolled her chair back and stood. She wore an over-sized button-down man's shirt over jeans that fit like they had an elastic waistband. Her smile was sunny, but her eyes remained lifeless. "So, this is the woman you talked about."

There was an odd inflection to her voice like she was on stage and over-acting. With Beau and his sister within feet of each other, the Charvet family resemblance was evident in the dark, arched brows which accentuated the siblings' amber-colored eyes like brown piping.

Beau smiled at the two women like they would soon become fast friends. He seemed oblivious that his sister viewed Grace in the same way she probably checked out fruit on a reduced price rack. "This is my sister, Genevieve Lundquist. I'm glad you two could meet. Too bad Grace's daughter, Lily, isn't here. We're going to lunch then I'm taking her to pick up the new car. Is her paperwork ready?"

Cathy brushed past them. "Gimme a minute to make copies of every-thing first."

Beau grasped Grace's elbow. "Let me show you something." He led her to a rear door and opened it. They walked to an asphalted area covering several acres where equipment was parked. "One day I hope to have an indoor storage facility here to house all but the biggest pieces. Now we try to schedule jobs so that the largest cranes go from one job site to the next."

"This is quite an operation you have."

"I've got plans for Charvet Crane to grow bigger than it is now."

When they returned to the main office, Cathy approached with an en-velope in her outstretched hand. "Here you go. Everything's inside. Too bad we had to meet under these circumstances. Since the accident this big guy can't stop talking about you and your little girl." She patted Beau's chest.

His cheeks darkened with color. "Uh, we should be on our way." His phone rang. Beau fished it from his pocket and checked the screen. "Excuse me a minute. It's Joe."

As he walked toward his office, Grace slipped the envelope into her purse. "Thanks, Cathy."

The older woman tilted her head. "Do you have a picture of your little girl? I'd love to see her. I have three grandbabies, but they're all boys and as wild as a pack of wolves. I love 'em to death but there are times I wanna cloud up and rain all over 'em."

Grace retrieved her phone and showed Cathy some photos of Lily. After a few minutes, Beau strode from his office, his face a mask of extreme annoyance. He ran a hand over his head. "Grace, I'm sorry but—"

Cathy stepped toward him. "What's wrong?"

"There's still a problem at the project in Delray. I gotta get back up there."

Grace opened her mouth to say she would call Tariq to come back. Before she could speak, Beau raised his chin and stared over her head. "Gen, would you drive Grace to the dealership for me?"

No. No. No.

Without waiting for an answer, Beau snatched up a thick ring of keys from a wall-mounted panel. "Come outside for a minute, Grace. Please." She followed him to his truck. He unlocked the door and turned to face her with a heavy sigh. "I'm sorry about lunch. I really wanted a chance to talk with you. Can I call you tonight?"

"Sure. We'll talk later."

Chapter 11

AFTER BEAU DROVE out of the parking lot, Grace waited in front of his BMW. She opened her purse to retrieve her phone and call Tariq who would come back for her. Before she could find it, Gen emerged from the building with an even deeper scowl.

In an abrupt and authoritative voice, as if she was about to lead Grace into battle, Beau's sister said, "Let's go. My car's the convertible."

As she walked to the passenger door, Grace prayed the top would stay up. Only dogs and bald-headed men looked good riding in an open car. After she was seated and belted, Gen jammed the key into the ignition and stomped on the gas. They headed out of the corporate park at a speed well above the posted limit.

Gen raced toward an intersection with a yellow caution light. "How old is your daughter?"

The red Camry shot under the red light.

Grace released her breath. "Lily is four."

"My son will be four next year. I also have a daughter who's seven." Gen didn't slow down when several lengths in front of them a car braked to make a right turn. "How long have you been divorced?"

Grace pressed an imaginary pedal in her foot well. "I'm a widow."

Gen's head cocked to one side as if she debated whether to believe what she heard or not. "When did your husband die?"

"Four years ago."

The convertible remained centered in the lane as it passed a bicyclist. The passenger side mirror came within inches of clipping the helmeted rider.

Beau's sister either ignored or didn't hear the man's profane shout. "Your little girl must have been a baby when that happened."

"Two months old."

They stopped behind a line of cars at a traffic light. Gen turned to Grace with a cruel smile. "Has Bojo told you about Megan?"

Beau's nickname is Bojo? "No, he hasn't."

"Their divorce was final three years ago. My brother gave her everything she wanted except his business. Neither of them has said why they didn't want to stay married, but since he was so generous, I guess it was his fault. I doubt he'll ever love another woman after Megan."

The light turned green, and the car lurched into the intersection. There was no more talk until they reached the dealership. Gen screeched to a halt under a portico where double doors led to the showroom. "Whether you want to hear it or not, I'm going to give you a piece of advice."

Grace sat for a moment to get her bearings. If the advice was to never accept a ride from her again, the woman didn't have to worry.

Gen draped both wrists over the top of the steering wheel and stared straight ahead. "Bojo has reached the age when he wants a child of his own. But once men have kids, they no longer desire the woman who gave birth to them. You're lucky your husband didn't live long enough to want a younger model, like you used to be."

Grace opened her door as a tall, slender man with reddish-blond hair rushed out of the showroom. His long strides brought him to the driver's side of the car. His knuckles rapped on the glass with rapid-fire taps. Beau's sister glowered and lowered the window.

The man bent to peer inside. Spots of color reddened his cheeks. "What are you doing here? I told you I'd be at work until eight tonight."

Grace slipped off the seat and stood on shaky legs outside the car.

"Like I should believe that." Gen's voice was heavy and cold. "You can leave any time during the day, and all of your employees would cover for you."

The man, who had to be Tom Lundquist, straightened and stared down at his wife. His head jerked toward Grace when she shut the car door, noticing her for the first time. He gawked as if she were an alien from another planet. "Who are you?"

Gen answered first. "That's Grace Stone, the woman you gave a friends and family discount to, although she's not family. Is she your *friend*?"

Grace gave Tom a weak wave. "Hello."

He looked away for a few seconds. When he faced her again, he had slipped into friendly salesman mode with an open, trustworthy expression, one intended to inspire confidence in buying a car from him. He circled the front bumper and grasped Grace's hand in his cool palm. "Nice to meet you. I'm Tom. Are you here to pick up your Highlander?"

She nodded.

In a softer voice, he said, "I'm sorry you overheard our argument. I wasn't expecting Gen to come here."

"Beau was called away, so he asked her to drop me off."

"Let's go inside and find Harry. We'll get this wrapped up then you can drive your new car home."

Despite the jolly veneer of his words, there was an undercurrent of stress in his tone. He inhaled a deep, cleansing breath through his nostrils. They rounded the hood of the car as Gen watched them through the windshield with narrowed eyes.

Grace stopped and leaned sideways toward the open driver's window. "Thanks for the ride."

Gen nodded, put the car in gear, and drove away without a farewell. When Grace looked up, Tom stood at the door of the showroom, holding it open for her. He smiled with an expression of equal parts friendliness and relief.

Chapter 12

BEAU CALLED AT nine PM that night. "Hi. Did you get your new car?"

"Yes."

"Great. I hope I'm not calling too late. I didn't want to interrupt you getting Lily ready for bed." After several silent seconds, Beau said, "Is something wrong?"

Grace bit her lip.

Before she could answer, he asked, "What happened? Was there a problem at the dealership?"

Grace fiddled with a pearl ring on the fourth finger of her left hand where she once wore a diamond wedding band. She attempted to speak with confidence, but her voice sounded tiny and scared to her own ear. "Now that our business with the car is concluded, I don't see any need for us to remain in contact."

A thread of anger punctuated his words. "Did Gen say something to you?"

No way would Grace add to Gen's troubles by repeating what she said about Beau's divorce and his desire for children. "No."

"Then why are you saying we don't need to talk anymore?"

"I know you're expecting I'll go out with you now that the car issue is settled, but today …"

All evening Grace had rehearsed what she would say when he called, but nothing sounded right. She was attracted to Beau more than any man since Michael. She observed him as a speed dater, as an employer, as the responsible party in an accident, and as a brother. In each situation he handled himself with humor, civility, and graciousness.

"Grace?"

"I'm sorry. My friends …" And Lily. "… think it's time I started dating again. Even though it's been four years since Michael's death, I don't feel ready to get romantically involved yet. Please understand." She stopped herself from saying: *It's not you. It's me.*

"I do understand." His voice softened which set up an inadvertent thrumming in her groin. "Like you, I did speed dating as a favor. I didn't expect to meet someone who interested me as much as you do. I'm also carrying around some painful baggage as a result of my divorce. That makes me somewhat wary to get involved too."

Painful baggage? Did Gen have it wrong? Was Beau, not Megan, the real injured party?

He said, "How about we take it slow?"

"What do you mean?"

"Let's be friends."

Did he mean following each other on Facebook? She already blocked former male classmates who messaged her about getting together for drinks to discuss old times. All they wanted was to hook up. "What would being friends involve?"

"We'll talk on the phone. If you need something, you can ask me to help, and vice versa. We can do things that friends do, as long as you don't make me go shopping with you. We can—"

"Wait a minute. Other than speed dating, every time we've been together shopping was involved. First it was a car seat then it was a car. We even spent two hours at a mall last Saturday."

"You're right. Okay, we can shop as long as it's automotive."

By the time, their phone call ended, Grace looked forward to speaking with Beau again. With the pressure of a romantic date tabled for now, she relaxed. He called her on Saturday with Facetime. Their conversation was light and effortless.

At one point, Lily came into Grace's home office. "Who you talking to?"

Grace turned the phone around so her daughter could see the screen. "Mr. Beau."

The little girl crawled onto her lap. "Can I talk to him?"

"Let's ask. Beau, may Lily say hello to you."

"Sure."

Grace held the phone, so he could see the little girl.

"Hi, Mr. Beau." She waved.

"How you doing, Miss Lily?"

The little girl hunched her shoulders in a coy posture. "Good. Guess what I did."

"What did you do?"

"I rode Maxi's bike. All the way down the drive. It's got training wheels."

"Hey, that's not bad for a four-year-old."

Lily frowned. "I'm not bad."

"No. Uh, I know you're not bad. I mean, you riding the bike. That's really good."

"You're a boy. Can I ask you a question?"

His eyes shifted left then right. "O-kay?"

"Adam said he likes me."

"Who's Adam?"

"A boy at school. With dots on his face. He scribbles. Can I wait?"

"Wait for what?"

"To like him. You know," Lily heaved a feminine sigh, akin to one many females use when explaining a simple concept to a man. "Till he grows up."

"I-I think that's a good idea. You should wait until he stops scribbling."

"Okay. Bye." Lily scooted off her mother's lap and ran from the room.

Grace smiled at the screen. "Welcome to my world."

Their next phone call was in the evening when Lily was in bed. After innocuous back and forth questions about their day, Beau asked one of the questions she had been dreading. "Do you have relatives who live around here?"

Grace blew out a deep breath. This was the information that may cause him change his mind about dating her. "I have no one."

"What do you mean?"

"I'm an orphan." This call was not on Facetime, so Grace couldn't see his reaction. Maybe it was for the best, considering what she was about to tell him.

"You never knew your parents?"

"I lived with my mother, but she died when I was twenty. I never met or knew any of her family. She told me there was none."

"Wow. I lost my mother when I was twelve. I still miss her, and I bet you still miss yours too. And your father?"

Grace swallowed. "I don't know who he is. All I know is that I'm the illegitimate daughter of a rich man. And my mother was his mistress."

There was a beat of silence. When Beau spoke, his voice had softened. "How did you find out about this?"

"Juliette told me when I was in middle school. Her latest boyfriend had ended their relationship. She said *the glass man* went back to his wife. I asked if she knew Mr. Glass was married."

At the time, her mother had snorted and looked at Grace like she qualified to win the Stupid Question of the Year trophy. Despite a string of broken romances, Juliette was all strength and certainty when it came to the men in her life. She never had a moment's doubt about their declarations of love or a future together.

Grace stared at her reflection on the black screen of the computer monitor. "She said Glass wasn't his name. It's what she called all men because their promises were easily broken. I made some smart remark then she told me what she did for a living. Given the relationship between girls that age and their mothers, ours didn't improve with my newfound knowledge. It was difficult for me to reconcile my mother's choice of profession. I worried about its effect on my life if my friends found out." To a degree, she still wrestled with it today. "Juliette died the day I graduated from college. I was upset she didn't show for my commencement. That evening, the campus police came to my apartment. My mother had been killed in a traffic accident on the way to UF. The day before she died, she had sent me an email, but I hadn't opened it since I was busy packing and getting ready for graduation. In it, she said the hardest job for a woman was prying a marriage proposal out of a man. I think she had finally found someone she could commit to in a long-term relationship."

At the time of her death, Juliette was in her mid-forties but looked a decade younger. Her competition for the wealthier sugar daddies were girls her daughter's age. When Grace had been home for Spring Break, Juliette told her, "I need to find someone and settle down while I still have my looks. No matter what I do, I'll never be young again."

Beau interrupted Grace's reverie. "Do you know anything about your father?"

"Before I left for college, I learned there was a trust he set up that paid our living expenses and covered my education. The terms required Juliette to never reveal his identity."

A flash of memory skittered across her vision like a strip of old film. Some scenes skipped ahead as if frames had been cut by an overzealous editor. Grace was about Lily's age and in the guesthouse with her nanny. Juliette entered with a man whose hair was either blond or gray. He wore thin, metal-framed glasses which glinted from the overhead light when he lifted her off the floor and asked her name.

When she didn't answer at first, her mother frowned. "Tell him your name."

"Grace Georgette Black. Mommy calls me Gigi."

The man smiled and bounced her on his arm. Her mother now looked happy, so Grace asked the stranger a question. "What's your name?"

"You can call me Mr. Mack."

Her remembrance vanished when Beau cleared his throat. "After losing your mother, it must've been tough not knowing, at least, your father's name."

"I do know he was called Mr. Mack."

"Like I'm called Mr. Beau?"

"Maybe. Mack could be his first or last name. The funny thing is, I don't even know who my mother was. After her death, I found out Juliette Black never existed until she moved to Florida."

"What?" Beau's deep voice raised a pitch. "Your mother didn't exist? Was she in the witness protection program or running away from someone?"

Grace shook her head in a weary gesture like a lost traveler who had been given one wrong direction after another. "I don't know."

"Are you sure she's your mother?"

"She is definitely my biological mother. We actually look quite alike. After her death, I was unable to find any of her records. I don't know where she was born. I don't know if she had any family. I don't even know if Juliette Black was her real name."

Beau breathed out a heavy sigh. "I'm sorry to hear you don't have any family. I can see why you're so protective of Lily. She really *is* all you have."

A sudden rush of emotion dampened Grace's eyes. "Yes, she is. Well, it's getting late, and I have a busy day tomorrow."

"Thank you for sharing your history with me, Grace. Can I call you in a couple days?"

"Sure. We'll talk again."

Chapter 13

THE NEXT EVENING Lily became feverish and complained her head hurt. Grace called Tariq.

He checked the little girl's temperature, examined her ears, and listened to her chest. "It could be a virus. If she's still running a fever in four hours, give her another dose of Tylenol. Check her temperature, and if it gets to a hundred and two, call me. If her headache gets worse, call me. If she exhibits any other symptoms, call me."

In the morning, Lily still had a fever but no headache. She was listless and cranky. The first clear blister appeared later in the day. By suppertime, Lily's face and chest were dotted with them.

Tariq confirmed the diagnosis. "It's chicken pox. Maxi and Erin were sick this morning. I expect they'll exhibit the classic symptoms soon. Have you had it?"

"Yes, but I wonder if Beau has."

"You better call him, and let him know about our little epidemic."

Beau answered on the second ring. "How is everything?"

"Lily has chicken pox. If you haven't had it, you've likely been exposed."

"I had it and was miserable."

Grace laughed. "Me too. It should be a fun week for me in quarantine."

At first, Lily loved being covered in pink calamine lotion, but the topical treatment and cool baths soothed her discomfort only a short time before the whininess and tears started anew. Tariq brought over a liquid antihistamine that helped Maxi's itching and an oatmeal bath product which provided temporary relief for Erin. The adults in the two neighboring houses were like mad scientists, consumed with finding the perfect chicken pox antidote.

Beau stopped by with DVDs for Lily that his sister lent him, as well as flavored water and sugar-free popsicles, a recommendation from his step-mother. He bought a jar of organic honey because an internet article claimed it was soothing when applied to the blisters. Grace was touched that he went to all the trouble to seek advice from other mothers and do online research.

"Thank you," she said at the front door.

"You're welcome." His teeth caught the light from the overhead foyer pendant as he smiled. "That's what friends are for."

After he left, a pressure valve in her chest seemed to release for the first time in over four years. Her relationship with Beau was different than any other she ever had with a man. It seemed to have its own specialness; sharpening her senses so that everything was more significant, more important, and essential.

After Lily was asleep on Christmas Eve, Tariq dropped off the presents Grace purchased for her daughter. Each December, she and Robert split one month's rent on a small unit at a nearby storage facility. After each shopping expedition, they would hide the kids' gifts there. Grace set up a table in the garage and worked until well after midnight to wrap everything for under the tree. She planned to make Lily's favorite pancakes for breakfast and bake a frozen pizza for lunch. The dinner menu was up in the air, depending on how the two of them felt.

Christmas morning dawned with neither Grace nor her daughter in the holiday spirit. Lily entered the master bedroom, shrouded in one of her mother's T-shirts, and threw herself onto the bed.

"Merry Christmas, sweetie." Grace leaned over and kissed the top of the little girl's head where any blisters were covered by hair.

Lily stripped off the socks she wore on her hands at night and sighed. "I shoulda told Santa I don't want pox."

"I wish you had too, but let's see what he did bring."

At four o'clock in the afternoon, Beau called. "Is Lily up for a visit? I have presents and leftovers from my family's Christmas luncheon."

"You do?"

"The gifts are the same ones I bought my niece, and the food is because my stepmother plans meals like the Atlantic fleet might drop in."

"Give us an hour. Lily needs her hair washed and another oatmeal bath."

While her daughter played in the tub, Grace readied herself. After a shower, she dried her hair, put on makeup, and dressed in a pair of light-weight linen slacks and a camisole top. The problem was finding something for Lily that didn't irritate her tender skin.

She pushed Grace's oversized tank top away. "I don't want to wear your shirt. It's too big."

"Ow. These panties hurt right here." She pointed to the elastic openings and skimmed the underwear down her legs.

"I look stupid." She pulled at the sheet Grace had safety-pinned around her like a toga.

At her wits' end and with Beau due any minute, Grace ran to the Christmas tree. Among the piles of presents Lily opened that morning, was a new pair of cotton pajamas. They were a little big which would not bind or chafe her skin.

When the doorbell rang, Lily smiled and clapped her hands. Grace opened the door to find Beau's arms full of packages and bags. A large cardboard box of plastic containers rested on the holiday poinsettia welcome mat. He was dressed in khakis and a white button-down. This time his shirttail was tucked into his pants.

"Merry Christmas," he said.

Grace smiled. "Merry Christmas to you. Let me help."

"Me too." Lily teetered on the doorsill in her bare feet, her arms out-stretched.

Two presents were put by the tree. In the kitchen, Grace unpacked an amazing variety of food. There were raw vegetables, ham, roast beef, side dishes, rolls, cookies, and slices of a red velvet cake.

She placed several containers in the refrigerator. "I hadn't decided what we were going to eat for supper, so this is wonderful, even though Lily hasn't had much of an appetite for days."

Beau leaned against the kitchen counter. "I can help you make a dent in it if you invite me to stay."

From the living room came a plaintive call. "Mommy, we need to open presents now." Once the adults were seated, Lily ripped the wrapping paper off the smallest box first. "It's a watch. And it's pink!"

Beau opened the case for her. "It's not just any watch. It's a smart-watch."

After fastening the plastic band around her wrist where there were no painful blisters, he showed Lily how to take photos, including selfies, and how to access pre-loaded games on the device.

The next present contained the Barbie Career Teacher and Playset. Lily smoothed the doll's long blond hair. "She's pretty and looks like Mommy."

"Your mommy is pretty and smart too. That's why I bought that doll for you." He slid a sideways glance at Grace and raised his eyebrows as a secret smile lifted the corners of his mouth.

A warm flush washed over her followed by a tingling sensation. She had been sitting on the edge of the sofa undisturbed until Beau's one look shook her. His warm honey-colored gaze caused her heart to flutter with secret excitement. She sat back before melting onto the floor.

Lily jumped up and threw her arms around his neck. "These are the bestest presents. Thank you." The little girl lay down on the floor with the doll next to her cheek. She raised her wrist and pushed buttons on the new watch to take a selfie with Barbie.

Grace gathered the crumpled wrapping paper and headed to the kitchen. Beau followed. After disposing of the discards in the trash can, she turned to face him. "Those are great gifts, the *bestest*."

Beau's smile wavered. "Is that bad?"

Grace shook her head. "I'm joking. Thank you for thinking of her."

"You're welcome. I didn't bring anything for you, except food."

"You brought me the best present of all, a happy child for the first time in days. How can I show my appreciation?"

Beau lowered his head and opened his arms. "I'll take a hug."

Grace wrapped her arms around his wide shoulders. His hands circled her waist, and rested at the small of her back, but he didn't pull her close. She was the one who stepped forward and pressed her chest against his. The side of her head rested against his jawline. Grace was in a blissful haze, lightly enveloped in his strong arms. It had been so long since a man had held her like this. Her senses heightened as if awakening from a long sleep. "This is nice."

"Yes, it is." His lips brushed against her ear.

Without conscious thought, Grace turned her head and placed her mouth on his. At first, the kiss was nothing more than a feather-light graze. Then his lips pressed against hers, gentle but exploratory. She quivered with the sweet tenderness of his touch, the thrill, the desire, the thawing of her heart.

"Mommy?" Lily stood in the kitchen doorway with her Barbie doll clutched to her chest, eyes wide.

Oh my God! Lily had never seen a man kiss her before. Grace swallowed hard and dropped her arms from around Beau. "What's the matter, sweetie?"

"When are we gonna eat? I'm hungry."

Chapter 14

AFTER DINNER, THEY watched the Christmas movie, *Elf.* Lily sat in Beau's lap and leaned against his chest like he was a man-sized recliner. He rested his feet on the large ottoman which doubled as a coffee table. Halfway through the movie, she was asleep.

Grace stood. "Let me put her in bed."

"I'll do it. Show me the way."

Beau rose in a lithe, fluid movement with the little girl curled on his chest. He followed Grace to the bedroom and eased Lily onto the mattress.

They returned to the kitchen where Grace rinsed out their mugs of hot chocolate. "I was wondering—"

"I should—" He opened his hand, palm up. "You first."

"I was wondering if you could put my license plate on the Highlander. I was having trouble with one of the screws."

"Sure."

He followed Grace to the door which led from the house into the garage. She retrieved a screwdriver for him. After removing the plastic Tri-City Toyota plate holder that had caused her such problems, he discarded the temporary paper tag then affixed the annual sticker to the corner of the new metal plate.

"Do you want me to put this plastic frame back on?"

"Is it needed?"

Beau shook his head. "It's just free advertising for Tom's dealership."

Grace shrugged. "Go ahead. He gave me a good deal."

When he finished, Beau rose to his feet and brushed his palms against his pant legs. "There you go. You're all set."

She held out her hand for the screwdriver, and he dropped it into her palm. "Thank you. I was afraid of stripping the screws. They were on so tight."

When she raised her eyes, Beau gazed down at her through half-closed lids. At first his stare was riveted on her face then moved down her neck to her chest. Her nipples seemed to come alive against the built-in cups of her tank top. Without a word, Beau curled his hand behind her head and captured her lips. He groaned a low, seductive sound. The muscles deep inside Grace's belly contracted. His hot tongue entered her open mouth as he pulled her against him. The flooding warmth made her lose focus. As she wrapped her hands around his neck, the screwdriver clattered to the garage floor. Their tongues jockeyed for supremacy.

His touch ignited sensations from her breast to her groin. With a gasp, she broke contact with his mouth and threw back her head. Beau's erection pressed against her abdomen. Without shame, she rubbed back and forth against it. With her lips pressed to his again, she ran her hands over his shoulders, down his arms, up his back. Grace was so lost in him she didn't hear him speak at first.

"We need ... Grace ... we need ... to stop."

She put her hands on his cheeks and looked into his hooded eyes. "I want you. I need you." Her heart thudded so hard behind her breastbone it was almost painful. The only sounds were their labored breaths.

Beau searched her face. "Are you sure?"

Was she sure? She wasn't. Not at all. Grace sighed with a regret fostered by four years of loneliness and hung her head. "No."

He pulled her close and rested his chin on top of her head. Together, they stood motionless as their breathing and racing hearts slowed. At last, Beau released her and Grace stepped back.

She raised her eyes to meet his. "I'm sorry."

He squeezed her shoulders. "It's okay. We both got carried away."

Grace gave a tiny shake of her head, one he didn't appear to catch or didn't question. Many men would never have asked her if she was certain about what was about to happen. They would have proceeded without concern. After all, she had said she wanted and needed him. Wasn't that all but a declaration of consent?

He was a big guy who could have easily forced her to follow through. Or he could have used a combination of verbal cajoling accompanied by wheedling to *turn her on* as some guys in high school and college had done. Instead Beau accepted her decision to change her mind midstream.

Maybe he was one of the good guys.

As a widowed single mother, she needed a good guy. Especially one who didn't act like Lily was an unwanted buy one/get one half off deal. If Beau showed up for a date on time, didn't ask her to pay half the check, or wouldn't demand sex in return, he might be a good starter boyfriend. The big question was if he still wanted to date her after what just happened.

"Grace? Are you okay?"

She hadn't moved or spoken for a while, just stared at him as if he was an unfamiliar phenomenon—which he might be. "I'm fine. It's getting late."

He checked his watch. "Yeah, I better go."

She walked to a pegboard where she slipped the screwdriver back into its designated holder. Beau followed her into the house. She unlocked the front door then turned to face him. "May I ask you a question?"

"Sure."

"Do you still want to go out with me?"

His neutral expression morphed into one of wide-eyed surprise. "You bet."

"Even after what just didn't happen?"

"I don't want you to regret anything we do. You're way more than a one-night stand. That's why I asked."

Once again, a feeling of warm liquid honey enveloped her. This time it had nothing to do with raging hormones, but was a genuine like for this man. "How about a date this weekend? We can get to know more about each other."

"Sounds great. I can pick you up around six on Saturday for dinner."

"I'll be ready." Grace prayed that emotionally she would be.

Chapter 15

THE NEXT MORNING Robert sent her a text. *Why was that BMW you had been driving in front of your house last night?*

Grace called him back. When he repeated his text question, she described Beau's visit, the presents he brought Lily, and all the leftover food. "Why don't you guys come over for supper tonight? I've got plenty."

"Okay, but we're not done talking about last night yet. I know Lily wasn't awake the whole time he was there. What did you two do after she went to bed?"

Grace told him about what almost happened in the garage.

Robert let out a deep breath that whistled over the phone. "Well, it's about time. But *the garage?*"

She shrugged one shoulder even though Robert couldn't see. "I wanted to—"

"Bump his bumper? Wet his dipstick?"

"Robert!"

"Bend his tie rod? Torque his nuts?"

"Stop." Her outrage was ruined when she giggled. "I can't believe I said I wanted and needed him."

"You were feeling like a woman again."

"I had forgotten what it was like, but you're right. Having sex in the garage would have been a terrible mistake."

"Not necessarily. If it's the right time and person, the place doesn't matter ... as long as it's not inside a display shed at Home Depot."

She was not sure she heard him correctly. "Ro-bert?"

He spoke in a rush. "Are you going to see him again?"

"We're going to dinner on Saturday. Would you be able to watch Lily?"

"Absolutely."

Now that she had agreed to the date, the beacon of her familiar life had suddenly shut off without a flicker. She would have to blindly navigate through an unknown expanse for potential hazards and avoid the perils of allowing a man into her world, even one as seemingly trustworthy as Beau Charvet.

Chapter 16

ON SATURDAY EVENING, Lily watched for Mr. Beau's car from the dining room window. She had recovered from her bout with chicken pox with only a scattering of scabs still dotting her body. "He's here."

Grace checked herself in the full-length mirror. She wore a red knit dress bought for this year's faculty Christmas party. Lily bounced up and down in the foyer. Her golden locks swung in a halo around her head. When Grace opened the front door, she discovered that, in addition to Beau, her neighbors and their children stood on the tiled front entrance.

Tariq completed the introductions. "… and my partner, Robert Chan."

Everyone entered the foyer. Lily wormed her way through the bodies to grab Beau's hand. Erin held Robert's while Tariq had Maxi's enfolded in his. Grace smiled. For once, Lily wanted to hold hands with a man who wasn't someone else's daddy.

Beau was dressed in charcoal gray slacks, a white open-collared dress shirt, and a black sports coat. He was so tall and masculine, especially next to Robert who still exuded holiday spirit with antler ears and a red Christmas shirt which read: *Reindeer are just gay moose.* Her neighbor carried a plate of cookies which had either been decorated by his children or by him while blindfolded.

She took the dish and headed to the kitchen. Robert followed with little Erin like she was a pull toy on a string. He studied Beau with backward glances.

Grace put the plate on the countertop. "Stop staring at him."

"He looks very dapper for someone in the building trades."

"What'd you think? He'd show up looking like the construction worker from The Village People?"

He arched his eyebrows. "I can dream, can't I?"

Tariq and Robert tag-teamed Beau and asked him pointed questions about his business (incorporated six years ago), his nationality (French-Canadian), his experience with children (a niece and nephew), and his level of education (a bachelor's degree in business).

While the adults chatted, the three little girls pirouetted as they held onto the men's hands. Grace was impressed with Beau's ability to carry on a conversation while Little Miss Ballerina dangled off him. At last, Tariq picked up Lily's overnight bag. The men and little girls waved goodbye and left.

Grace locked the house, and Beau escorted her to his car. "Did I pass inspection?"

She laughed. "You must have. They're letting me leave with you."

At the restaurant, patrons were seated outside in the pleasantly cool December weather among big-bellied pots of blooming multi-colored impatiens. She and Beau were escorted inside to a table next to a large window. The immediate aromas of earthy truffles, pungent garlic, and sweet basil assailed Grace when she sat on the wooden chair. Strands of white lights hung in swags from the building to the edge of the canvas awning and reflected on the glass like silvery ribbons. The waitress set down two filled shot glasses as they studied the menu.

Grace pointed to the pale, yellow drinks. "What's this?"

"Limoncello. It's a lemon-flavored liqueur the owner makes."

She sipped the fresh and surprisingly strong drink. "I like it."

They ordered a Caprese salad to split. While they waited, Grace counted out twenty sugar packets from the ceramic holder on the table.

Beau watched her with a puzzled expression. "Are you doing inventory?"

"They're for a get-to-know-you activity since that's the purpose of this date." She pushed ten packets toward him. "Every time you ask a question, you lose a packet. Once they're gone, you can't ask any more."

"Sounds like fun. Who goes first?" Grace reached over and returned one of his packets to the white ceramic container. Beau covered the nine he had left. "Hey! I didn't know we started."

"Now you do. My turn." She put one of her packets in with the remaining sugars. "Why did you and Megan divorce?"

"How do you know my ex-wife's name?"

She grabbed a second packet from his pile. "Gen told me."

He waited a beat and wiped his hand across his mouth. "Obviously, she didn't tell you I found her in bed with someone."

Grace winced. His sister had theorized the exact opposite. "No, she said she didn't know the reason for the divorce."

He sat back when the waitress placed a basket of warm yeasty bread on the table. As soon as she left, he said, "Yeah, I haven't shared that information with her. She and my ex-wife were friends from high school. I guess Megan hasn't told Gen what really happened either. The only person who knows the truth is my stepbrother ... and now, you."

Grace recalled Gen's words about Beau's generosity with the settlement. Regardless what his sister believed was the reason for his divorce, Grace would not inform him that Gen placed the infidelity on him.

"Okay, my turn." Beau's words drew Grace's attention back to the game. "How did your husband die?"

She took his third packet away. "He was killed in a traffic accident in Thailand."

"Why was he in Thailand?"

She removed Beau's fourth packet. "Michael said he had meetings in Bangkok the entire week of Christmas. He was going to miss our first holiday with Lily. I began to panic when I couldn't reach him after he missed his return flight."

Their waitress set a bottle of wine and two glasses on the table. Grace buttered a slice of crusty Italian bread, took a bite, and set the rest on her small plate.

Meanwhile, Beau poured the wine. "What did you do?" She slipped his fifth packet into the container, and he smiled at her. "Am I going to have any questions left by the time you finish your story?"

"Probably not." She took away his sixth packet. "First, I called his employer. That's when I received my next surprise. They said he was on vacation, not a business trip and expected back in the office the day after New Year's."

Beau handed her his seventh packet. "What was that all about?"

"At the time, I didn't know. I was angry and frantic, but all I could do was wait." She shook her head with a duh-stupid-me laugh. "I hadn't asked him for the name of his hotel because I always reached him by cell phone or email. I contacted the State Department, but it took another week before I heard back from anyone. I already suspected Michael was dead, but then I was hit with my next surprise."

Beau had a mouth full of bread, so he gestured for her to continue.

Grace smiled. "Do you know your bread just saved your next sugar packet?"

His eyes lit up. He reached across the table, grabbed one of hers, and put it in the container as if it was a tie-breaking ballot in a voting box.

She laughed then grew pensive. "The official on the phone thought I was Michael's mother. He said they had just received notification from the Thai government that the bodies of Mr. and Mrs. Stone had been identified by the manager of the resort."

Chapter 17

BEAU CHOKED AND covered his mouth. He gained control with a quick swallow of water. "You have great timing, Grace. Now I know where Lily gets it. Here are my last packets." He pushed them towards her. "Finish the story."

Before more could be said, the waitress laid a plate of tomato slices, basil leaves, and fresh mozzarella on the table. As Grace divided the salad between their two plates, she said, "I informed the official *I* was the real Mrs. Stone. Talk about an awkward silence. It turned out Michael and his personal assistant had registered at the seaside resort as husband and wife. I stormed to his office and dropped the bomb about my husband and Deirdre being dead and vacationing together while I was home with a newborn. I received an apology and condolences from his boss and was sent on my way."

"Did Michael's family help you out? You had none of your own."

"His father, stepmother, and sister showed up for the funeral and wished me well. They live all over the country. Robert and Tariq were my lifesavers. Within a year, I finished my dissertation and was hired at the university. Work and a baby helped me through the nightmare."

Beau shook his head. "How old were you?"

"Twenty-five."

"I'm amazed you did all that."

She shrugged. "Both you and I had to carry on after being blindsided by the people we loved."

"Yeah, but I wasn't as young as you, with no other family, and a small baby. You had every right to be hit hard by your husband's death and cheating."

Grace took a sip of wine. "After watching my mother's many failed relationships, there's one lesson I learned. It's a waste of time figuring out a philanderer's motivations or agonizing over the clues you missed. The best thing is to drive away and not look back in the rearview mirror."

Beau nodded with a small smile. "You're right. And after four years, going on this date is putting a little more distance between then and now. Tell me about your neighbors. They seem like a great couple."

When their entrees arrived, Grace had just finished relating the trip Tariq and Robert had taken five years ago to pick up Maxi from a Chinese orphanage. She studied the plate of pasta and seafood set on the table. Her first bite of the Frutti di Mare was ambrosia. She ate several more mouthfuls in silence. The small pile of eight sugar packets beside her wine glass beckoned her.

She placed one in the container. "Is your business insurance going to go up because of the accident?"

He sighed. "It might. Likely, it will. You know how insurance companies are. But I'm more concerned with the OSHA ruling."

She deposited her fourth packet. "Do you have family in the area other than your sister and brother-in-law?"

"My dad owns a company called BC Construction. He and my stepmother, Marilyn, live in Deerfield Beach. I have a younger half-sister, Zoe, who's a freshman at Duke."

Grace watched his face and listened to how he talked about his family. The only relative for whom Michael showed affection was his mother, Lillian. She died of cancer when he was in high school. He wanted their baby girl given the old-fashioned name. They compromised on Lily Anne.

Beau chewed his lip. "I also have a stepbrother. He's the one who made me try speed dating."

"Yes, I remember you saying that."

"Skip and I were both there that night. Unlike you, *Gigi*, he went by his real name. Do you remember Scott?"

The blond lawyer. "I do."

"We were both disappointed you didn't put our names down."

"Does your stepbrother know we've met again?"

Beau removed one of her sugar packets. "No, he left the country a month later."

Grace smirked. "Wow. He really was disappointed I didn't match him. All you did was total my car."

Beau laughed aloud. "A week after the speed dating he was notified of a transfer to Dubai for a big construction project. He'll be there for six months to a year. I've told him I'm seeing a woman named Grace Stone, but not that you're Gigi. No sense rubbing salt into the wound, seeing how he's miles from home in a foreign country."

She pushed another packet across the table to him. "Where do you live?"

"I have a townhouse in Pompano Beach. I gave Megan the house we had in Boca."

Grace waved a sugar packet back and forth as she thought of her next question. "What was your first thought when you realized I was the owner of the wrecked BMW?"

Beau's intense gaze made her wobbly around the edges. "I wondered what it would feel like to kiss you."

His answer gave her a tiny shock, like proof that fortune tellers were real and some people could talk to the dead. Both of them had the same thought at the same time. To cover her fluster, Grace scooted her ninth packet toward the sugar container. "When you kissed my cheek the day of the accident, was it because *you* wanted to or because my daughter asked you?"

"That one was for Lily. The ones in your kitchen and garage were for me." His eyes darkened.

Heat gathered between her thighs. "If you kiss me tonight, who's that one going to be for?"

He gave her a wicked smile and reached for her last packet. "There's no if, and that one will definitely be for you."

In Beau's car driving home from the restaurant, Grace studied his profile. What was it about him that made her want to date again? He was bigger and bulkier than Michael or any of the other *boys* she had gone out with before her marriage. Although he was a college graduate, he didn't pursue his degree as a career. He was so different from the suave, preppy guys she had been attracted to in the past. His stepbrother was more her style, but Lily approved of Beau, as did Robert and Tariq. Had she dated and been married to Mr. Wrong in the past?

At her front door, she turned to Beau. "Would you like to come in?" Her voice was breathless with nervousness.

He glanced up at the overhead outdoor light. "Just long enough to say goodnight in private."

Once inside, they embraced and his lips found hers in a long, earth-moving kiss. She quivered under its impact. The glacier which had been her armor and protection for years melted. The mutual exploration of each other's mouths and bodies continued until Beau pulled away.

He spoke between breathless pants. "If we don't stop, blue balls won't just be on your tree."

"You're right," she said with a touch of sadness. It seemed her default state with Beau was often one of regret.

He stepped back but his hands continued to encircle her upper arms. "What are you doing for New Year's Eve?"

"Babysitting three little girls." Grace grimaced as she delivered the bad news. "Weeks ago, I promised to watch the girls, so Robert and Tariq could attend a friend's party."

"How would you like an assistant?"

Chapter 18

BEAU ARRIVED AT seven PM on New Year's Eve with the items he was instructed to bring. From his car he removed three trash bags filled with inflated balloons, a large net, and his camping tent. When the neighbors entered with their daughters, the pop-up shelter was laid out flat on the family room floor.

Robert checked out the snack food on the table, the fixings for s'mores, and plastic champagne glasses in a line on the counter. He spooned some trail mix into his palm. "Looks like there'll be a party here too."

Grace handed him a napkin. "I've planned several activities for the kids. I don't know if we'll get to them all."

Childish squeals sounded from the family room. Beau had pulled the strings which caused the tent to rise in the air. The girls clapped, danced, and hugged each other.

Robert flashed Grace a wicked smile. "Beau seems to be good with getting things to go up."

Tariq took his partner by the arm and led him out of the kitchen. "We have to go. Bye, girls, we'll see you tomorrow."

Distracted farewells sounded from the family room. At the front door, Grace kissed each man's clean-shaven cheek. "Drive carefully. If you need a ride, call. I can send Beau."

"Don't worry." Tariq hugged her. "We're picking up four friends in the minivan, and I'm the designated driver."

When Grace returned to the family room, the comforters she piled on the sofa were inside the tent with pillows and toys. Beau unzipped the last of the side panels to expose netted openings for ventilation. Three little faces propped on their palms peeked out the tent's main entrance as the DVD, *My Little Pony: The Movie,* played on TV.

Beau joined her in the kitchen after he hung the large net high on the living room wall and filled it with the balloons he brought. Grace punched buttons on the microwave panel.

He stood beside her. "Why are you changing the time?"

"Shhh." She glanced into the family room where the girls were still inside the tent. "Take off your watch. We want midnight to arrive at nine o'clock."

Beau put his watch in the front pocket of his jeans.

Grace moved to the oven and changed the readout from seven-thirty to eight-thirty. "Erin and Lily can't really tell time yet, but Maxi is pretty sharp. I've unplugged all the other clocks in the house and put electrical tape over the display on the cable box. Every half-hour I'm moving the time up an hour."

When the DVD ended, everyone trooped outside to the fire pit and melted marshmallows. S'mores were assembled and eaten. The Three Missketeers ran inside to play while Grace and Beau sat on patio chairs as the red-gold embers flickered in the night air.

He licked sticky residue from his fingers. "What's next on your agenda?"

"I have a couple of games planned if we need them. I've learned from Robert's mistake to not force activities on little kids. At Maxi's fifth birthday, she revolted when all she wanted to do was open her gifts, play with them, and eat."

"What's the plan for the balloons?"

"At midnight, or nine PM real time, I have two alarm clocks set to go off in the living room. The girls will stand under the net while you release the balloons. I may regret it, but I bought noise makers for them. Then we'll have 7Up in champagne glasses and make toasts. It'll be the kiddie version of ringing in the New Year."

When the clocks buzzed all at once, the little girls jumped and squealed. They blew into kazoos and giggled with abandon when the net was released and multi-colored balloons rained down on them. Grace and Beau laughed as the children sat on the inflatables to pop them. Erin and Lily were more successful than tiny Maxi.

Grace carried a tray into the living room with plastic stemmed glasses, two of which contained real champagne. "Everyone sit down so I can give you your drink."

It took a minute to settle the excited youngsters. They sat on the floor with their legs crossed. Grace handed them each a glass. "Hold still and don't drink yet. Everyone will make a toast about the New Year."

Lily looked around. "We're having toast?"

"A toast is when you say something nice about someone or something then take a drink. It's like making a wish before blowing out birthday candles."

Beau raised his glass in the air. "I'll start. Here's to all the beautiful girls I'm lucky enough to be with on New Year's Eve."

All the beautiful girls smiled, some giggled.

"Now everyone sip your drink." Grace demonstrated with a delicate taste of the crisp, bubbly Brut.

Maxi raised her hand. "Me, next." She waited until everyone quieted. "Here's to the best New Year's Eve party ever."

After more sips and noisy slurps, Erin spoke up. "Me now, Gwace?"

"Sure, honey."

"No moah chicken pox."

Grace raised her glass. "That's a good toast, Erin." Everyone drank their libation. "Do you want to go next, Lily?"

"No, you go, Mommy. I'm still thinking."

Grace's smile faltered as trepidation crept through her. Maybe Lily won't say something inappropriate to Beau. Then again, who was she kidding? "I wish a healthy and happy New Year to everyone we care about and love."

While the others sipped, Grace braced herself with a healthy swallow and tried subliminal mind control on her daughter. Please, please, please don't wish Mr. Beau will be your daddy. She glanced over at him. He watched Lily with the corners of his mouth lifted in amusement.

The little girl raised her glass in the air like Grace and Beau when they toasted. "My friends, Mommy, and Mr. Beau. I love, love, love, love you." She looked at each one as she repeated the word.

Grace breathed a sigh of relief and drained her glass. "Okay, girls, now that we've welcomed in the New Year, it's time to get ready for bed. Finish your drinks then you need to brush your teeth."

Two hours later, Beau and Grace sat on the family room sofa and waited for Erin to fall asleep while *Enchanted* played on TV. Maxi and Lily slumbered within minutes of lying down. Several times as the movie played, Beau leaned forward, peeked through one of the netted openings at Erin, sat back, and shook his head. When the film ended, the three-year-old lay down, closed her eyes, and she was asleep.

"I thought she would be up all night." Beau switched off the DVD player with the remote.

"Erin's been that way since infancy. She's also a very light sleeper, so let's talk elsewhere."

They sat on the patio in a two-person glider. The air was nippy, and gooseflesh stippled Grace's arms. She leaned close to Beau and patted his leg. "Thank you for your help tonight. I know it wasn't exactly a thrilling party for you."

He wrapped a warm, weighty arm around her. "It was better than being alone or with annoying drunks."

She rubbed a bump on his thigh. "Is that your watch I feel?"

"Maybe, or I'm just happy the kids are asleep."

Grace gave him a soft punch. "I was wondering what time it really is."

He removed his arm from her shoulders, straightened his leg, and with effort pulled the timepiece from his pocket. "Fifteen minutes until the new year."

He strapped the watch onto his wrist. They sat in comfortable silence. At midnight, cheers sounded from a nearby house where an adult party was in full swing. Beau stood and pulled Grace to her feet. She intertwined her fingers behind his neck.

He held her flush against his body. "Happy New Year, Grace."

"Happy New Year, Beau."

As the revilers' noisy celebration continued, he kissed her with passion. His body radiated heat and was granite-hard against hers from chest to knees. The whistle shriek of a bottle rocket climbed into the air then exploded with a concussive bang.

Grace jumped. "Oh, my God! That's going to wake Erin."

They rushed to close the open sliding doors. She tiptoed to the family room, bent down, and peeked into the tent. The youngest child was still asleep. With the doors closed, the neighbors' fireworks were audible but muted.

When she joined Beau in the kitchen, he stifled a yawn. "Sorry."

Grace patted his back. "I think it's time we went to bed too. The kids wake up early."

He hugged her and headed to the guest room down the hall where she had him put his overnight bag. Grace changed into a knee-length football jersey, washed her face, and brushed her teeth. She carried a bedsheet into the family room and told herself she was not concerned with Beau sleeping on one side of the house, her on the other, and the three little girls in the middle. Still she unfolded a sheet, put half of it on the family room sofa, lay down, and covered herself with the rest.

The three little girls, who were tumbled together inside the tent like a litter of puppies, made a variety of snorts, snuffles, and squeaks as they slept. Through the walls of the house, fireworks or, God forbid, gunfire sounded at intermittent intervals. But, these noises were not what kept Grace awake late into the night. Instead the handsome, charming, intriguing, and passionate man in the bedroom just down the hall was the reason she was restless and unable to fall asleep until well into the New Year.

Chapter 19

"IS GWACE ASWEEP?"

She opened her eyes then squeezed them shut against the too-bright sunlight.

"Mommy's awake."

"Just barely." The masculine voice jolted her into full consciousness.

Beau stood at the end of the sofa by her feet, a coffee cup in his hand. Next to him was Erin with a spoon clutched in her fist. Maxi held a glass half-filled with milk. Lily cupped a bowl of cereal in her palms. Everyone grinned at her.

Beau looked way too attractive so early in the morning. "We have your breakfast ready, Sleeping Beauty."

"Eat, Mommy. We made you food."

Maxi stared at the glass in her hand. "Mr. Beau and us already ate."

Erin piped in. "Outside."

Grace's eyes bounced from Beau to the girls and back to him again like a criminal surrounded by police. Her now-thwarted plan had been to wake up early, get dressed, and put on makeup. She patted the lopsided ponytail on top of her head and scrunched under the sheet until only her eyes and hair showed. "Why don't you put everything on the table? I'll come to the breakfast room after I get dressed."

Beau frowned. "C'mon, Grace. We went to all the trouble to bring you breakfast in bed."

The bowl of cereal and glass of milk became less stable in the children's hands. With reluctance to reveal her morning self, she pulled down the sheet and scooted into a seated position. Lily handed her the bowl. Maxi stepped forward and poured the milk. Erin plopped in the spoon.

She took a mouthful, chewed, and swallowed. "It's good."

The girls beamed and watched her take one more bite then spun around as if cued. Before racing from the room, Maxi handed the empty glass of milk to Beau.

Grace gave him a wry smile and patted her hair. "I must look like a one-eared albino bunny."

"I love albino bunnies."

She eyed the cup of coffee he held in his one hand. "Is that for me?"

"It's probably cold now. Let me get you a fresh one."

When he had taken several steps, she set the cereal bowl on the side table and tossed the sheet aside. "I'll get dressed first." She hurried past him, pulling down the hem of her football jersey.

An amused chuckle sounded behind her. "If you're trying to hide your cute little tail, it's not working."

Grace grinned and hustled to her bedroom.

Chapter 20

THE FOLLOWING WEEKEND the Mahmoud/Chan clan went to Tampa for a birthday at Tariq's sister's house. That meant Grace didn't have a babysitter for Lily. She tried contacting several people without success.

On Friday, she called Beau to decline his invitation for a second weekend date. "I'm sorry, but I can't get a sitter for tomorrow night."

"Then let's take Lily with us."

"She needs to be in bed by nine o'clock at the latest, so we'll need to eat early."

"I have an idea. See what's playing at the Swap Shop."

The daytime flea market in Sunrise was located on the grounds of a nighttime drive-in theater. They found a G-rated film suitable for Lily. Grace lowered one of the rear seat backs in her Highlander, fixed up the now-flat section with a comforter, pillows, and toys. Lily climbed into her booster seat dressed in pajamas and slippers. On the way, Beau picked up pizza and soft drinks.

When the movie started, Lily sat cross-legged on her makeshift bed and munched a square of pizza. "This is fun. I love my first date."

Halfway through the movie, Beau twisted in the driver's seat. "She's asleep."

Grace checked. "I thought she would last longer. She really wanted to see *Paddington 2*."

Facing the screen again, Beau asked, "Should we stay until it ends, in case she wakes up?"

"That's not likely. I'm ready to go if you are."

After Grace secured Lily who remained half-asleep into her booster seat, Beau replaced the speaker on the stand outside his door, started the engine, and drove out the theater gate. "Do you want to stop anywhere on the way home?"

Grace shook her head. "I have wine chilling and tiramisu in the refrigerator. Let's head back to my house."

After settling Lily in bed, Grace returned to the kitchen. Beau had decanted the Prosecco, added ice to a wine bucket, poured out two fluted glasses, and carried everything into the living room. Grace followed with the dishes of the Italian custard, forks, and napkins.

The only illumination was from the lights on the Christmas tree, the Dickens village on top of a glass-fronted bookcase, and the kitchen high hats. After she placed the dessert tray on the coffee table, Grace dropped onto the sofa and patted the cushion next to her. Beau sat, and she handed him a dish and fork.

He glanced at the Christmas decorations around the room. "My stepmother had my father take down their tree before New Year's Eve. Of course, it was a real pine and drying out. How long do you keep your artificial one up?"

"I had planned to put all the decorations away last week, but Lily insisted it was too soon. She hates for the holiday to end, but I'll have to start tomorrow. Since I'm back to work on Monday, it'll probably take me until next weekend to get everything packed up and into the crawl space over the garage."

Beau dug into the tiramisu, took a big bite, and swallowed. "I don't have any plans for tomorrow. If you want, I can help."

His offer touched her. She hadn't expected him to volunteer when she told him about the delayed takedown. Michael rarely assisted with around-the-house chores, even when she asked. Grace either had to do them herself or hire someone.

"Thank you. I can only give Lily small jobs to do." She studied his long legs and the eight-foot-tall tree. "Your help would speed the packing along."

They drank wine, finished the dessert, refilled their glasses, and talked.

He told her about his early childhood in a small town outside of Quebec and his own mother's death. "Our family came here because of the booming construction industry when I was eight, and Gen was five. The move was harder on her than me. She missed our Canadian relatives. Less than a year later, *ma mère* was diagnosed with cervical cancer and died. We were all devastated, but Gen didn't get over her death for a long time. That's when she became so protective of *her family*."

"What do you mean by protective?"

"Dad began to date about two years after *ma mère's* death. I guess he was lonely. You can't blame him since he was a single father with two kids and away from his own siblings. He said when he met Marilyn, he fell in love and knew she would be a good stepmother for us. She was divorced and her son, Skip, was between my sister and me in age. But Gen wasn't having any of it. A stepmother and a stepbrother, I mean. It took a lot of persuasion on my dad's part to convince Marilyn to take us all on. Thank God, she did."

"Did Gen finally accept her and Skip?"

Beau's knee jiggled. His big hand cupped the joint to still it. "It was a rough couple of years at first. Gen was pretty hostile. When she was a little older, I think she was glad to have another female in the house. Then Marilyn had Zoe, which finally made her family in my sister's eyes."

Time passed, and the level of wine in the bottle lowered quite a bit. The alcohol seemed to raise Grace's body temperature more than usual. She shrugged out of the cotton blouse she wore over a tank top. For the next hour, not once did the conversation between them lag. One topic flowed into the next with the ease of people who had been friends for years rather than acquaintances for a few weeks.

Grace stared at Beau in the flickering light. As he talked, she categorized him as a man of four letter words: duty, care, work, and home. Was love another of those words, despite what his sister said?

Beau frowned at her fixed gaze. "What?"

Grace shook her head. "Nothing. It's just that you're an easy guy to talk with. I haven't had this long a conversation with a man in years."

He raised an eyebrow. "Yeah, I'm a regular Dr. Phil."

She tipped back her head and drank the last of the wine in her glass. After she placed the goblet on the coffee table, Grace slipped off her sandals and tucked her legs under her. She scooted towards him and curled against his side. Beau lifted his arm and placed it around her shoulders. She snuggled closer. His firm palm caressed the bare skin above her elbow in an absentminded manner, like the soothing stroking of a beloved pet.

She, in turn, was mesmerized by the twinkling lights and his solid body, imprinting itself against her own softer, more malleable one. He had such a strong sensual and sexual effect on her at the oddest times. When she folded laundry just out of the dryer, she recalled his gaze on her, warmer than the heat of the sun on her skin. Even the smell of lemon Pledge reminded her of the limoncello on their dinner date. When the house was quiet, the deep, sexy timbre of his voice sounded in her head.

Get a grip, Grace. You're the twenty-nine-year-old mother of a pre-schooler. Next, you'll be dotting i's with little hearts.

But being a mature, level-headed professional didn't make her smile at odd moments, which she caught herself doing lately. It was like her life was now a shaken snow globe and glittery bits of excitement floated in the space around her. Nearly a month ago, she almost forgot her scruples and ignored the strict control she maintained for herself in the garage with Beau. Since that night, sex had been on her mind almost constantly, like she was a teenage boy with out-of-control hormones. Slightly pornographic images flitted across her thoughts at the least expected times, leaving her unsettled as well as damp. Her rusty, ignored femininity creaked back to life as she caught herself looking at men, not in a sexual manner, but in an appreciative, aesthetic way.

Beau's hand moved under her arm and rested on her ribcage, just below her left breast. She slid her hand across the muscles of his abdomen and lifted her face to his. He sealed his mouth to hers, and his tongue slipped inside. Their kisses grew wetter and hotter until low moans of need spilled from both of them.

Without warning, Beau sat up straight which forced Grace to put out a hand to prevent toppling over onto his lap. He picked up the near-empty wine bottle, tipped it over her glass, and with a husky voice said, "Would you like more?"

"Why? Are you trying to get me drunk?"

"Absolutely not." He set the bottle back into the bucket. "I want you to know what you're doing at all times."

She didn't move or speak for several seconds, then straightened her legs, and put her feet on the floor. Grace rose to her feet in a decisive manner, as if a troublesome conclusion had been reached at last. A slight wobble caused her to lilt a bit to the side. She attempted to cover the rush to her head by bending forward and placing her wine glass on the wooden tray with one hand while the other lay flat on the glass-topped coffee table. The delay gave her a second chance to rethink her decision. When she stood again with her chin up, the fogginess had dissipated enough for her to be fully aware of what she was about to do. Grace stepped over Beau's feet and patted across the living room.

At her bedroom door, she stopped and looked over her shoulder. "Are you coming? That couch isn't big enough for the both of us."

Beau's face was in shadow and prevented her from reading his expression, but his words were loud and clear. "Are you sure about this, Grace?"

I want this. I need this. "Yes, I am."

Chapter 21

IN HER BEDROOM, moonlight beamed through a high window and a night light glowed near the floor. Beau's footsteps across the tiled living room muted when he stepped onto the bedroom carpeting. Grace reached the bed and turned to find him a step behind her. She lifted her arms and wrapped them around his neck. He bent forward, slipped one arm behind her back, the other behind her knees, and lifted her into his arms. She was lowered to the bed, one foot at a time, as if to give her an opportunity to call a halt. He needn't worry. Her slight buzz wasn't false courage, but relaxed confidence.

Beau followed her down, lying on his side next to her. To Grace's surprise, he seemed somewhat nervous. His free hand rested on her abdomen. He inched it closer to her breast but retreated back to her navel before making contact. He lowered his head. She raised her chin. He leaned closer. Grace waited for the soft brush of his breath on her face, but it never came.

Except for his awkwardness at speed dating, Beau always appeared certain and confident, in contrast to her own fear and indecision. Now his reluctance to take control was disconcerting.

Their lips finally came together with whisper softness. The arm beneath her neck tightened, and Beau deepened the kiss. Soon their breathing became ragged as air was dragged in and released with sharp puffs against each other's cheeks.

Beau broke the kiss. His hand moved to her face and stroked her skin with the backs of his fingers. "Are you sure about this, Grace?"

How many times is he going to ask? "Are you?"

He swooped in and kissed her, as if in answer to her question.

Chapter 22

AFTERWARDS, GRACE LAY with the heavy warmth of Beau's body covering hers. It had been so long since the weight of a man encompassed her, and she couldn't help comparing the feel of Beau to that of her dead husband. Michael was not as tall, and he had less bulk; at least, when they first became lovers. After they were married, he added some pudginess to his mid-section. He attributed it to working longer hours at the office, but Grace pointed out his increased beer and alcohol consumption. Michael's reaction had been to lash out at her expanding waistline. She was four months pregnant at the time.

Beau bent his elbows and raised himself off her. "Talk to me, Grace."

She didn't answer, unsure what to express to a new lover.

The rumble of Beau's chuckle vibrated on her chest when he said, "The English professor has nothing to say?"

"Do you want me to talk nerdy to you?" She giggled and ran her hands up and down his muscular back. Without thought, she curled her fingers and brushed his skin with her nails.

He moaned. "Do it again."

"Do what again?"

"Scratch my back."

"Are you sure?" She didn't wait for his reply and smiled at his groan of pleasure.

Eventually, they crawled up to the pillows. Grace lay curled in his arms with his front pressed to her back. They spooned for several minutes.

Beau checked his watch. "I better get dressed."

Grace lowered his wrist and looked at the illuminated dial. She pulled his hand to her chest again. "Yes, but this feels so nice."

"I take it you wouldn't want Lily to find me here in the morning."

"One thing I learned from my mother was that a woman needs to keep her sex life and her child separate. But let's snuggle a little, and maybe …" She wiggled her bottom against him.

Chapter 23

THE MORNING LIGHT awakened Grace. She lay on her side, curled like a cat in a quivering sunbeam streaming in from a window near the bedroom's slanted ceiling. She squinted at the clock which read six-thirty. Lily would be awake soon. The sheets touched her bare skin everywhere. She rolled over, and her arm bumped against a hard object.

Staring at a broad, bare back, she jumped out of bed onto a pile of discarded clothes. Grace grabbed her pants and pulled them on. She spun in a circle and spotted her tank top lying against the wall.

Lily's voice came from the direction of the kitchen. "Mommy."

As Grace hurried to her bedroom door, she turned the tank top right side out and pulled it over her head. She blocked the doorway as Lily was about to enter. "You're up early, honey. Are you hungry?" She spun her daughter around and herded her away from the bedroom.

The little girl looked at her mother over her shoulder. "You're not wearing pajamas."

Grace glanced down at her wrinkled outfit. "I laid on my bed to rest and fell asleep with my clothes on."

"Uh-oh. You didn't brush your teeth."

"Look who's talking. You fell asleep during the movie and didn't brush *your* teeth either. You know what? We should do that before we have breakfast." She followed Lily to her bathroom. The little girl stepped up on a stool. Grace squirted a line of toothpaste onto the child-sized brush and set a timer for two minutes.

Once Lily's mouth was full of toothpaste, Grace said, "I'm going to brush *my* teeth now."

She strolled out of the bathroom and flew to the other side of the house. In her bedroom, Beau was dressed. He looked up from tying his shoelaces.

"We've got about ninety seconds." She grabbed his hand and pulled him to the front door. With cautious slowness, she unlocked it without a sound.

He stepped outside and turned. "Grace, I—"

"Go drive around for twenty minutes then call me." Before he could say anything else, she shut the door and raced to her bathroom. Her cell phone rang five minutes later. She fished the device out of her purse as she pulled a brush through her tangled locks. "I need another ten minutes."

"Is that all it takes?" Robert replied in a sardonic tone.

"Oh, it's you."

"Good morning to you too, Sunshine. Was that Beau's car still in your driveway this morning?"

"You know it was. We fell asleep. I got him out of here before Lily saw him. He's coming back to help me take down my Christmas decorations."

"We're on our way to your house with pancake mix and coffee. The girls decided we should visit and have breakfast with you guys."

"The *girls* decided?"

"Who else?" Robert's voice was syrupy.

"Who else indeed."

Beau called Grace ten minutes later. "Hi. Is it okay to come in now?"

"Sure. The more the merrier. Robert is making waffles and Tariq is brewing his famous coffee. The front door's unlocked."

An hour later, Lily followed the neighbors out of the kitchen as they headed home.

"Hey," said Beau. "I thought you were going to help me take down the tree."

Lily waved. "I will. But I have to play first."

When the front door slammed shut, Beau looked at Grace over the rim of his coffee cup. "When will she be back?"

"Probably around lunchtime."

"I'm sorry I didn't go home last night."

Grace shrugged. "It's as much my fault as yours. I'm just glad I woke up in time. We need to ensure our privacy in the future."

As a child, she often stayed in the guesthouse on her mother's property with a babysitter. For Juliette, the separate cottage wasn't a luxury, but a necessity. Her lovers didn't have to be hustled off the premises like an informant after giving testimony at a mobster's trial.

"I'll do whatever you decide is best." Beau rose from his seat and carried his coffee cup to the sink. "Now let's get busy taking down that tree since Lily is hoping we'll have it done before she gets home."

Chapter 24

WHEN GRACE RETURNED to work, it had been almost four weeks since her car was totaled. Although it was old news to her, people in the English department inquired about the accident as if it happened yesterday.

Alice came into Grace's office at lunchtime. "Do you want to grab a bite to eat?"

"Sure, but I have to be back for a meeting at two."

They headed to the Faculty and Staff dining room. After getting their food, they found two empty seats. Alice tore the plastic off her prepared salad. "Will was gloating this morning about your ill-fated parking spot."

Grace tore open the cellophane around her sandwich. "I expected Whine-Hard would have something to say."

She and Dr. William Reinhardt had been hired the same year. He was a beanpole of a man with Draculean skin. Reinhardt complained without success when Grace was assigned to the parking lot across from the Arts and Humanities building. His second gripe, which reached her ears, was after she received her associate professorship. It was unusual, although not unheard of, to achieve that level in academia after only three years of employment.

When her tenure approval was announced at the beginning of the fall semester, he had flashed a smile thick with mock charm. "Dr. Black-Stone, I guess congratulations are in order. You should be aware, however, of a rumor that you're dating one of the trustees. Of course, no one intimated your social life influenced your good fortune, but I'm just sharing with you what is going around."

Grace maintained a cordial working relationship with the man by util-
izing avoidance techniques. When forced to interact with him, she would
smile, suppress an eye roll, and reply with a veneer of polite civility.

Alice, on the other hand, urged her to deal with his passive aggressive-
ness head-on. "One day, you're going to need to confront Whine-Hard. His
less-than-subtle digs will only continue and worsen over time."

Grace suspected her friend was correct. So far, his gripes and complaints
only created negative reactions which reflected poorly on him, rather than
her.

Alice poured dressing on her salad. "How did you get home after the
accident?"

Grace lowered her eyes as a secret smile lifted the corners of her lips.

"Ha!" Alice's exclamation caused nearby diners to look their way. She
softened her volume. "I know some man is responsible for your grin."

"The owner of the crane company gave me and Lily a ride back to our
house."

Alice cocked her head and studied Grace. "There's more to this story.
C'mon, talk."

"Do you remember Beau from speed dating? The Republican with the
shirttail."

"Oh, my God. He's the guy who totaled your car?"

"Someone who works for him did. Since the accident, he and I have
been seeing each other."

"Naked?"

"That too."

"Hot damn. It's about time. I want details."

Grace's cheeks burned as she chewed her chicken salad sandwich and
avoided eye contact with her friend.

Alice extended her hand across the table. "Why are you embarrassed?
You've been a widow for the last four years and are in the prime of your life.
Now tell me all about it."

Grace put down her sandwich. She recounted the day of the accident
and her involvement with Beau since then. "He's very different than Michael,
but I'm really attracted to him."

"How does he feel about Lily and vice versa?"

"She's thrilled having a man in our lives, and he seems to enjoy her company. On New Year's Eve, he spent the night helping me babysit the three Missketeers."

"He slept over?"

"In the guest room."

Alice sat back in her chair. "Maybe this guy is a keeper."

Grace hoped he was too.

Chapter 25

THE CHARVET CRANE equipment had been in place at the construction site when Grace parked her car in the faculty lot that morning. But when she left work, it was gone. Of course, Beau and his crew would not remain across the street forever. Once they lifted whatever needed raised, they moved on to the next job. The disappointment of not seeing his name in large blue letters surprised her.

On Friday after her yoga class, she sat down with Robert and Tariq for their usual morning coffee. "I need to talk to you two about something."

Grace had an agreement with them for babysitting services on her workdays when Lily wasn't in preschool. Both men insisted since there were two of them and they had two kids, they owed her more than twice the amount of babysitting time she owed them. But Grace was always cognizant of not abusing Robert's status as a stay-at-home dad/trophy husband.

Tariq put down his cup. "That sounds ominous."

"Now that I'm seeing Beau, I don't want to always impose on you to watch Lily. I'm thinking about looking for a high school student to babysit her, but I wanted to talk to you two first."

The men looked at each other and said nothing.

Grace continued in a rush. "I can even hire somebody to watch all three girls on the same night, so you can go out too. What do you think?"

Tariq patted her arm. "We love having Lily here, and you've never imposed."

"But my weekends won't be as free as they've been in the past. I don't want to offend you by hiring an outside sitter."

Robert laid his hand on top of hers. "When you have a date with Beau, just tell us. If we can watch Lily, we will. If not, you can get some hare-brained teenager who has a meth-head boyfriend to do it."

The plan was for Maxi and Erin to sleep over at Grace's house on Friday evenings so their fathers could go out to dinner and have the house to themselves until late Saturday morning. Lily would stay with them Saturday night and Sunday morning. The arrangement would start that evening.

Grace called Beau when she got home. "We're on for tomorrow night. What if I meet you at the restaurant and follow you home? Then you don't have to drive me back here on Sunday."

"That cuts down on the time we spend together. Besides I won't get to see Lily. I don't mind picking you up and taking you home. My stepmother pounded into me and Skip that a gentleman always picks up his date and sees her safely to the door."

"Just promise you won't be too much of a gentleman."

"I can't help it since you're such a lady."

"A lady doesn't do the things I've done with you."

Beau's voice went low and husky. "Mine does."

Chapter 26

WHEN BEAU ARRIVED on Saturday evening, Lily greeted him at the door with a drawing she made. She held it to her chest and squirmed in place.

He squatted on his heels in front of her. "What have you got there, Miss Lily?"

"I drawed a picture for you."

As soon as Lily handed him her artwork, Grace spun around and went into the kitchen.

Behind her, Beau said, "Oh, wow."

Grace wiped the counter and drank a glass of water until her daughter bounced into the room and hugged her around the legs. "Mr. Beau likes my picture."

"I'm sure he does. It's wonderful. I've got your clothes ready, but you need to put the toys you want in your backpack." As Lily hustled to her bedroom, Grace forced a smile and turned to face Beau who now stood in the kitchen doorway.

He waved the paper at her. "You are a cruel woman, Grace Stone."

"I'm sorry. I just couldn't be there when she gave it to you." She walked forward, laid her head on his chest, and hugged him around the waist. They viewed Lily's drawing with snorts and chuckles.

"I get that I'm the guy. She explained this," he pointed to the drawing, "is your flattened BMW and the erection on it is the I-beam. But what is the ejaculation coming out the end?"

"It's the broken chain that dropped the giant penis on my car."

Beau's chest rumbled with laughter. "I told Lily I'm going to frame this and hang it in my office."

They walked the little girl next door, and when she ran off with her friends, Beau turned to Robert and Tariq. "Lily did a drawing of me and the wrecked BMW. You want to see it?"

Grace covered her mouth with her hand. Beau gave the drawing to Tariq who doubled over with laughter.

Robert snatched it from his partner's hand. "Oh my God."

All four adults hooted and giggled.

"Stop." Grace swiped her index fingers under each eye. "Or I'm going to have to redo my makeup."

Robert shook his head. "Well, *I'm* going to have to redo my impression of your accident."

After Beau and Grace left the neighbors' house, they drove to a sushi restaurant for dinner then headed to his townhouse. He parked and grabbed her overnight bag from the trunk. "Now don't expect too much. Megan got all the good stuff in the divorce."

He unlocked the front door and hit light switches to illuminate the tiled entryway. On the left was a kitchen which consisted of builder grade cabinets, white appliances, and laminate countertops. Straight ahead was a large room which doubled as a dining and living room. A brass light fixture hung over a rectangular wood table with four chairs. Oversized faux-leather furniture and a three-piece, veneered entertainment unit filled the living room.

Beau walked through an opening across the hall from the kitchen and pointed to his right. "That's my office. In the middle is the only bathroom. To the left is the bedroom."

Grace headed that direction. A king-sized bed was against one wall with a flat screen TV mounted above a low dresser.

Beau laid her overnight bag on a canvas chair in the corner. "What do you think?"

"I thought it would look like a frat house, but it doesn't, although the furniture in the other rooms is a bit dated."

"I bought it furnished."

She pointed at the large TV on the wall. "Including that?"

"The TV, the bed, and the office furniture are all new."

Grace sat down and bounced on the mattress. Beau stood in front of her. She rose to her feet and unbuttoned his shirt. Her hands glided over his rock-hard chest and tight stomach muscles. He had told her his beard required him to shave twice a day, but his skin could only tolerate it once. By mid-afternoon his face was always shadowed in dark whiskers. Despite his hirsute cheeks, his chest, back, and abdomen were almost hairless. His body was her new secret fantasy.

She kissed his neck. "I want you naked."

He toed off his shoes and stepped out of his pants and boxers. His hands roved up and down her back. "You're still dressed."

Grace kicked her shoes off and shimmied out of her pants and panties. When she straightened, Beau picked her up and tossed her into the middle of the mattress.

He climbed on the bed and pulled her on top of him. "You still have on too many clothes."

She sat up, straddled his waist, and grabbed the hem of her shirt. With incredible slowness, she raised her top inch-by-inch until it cleared her head. Leaning forward, she teased the corners of his mouth with light kisses. Beau reached behind her and fumbled with the bra clasp while she licked his ear and feathered kisses along his jawline. When the fastener loosened, she sat upright again and the lacy pink bra slipped down her arms. Beau cupped her breasts. She closed her eyes and sighed.

"You're beautiful. So …"

Grace leaned forward and kissed him. One of his hands tunneled through her hair. The other slid between their bodies. He turned her to liquid with the light caress.

As she rose onto her knees, his fingers closed around her wrist and guided her. "You do it. You're in charge."

Later, Grace propped her elbows on Beau's chest and studied his tattoo. It started above his left nipple and finished on the right in dark blue lettering.

Aimer toutes les femmes   *Faire confiance à um peu*

She ran her fingertips over the words. "What does this mean?"

Beau dipped his chin. "Love all women, trust few. A word of advice: never get a tattoo right after a divorce."

"It's similar to something from Shakespeare's *All's Well That Ends Well*. But, I think, the quote says *love all, trust few, do wrong to none*."

"It hurt so much I told the guy to just do the first two parts." He lifted his head with a droll smile and captured her lips.

Although Grace kissed him back, she was troubled Beau didn't add the last four words, despite the pain additional inking would have caused him.

Chapter 27

ON MONDAY THE university was closed for the Martin Luther King holiday. Months earlier, Grace had scheduled an appointment with her gynecologist on this day off. During the exam, she told her doctor she was sexually active again. The two women discussed methods of birth control and chose the Depo-Provera shot.

Dr. Devaney stopped at the door of the exam room before she exited. "D-P will provide immediate protection and lasts for three months, but you have to remember to get the injection. I recommend you schedule your next appointment before you leave today."

Grace invited Beau for dinner Saturday night with her and the three little girls. Robert and Tariq had tickets for a Broadway musical at the Broward Center for Performing Arts. Lily begged for another weenie roast since her friends were spending the night. After the kids were fed, the adults sat alone on the patio with the doors open.

Beau smiled at her. "The last time we did this, I had no idea of all the great things you could do with a weenie."

Grace laughed. "Since we're on the subject, I went to my gynecologist this week. I'm taking the D-P shot instead of going back on The Pill."

"So, no more—"

"That's right."

A wide smile split Beau's face but disappeared when squeals came from inside the house. "Did you have to tell me this weekend?"

"It wouldn't matter. It's my time of the month. You're going to have to wait no matter what."

A week later on their regularly scheduled Saturday evening, they lay in satiated exhaustion on Beau's bed. He rolled over to face her. "How would you like to be my date next month for The Discovery Ball?"

"What's that?"

"It's a fancy fundraiser at The Breakers hotel in Palm Beach. They raise money for cancer research. My dad and I have our two companies buy tickets every year in honor of my mother. I haven't gone since my divorce, but I'd like to take you. Dad and Marilyn will be there. Gen has Tom's dealership buy tickets also. I don't know if they're going, or if he'll give them to one of his managers. It's a nice evening event with dinner, dancing, and auctions."

Grace remained silent.

Beau pushed up on an elbow. "What's wrong?"

She dropped her gaze to his chest as her finger wrote in invisible script across his pectoral muscles *do wrong to none*. "Do you think it's a good idea for your parents to meet me at this charity ball for the first time?"

"They're going to have to meet you somewhere. We'll only have dinner with them. Besides, I want to show you off. You'll be the pretty professor on the arm of a rough construction guy."

A paradoxical picture flashed through Grace's mind in which Beau wore a hard hat, jeans, and work boots while the Palm Beach elite in tuxedoes and ball gowns stared at him. She studied his hopeful expression. "How fancy is this fundraiser?"

"I have to wear the tux I bought for my sister's wedding. Will you go with me?"

"I'd be proud to be your date."

"It'll be our version of The Lady and the Tramp."

A thought flitted through her mind as she lay naked beside her lover. Would his family wonder which one she was? For the first time in a long time, she enjoyed being pleasantly promiscuous. Like a character from *Sex and City*, she was a young career woman with a lover. The one difference being she had a child and a respected teaching position at a university.

When Grace told Robert about the event, he offered to help her get ready. "I was born to be a stylist. Maybe one day when the girls are older, I'll pursue that as a career. You know, I have subscriptions to all the best fashion magazines."

She showed him several of her mother's gowns stored in the back of her closet. "Maybe one of Juliette's dresses might work, and I won't have to buy a new one. I kept three and sent the rest to a consignment shop." She unzipped the plastic cover on a royal blue Versace dress. "I'm sure she didn't pay for any of these."

Robert chose a floor-length, amethyst silk chiffon by Dior with a knotted one-shoulder strap. The gown fit close to her body through the bodice and drop waist. "It's perfect and reminds me of a Princess Diana dress. I remember the comments because she wore a jeweled choker as a headband."

Grace held the gown at arm's length and viewed it with a critical eye. "Are you sure it doesn't look dated?"

"Couture never goes out of style. Celebrities wear vintage designer pieces on the red carpet all the time." He lifted a handful of fabric and sniffed. "It smells a bit musty. Hang it outside in a shady spot for a day or so, and it should be fine."

On the day of the ball, Grace used a birthday gift certificate Robert and Tariq gave her for a manicure, pedicure, and massage at a nearby day spa. While she lay on the heated table with her face cradled in a cushioned ring, the masseuse told her to relax several times. All her muscles were tense with the anticipation of meeting the parents of a man she was dating. Added to that was the knowledge that Beau's sister and brother-in-law would also be in attendance.

Robert came to the house two hours before Beau was to pick her up. He pulled her hair tight to the back of her head and wove the long ponytail into an intricate bun. The makeup he applied was much heavier than she usually wore.

Grace searched through her jewelry box. "Chandelier earrings, gold hoops, or pearl studs?"

He tilted his head to the side. "Hmmm. I think you should stick with the pearl studs. Put on the diamond tennis bracelet Michael gave you then it'll be perfect."

It was six-fifteen and Beau was due any minute. Grace's heart stopped when she saw her reflection in the full-length mirror. "Oh, Robert."

"Beautiful, isn't it?" He clapped his hands to his chest.

My God! She looked like her mother had come back from the dead.

The doorbell rang.

Robert air-kissed her near both cheeks and headed to the French doors in the bedroom. "Go and have a great time."

Grace stared at her reflection until an impatient knock sounded. When she swung the front door open, she gaped. Beau was dressed in a traditional black tuxedo and white tucked shirt which made him appear suave, sexy, and debonair. His face was the most clean-shaven she had ever seen it. With his long legs, broad chest, and shoulders, he was a splendid specimen of masculine civility overlaid with sheer magnetism. His looks were far too rugged to be considered classically handsome, but her heart beat faster with his blatant masculine appeal. His eyes scanned her with a heat that could have melted glass.

Grace recovered first. "Aren't we pretty?"

Beau stepped inside. "I don't know about me, but *you* certainly are." He wrapped his arm around her waist and pulled her to him.

"Don't mess me up. I'll never be able to fix my hair and makeup without Robert's help."

He lightly touched his lips to hers. "If I hadn't shaved so close and dusted off this monkey suit, I'd say let's forget about going, but Dad and Marilyn are expecting us. Are you ready to leave?"

"I just need to get my purse from the bedroom. I'll be right back."

Grace grabbed her satin clutch from the bed and went to the French doors to lock them. She gasped when Robert's face appeared. He sported a wide grin and gave her two thumbs up. She waved goodbye, turned out the lights, and left for her first charity ball.

Chapter 28

GRACE HAD NEVER been to the landmark Breakers hotel, although she lived less than an hour away all her life. Its lighted twin towers were visible in the night sky when they crossed the bridge which spanned the Intracoastal Waterway onto the island of Palm Beach. The drive to the entrance was an avenue of tall palms, swaying in the evening's ocean breezes. They waited several minutes until a valet was available to take Beau's car. Grace's stomach was fluttery with the feeling one gets at the top of a roller coaster's largest hill, scared but excited.

Inside the hotel, the lobby stretched a football field long and resembled the hall of a great Italian palazzo, adorned with a barrel vaulted ceiling and tall arched windows. Large floral arrangements of fragrant dahlias and colorful chrysanthemums were combined with silvery grasses and greenery on tables and credenzas.

The gala event was in the Venetian Ballroom where Grace stifled the urge to gawk at the massive chandeliers and both woodwork and fabric in a glowing gold hue. The windows looked onto the Atlantic Ocean, but at this time of night, the scene was a palette of moonbeams on inky velvet beyond the landscape lighting.

"I see Dad." Beau pointed to a distinguished man in a tuxedo who approached them.

Mr. Charvet was not as tall as his son, but had the same whiskey-colored eyes and arched eyebrows. Spikey gray hair covered his head. "Bojo! You're here." He clapped his son on the back like he expected him to giddy up. He put out his hand, palm up. "And you must be Grace."

She laid her hand in his. "I've been looking forward to meeting you and your wife."

"How's your daughter feeling? Bojo told us she came down with chicken pox right before Christmas."

"Lily's fine now. Thank you for the food from your family's dinner. It was very much appreciated since I had been housebound with an itchy child."

"We had plenty. I'm glad you enjoyed it."

Beau scanned the room. "Where's our table, Dad?"

His father shrugged. "No idea. Marilyn knows. I guess we'll wait for her to find us and lead the way." He turned back to Grace. "We've gotten a big kick from how you two met."

Grace was unsure if he meant speed dating or the car accident. "It was certainly unusual, Mr. Charvet."

"Call me Beau."

The younger Beau squeezed her elbow. "It's why I'm called Bojo, short for Beauregard Joseph, Junior."

A woman joined them and linked her arm with Mr. Charvet's. She had chin-length blond hair and dark brown eyes. Her dress was a black, knee-length sheath with a satin tuxedo jacket. A discreet diamond crucifix on a silver chain encircled her neck.

"Here she is." Beau's father patted the hand on his elbow. "Grace, this is my wife, Marilyn. Marilyn, Grace."

Mrs. Charvet smiled then her face went slack, eyes wide. "Y-you're Grace?"

The men glanced at each other with puzzled expressions. Beau said, "I told you about her and Lily."

To break the awkwardness, Grace smiled at the woman. "It's nice to meet you, Mrs. Charvet."

Beau's stepmother recovered with a little shake of the head. "Please, call me Marilyn. It's wonderful to meet you too. We've heard so much about you and your daughter."

"Where are we sitting, *ma femme*?" Her husband turned to look into the vast room.

"Come on, you guys follow us girls." Marilyn took Grace's arm and led her away. When they were several feet in front, Beau's stepmother leaned toward her. "You look so familiar. Have we met before?"

"I don't think so."

Marilyn Charvet cast surreptitious glances at her as they walked the aisles of beautifully decorated round tables. When they stopped at their assigned table, Beau and his father pulled out chairs next to each other. The two women sat down. Beau took a seat on Grace's right. Mr. Charvet waved at someone before he sat on his wife's left.

Marilyn put her lips close to Grace's ear and lowered her voice. "Bojo said you teach at FAU. I serve on a building committee for the university. Maybe I've seen you on the campus."

"That must be it."

From behind Grace's back, Tom Lundquist spoke in his cheery, salesman-like voice. "Hi, everyone."

Beau and his father stood and Tom shook their hands. Grace smiled at Gen when they made eye contact. The woman's nose wrinkled like she picked up the whiff of something rotten.

Like Beau and his father, Tom was resplendent in a black tuxedo. With his pale skin and reddish hair, he looked like a model in a newspaper insert from a local department store. In contrast, Gen's brunette locks hung straight from a center part. Her makeup was heavy with eyeliner and blood-colored lipstick. She wore a floor-length, black jersey dress which appeared to have been purchased when she was thinner. Grace was thankful the Lundquists seated themselves next to Mr. Charvet. When the remaining two attendees arrived, they sat in the chairs to Beau's right. Tom introduced them as Tri-City Toyota's sales manager and his fiancé. Gen greeted the young couple with cool politeness.

After a short welcome speech from the husband and wife who were this year's chairpersons, the wait staff began to circle with salad plates followed by entrees of either beef short ribs or sea bass. The talk at the table centered on what kind of work everyone did, who they knew in common, and where they had traveled recently. Grace's face ached from smiling.

During dinner, Mr. Charvet referred to Beau several more times as Bojo. Grace could not get used to the nickname. Maybe it suited him when he was a boy, but as an adult he was too masculine for such a cutesy name.

For the final course, she and Beau chose the raspberry mousse and pistachio cake. He placed a forkful of his nut-laced dessert in her mouth then leaned close to lick a dab of pale-green icing from her lips. Somewhat embarrassed by the sensual public gesture, she looked around. His parents smiled at her. Beyond Marilyn and her husband, Gen stared with the blank, flat eyes of a shark.

Following dessert, speeches were given about the Dana Farber Cancer Institute. Presentations and awards were handed out to the benefactors, patrons, and sponsors of the event before a live auction commenced. Grace sat in awe as donated items, such as a flight in a Lear jet, received bids in the tens of thousands of dollars.

She looked around the room at women in current designer gowns. Many of the wealthy spinsters, wives, or divorcees were covered in precious gems and several even wore tiaras. They were escorted by handsome, young to middle-aged men, or elderly husbands. The more obvious trophy wives or girlfriends had companions who were decades older.

How many of the younger women and, for that matter, the men also, were likely someone's mistress, gigolo, or walker? Her mother had schooled her in the difference between male escorts. Walkers were often homosexual and paid only to accompany well-heeled women to society events. Gigolos were compensated for their sexual services as well as their company. Grace had once asked Juliette why she didn't become a female walker.

Her mother laughed. "Don't be silly. Men always want sex, and it pays better."

The wealth of the guests here tonight probably drew her mother to attend similar charity functions on some man's Armani-suited arm. This was the perfect venue for scoping out, not only the competition, but the next wealthy prospect. For Juliette, this wasn't a ballroom. It was a showroom.

All evening Grace remained unsettled by Marilyn's certainty they had met before. During dinner, Beau's stepmother asked questions about people, places, or events which might be the link to explain her familiarity. At one point, Grace's breath caught in her throat with the realization that perhaps

Marilyn knew Juliette. Adding to her discomfort were the narrow-eyed stares Gen cast her way.

After the auction, the orchestra began to play. A number of guests, both young and old, jostled for position on the parquet dance floor. Beau squeezed Grace's shoulder. "How about a dance or two before we head home?"

"Why don't we just say goodbye to your parents and leave?"

Before Beau could answer, Mr. Charvet leaned forward in his seat. "Bojo, there's someone here I think you should meet. He's putting out bids for a multi-story construction project in Martin County."

Beau turned to Grace. "Do you mind?"

"Not at all. I'll go to the ladies' room and meet you back here."

Grace exited the ballroom. Across the hall from the restroom was The Seafood Bar. A turquoise glow drew her to peer inside. Large windows, lined with rows of linen-covered tables, looked out to the dark Atlantic. Most of the patrons were seated at two L-shaped bars made of aquarium glass. Small fish darted beneath their drink glasses. The bubbling sound of filtered water and the hum of air pumps punctuated conversations at the unique counter.

When she entered the restroom, there was a line of women in place. As she waited, the conversations around her were a sneak peek into a lifestyle very different from her own.

In front of her stood a woman who would have been attractive except for grotesquely plumped lips. "We wanted to go to our condo in Aspen last month, but the Winter X Games were there. Howard said the slopes would be simply *clogged* with athletes."

Farther up the line, a tall, surgically enhanced Barbie doll spoke to a woman with impressive cleavage. "I've been having a terrible time finding another housekeeper. They either don't want to live-in or don't speak enough English to communicate."

A nasal voice droned behind her. "Did you hear the Ashbury's house was broken into over Christmas? They took a small Degas and a Picasso. The police think it was an inside job."

Grace bit her lip to keep from asking one of these women if they preferred Sam's Club or BJ's.

The door opened again. "Oh dear, I should have had you girls bring me earlier."

A frail woman with a walker entered from the hallway. She was trailed by two younger females in their late teens. No one spoke up.

Grace turned to the elderly woman and indicated her spot in line. "Take my place. There's only one person ahead of me."

She moved out of the queue. The disappointed Aspen skier retreated to the space Grace vacated. "You can go ahead of me, Mrs. Gunderson."

As one of the young women accompanied her relative to the front, she mouthed a *thank you* to Grace. The art theft reporter maintained her position and stared straight ahead. With a wry smile, Grace walked to the end of the line.

The second girl, who had escorted the aged woman, smiled at Grace and slipped into place behind her. "My great-grandmother isn't able to stand very long. Thank you."

"You're welcome."

The girl cocked her head. "Do I know you?"

Not again.

"Do you work at FAU?" the girl said.

"Yes, I teach English there."

"I haven't had you for a class but I've seen you in the building. My name is Lindsay Archer. I'm a freshman, majoring in elementary education."

"Grace Stone. On campus, it's Dr. Black-Stone."

Several heads turned when she said her professional name. Grace and Lindsay talked about the university until her sister and great-grandmother returned. More introductions were made and gratitude expressed.

Ten minutes later, Grace returned to the hall outside the ballroom. As she neared a set of double doors, a tall spare man leaned against the wall and tracked her approach. He had thick, steel-colored hair and black eyebrows which looked like hedges across his forehead. His purplish lips lifted in a savage smile. When she came abreast, his hand shot out. He grabbed her elbow and pulled. Grace fought for balance in her stiletto heels.

"Hello, Juliette. Where have you been?"

Chapter 29

GRACE LOOKED AT his gray, gimlet eyes and stony face. "That's not my name."

"Well, whatever you're calling yourself now, you look beautiful. It's like you haven't aged a day." His voice was thin and sarcastic. "Where have you been hiding?"

"Please let go of my arm."

"Who's your daddy now? Are you here with him tonight?"

She struggled to wrench her arm from his talon-like grip. "Sir, you're hurting me."

"I've missed you. I drove to your house several years ago, but there's a Hispanic family living there now."

A middle-aged woman with soft brown hair and an anxious look opened one of the ballroom doors. "Preston?" The woman's expression changed to alarm. "What are you doing?"

The man pulled Grace closer. "Go back inside, Maura. This doesn't concern you."

The woman stepped into the hall and shut the door behind her. Her voice was low and soothing. "Dear, we don't know this woman. You need to say goodbye. The Kincaids are waiting for us."

Preston's fingernails bit into Grace's flesh like sharpened claws. "I want to talk to her."

Grace turned to the woman. "Please tell him to let me go."

Maura put her hand on her husband's and tried to pry his fingers loose. She continued to speak in soft but urgent tones. "Preston, you promised everything would be fine tonight. You said seeing old friends would be good for you. Our friends are waiting inside. You need to come with me now."

He shouldered his wife away and spun Grace and himself to face the opposite direction. "I want to talk to *her*, not you, or the Kincaids."

Several women stood frozen in the hallway which led from the ladies' room and restaurant. Lindsay Archer was one of them. She turned and disappeared toward The Seafood Bar.

Maura hissed in the space between her husband's cheek and Grace's. "Why are you doing this to me? Haven't I suffered enough? I'll never be able to show my face here again if you don't stop this nonsense. Do you hear me, Preston? People are watching."

Grace sobbed with relief when Beau came through one set of ballroom doors. In desperation, she mouthed the word *help*.

"I saw her first," Preston shouted when Beau rushed over. He spun her in a half-circle.

Grace lurched. The man's hold on her arm brought her upright as a wrenching pain shot through her shoulder and up her neck like a lightning bolt.

Beau put his hand around her other arm. "Who is this guy?"

Her voice broke. "I don't know."

The world had gone from composed to calamitous in an instant. The stunned faces of spectators spun past Grace like a crazy carousel as she was twirled around again.

Preston screamed close to her ear. "You whore! Is he your new john?" His spittle hit her cheek like hot acid.

Beau growled with menace. "Sir, you need to let her go. She's here with me."

"Fuck you!"

Beau's face hardened. His free hand rose and curled into a fist. Grace could not allow him to suffer legal repercussions if he hurt this deranged old man. She caught his eye and shook her head.

A security guard pushed his way into the fray. "What's going on?"

Maura cried out, "My husband thinks he knows this woman, but he doesn't. Please, don't hurt him. He's sick." She plucked at Preston's tuxedo sleeve.

The guard planted himself in front of the wild-eyed man. "Turn the woman loose, sir."

"I want to talk to the bitch. Leave us alone." Preston whirled himself and Grace to face away from the guard.

Beau's grip righted her when she stumbled. They were closer to the doors which opened onto the ocean side of the building.

The security guard ran around and stood in front of them with his hands raised, palms up. "Let's everybody calm down."

Preston continued to clutch Grace as he spewed invectives at his wife, Beau, and the security guard. The crowd in the hallway grew as patrons from The Seafood Bar stepped out to view the commotion.

Maura looked past her husband and keened. "Oh, my God, the police are here."

Two Palm Beach patrolmen cleaved their way through the spectators. Preston spun around again and faced them.

A bald officer with a gray mustache approached with his hand on his holster. "Sir, you need to release the woman, so we can talk."

"Fuck you!" Preston screamed.

With tears running down her cheeks in powdery rivulets, Maura begged, "Don't shoot. He has Alzheimer's."

The other officer nodded at Beau. "Stand back, sir."

"No. She's with me, and he's hurting her."

Preston turned to his hysterical wife. "Maura, tell them to leave me the fuck alone."

Hotel staff positioned themselves at the closed ballroom doors to prevent people from exiting. Three others held their arms out to keep onlookers bunched together at the lobby end of the corridor. Even with the police on the scene, Preston twirled Grace in a violent pirouette down the hall toward the exit doors. Then the macabre dance repeated itself back toward the ballroom. Younger people had their cell phones raised and photographed or recorded the scene.

Grace prayed. This has to end now. She summoned her inner Juliette, stiffened her spine, and shook Beau's hand loose from her elbow. She swung her arm back and, in a dominatrix voice commanded, "Let go."

With all her strength, she smacked Preston hard across the face with her satin clutch. His head snapped back. His grip eased. Grace pulled her arm free. Beau put his body between hers and her attacker. Preston let out an inhuman howl as the police wrestled him to the ground with their knees on his back.

Maura wrung her hands. "Don't hurt him. Please, don't hurt him."

The man on the carpeted floor blubbered as handcuffs manacled his wrists. Beau picked up Grace and bullied his way through the crowd to the main lobby.

Two paramedics with a stretcher stopped him. "Does she need medical attention?"

"No. The guy who needs you is with the police back there." He jerked his head toward the hall.

A young woman in a skirt and blazer came alongside Beau. "Excuse me. I'm Ms. White, the assistant manager. You can follow me to my office."

"I'm taking her home." He swerved around the woman and headed to the entrance doors.

She sped up and planted herself in front of him. "I'm sorry, but you can't leave until the police say you can. They'll need to speak with both of you."

Grace pointed to a nearby loveseat. "She's right, Beau. Put me down over there."

He placed her on her feet. Grace took two steps and sat with a deep, broken sigh. She leaned her head against the high back and closed her eyes.

Ms. White said, "I'll get you some ice."

Grace opened her eyes. "Ice?"

Beau sat next to her. "Your arm is bleeding and swollen."

Three half-moon cuts above her inside elbow oozed blood. There was also the dark imprint of four fingers and a thumb which blossomed through angry red welts. She trembled. Beau shrugged out of his tuxedo jacket and wrapped it around her.

Ms. White returned a few minutes later with an ice pack in a linen napkin. "Excuse me while I check on things."

After she left, Beau put his arm around Grace and pulled her close. They sat without speaking. The paramedics wheeled a strapped-down figure out the front entrance. Maura followed with a man and woman on each side as she held a handkerchief to her mouth. One of the paramedics returned with his medical case. He stopped at the front desk, and the concierge pointed their way.

The EMT squatted in front of Grace. "Do you need medical attention?"

"I think I'm okay."

"May I take a look?" He did a quick examination and confirmed nothing was broken. He swabbed the cuts with antiseptic and placed a bandage over them. "You're going to be badly bruised. If you start to feel severe pain in your arm or shoulder, go to a doctor." He packed up his bag and left.

With the floorshow over, partygoers flowed toward the exit. The chatter of the young adults was sprinkled with laughter as they pointed to their cell phone screens. Older guests looked upset and talked in hushed tones.

One of the police officers approached and the other stood guard. "I need to get a statement from you." Grace provided her contact information and an account of what happened. The officer scribbled in a notebook. "Do you know Mr. Carlisle?"

"I'd never seen him before tonight."

"Do you want to press charges?"

"No." She shook her head with weary resignation. "His wife said he's sick. There would be no reason to have him arrested."

The policeman snapped his notebook closed. "You're free to go, Ms. Stone. If we need anything else from you, we'll be in touch."

Beau stood and held out his hand. Grace wobbled to her feet. His father and stepmother hurried over with Tom and Gen.

Mr. Charvet looked back at the officers who now spoke with Ms. White. "Why were you talking to the police?"

Gen eyed Grace in Beau's jacket like she had been covered up for stripping down to pasties and a G-string. "Everyone was talking about a brawl between a man and a woman outside the ballroom."

Beau glowered. "Some guy with Alzheimer's thought he knew Grace. He grabbed her and wouldn't let go. No one could get her away from him."

Marilyn's brow wrinkled. "Are you hurt?"

Grace cradled her elbow. "I'm fine."

A muscle pulsed in Beau's jaw. "He nearly ripped her shoulder out of the socket."

"How did she get free?" Tom asked.

Beau hugged her close. "Grace slugged him in the face with her purse."

A tuxedoed man with curly black hair squeezed between Mr. Charvet and Tom. "Excuse me. Could I speak to the young lady? My name is Daniel Bernardi. I'm a personal injury attorney."

Beau planted himself in front of Grace.

"I just wanted to give the lady this." The man pulled a business card from his pocket and held it out. "Preston Carlisle is loaded. You've got a documented and witnessed claim against him."

Beau shielded her as they walked toward an exit.

Behind them, Mr. Charvet said, "Leave them alone."

Rather than go out the main entrance, Beau hustled past closed shops to a darkened patio. He sat her in a shadowed chair. "I'm going to get the car. Wait here."

Despite the cool ocean breeze, her face burned. She breathed in the salty night air. Within minutes, Beau returned and led her through an opening in a tall, dense hedge. His BMW idled curbside. As they drove home, she pretended to sleep to avoid conversation. When Beau pulled up to her front door, she opened her eyes.

With the engine still running, he turned to look at her. "You're awake. How do you feel?"

"Embarrassed."

"It wasn't your fault."

"Yes, it was. This is my mother's dress, and she wore her hair like this." Grace opened her purse, found her door key, and fisted it in her palm.

Beau inhaled a sharp breath. "What are you saying?"

"Preston Carlisle called me Juliette. I told him that wasn't my name, but it made no difference. I thought about telling him she was my dead mother, but didn't get the chance before his wife arrived on the scene." Grace unhooked her seatbelt. "Your father and stepmother are probably wondering who you've gotten yourself involved with."

Beau cleared his throat. "Since Marilyn was sure you looked familiar, do you think she knew your mother?"

"I don't know. But you can't tell her about Juliette."

"But, Grace, no one can accuse you of being like her."

"Are you kidding? Of course, they do. In the past, I've had jealous classmates and colleagues accuse me of using sex to get ahead. I've worked hard and didn't get where I am today by sleeping around."

She hated the misconception that her gender, sexuality, or looks were a springboard for her achievements. Did children of other flawed parents fight hard to distance themselves from the inevitable comparisons? She didn't dress or act provocatively. She had been committed to her education and applied the same drive to her career. She interacted with everyone in the same manner. And yet, often her success was attributed to her femininity, not her intelligence and determination.

Beau sighed. "If they ask, what should I tell my family?"

Grace jerked her head toward him. "You don't have to tell them who Preston Carlisle thought I was."

"But Marilyn thinks she's seen you before."

A headache throbbed behind Grace's eyes. She opened her car door and put one foot on the driveway. "You know what? If this is a problem for you, tell everyone you won't be seeing the woman in the *brawl* anymore."

She rushed to the front door. The key slipped into the lock and turned. She stepped inside, shut the door, and twisted the deadbolt with a loud click.

In seconds, Beau rattled the knob. "Grace, open up. Grace."

"Go home, Beau. I want to be alone." Grace closed her eyes and sank to the cool tile floor, her back against the door.

She'd deal with the fallout by herself, like always. Would the incident be reported in the paper or on TV? Will a video end up on the Internet? Would Lindsay Archer tell someone at the university? A sick feeling rose in Grace's stomach like boiling acid. She folded her arms across her middle and squeezed.

Chapter 30

TIME PASSED. A hand on her head startled her. She must have fallen asleep.

Tariq's voice was soothing. "Let me help you up." He pulled her to her feet. "Beau told us what happened. I want to look at your arm." In the bedroom, she sat on the mattress while he probed, moved the joint, and asked questions. "Do you have any Advil or Motrin?"

She nodded.

"Take two tablets tonight for the inflammation and more tomorrow. Is there an ice pack in the freezer?"

She nodded again.

"Let me unzip you, and I'll get it."

Grace slipped out of her mother's dress and laid it on a chair. She put on a long T-shirt and went into the bathroom. When she returned to the bedroom, Tariq had pulled back the duvet and sheet.

After she got into bed, he applied the ice pack. "I have to go to work in the morning. If you're in severe pain, call me. Sleep as late as you want. Robert can keep Lily all day, if necessary."

"I don't know what I'd do without you guys." Tears filled her eyes. "I love you both so much."

"We love you too. Everything will work out. Rest is what you need right now."

He turned off the light. The bedroom door gave a soft click when it closed. For a long time, Grace stared at the ceiling.

In the morning, she came awake with the throbbing in her shoulder. Grace ran her hand through tangled hair as the memory of last night's fiasco replayed like a drunken dream. She went into the bathroom and checked her arm. The redness was gone, but purple bruises stained her skin. She peeled off the Band-Aid applied by the paramedic. The crescent-shaped cuts were tender to the touch. As she applied more antiseptic ointment to them, she winced. Her right side from neck to waist was stiff and sore. She needed strong coffee and more Motrin.

Cradling her arm, she passed by the living room and came to an abrupt stop. Stretched out on the sofa, asleep in his tuxedo pants and unbuttoned dress shirt, was Beau.

Grace put her hands on her hips. "What are you doing here?"

His eyes opened. "Good morning. How does your arm feel?"

"Did Tariq let you in?"

He sat up and stretched. "Were you able to get some sleep?"

"Why didn't you go home last night?"

Beau stood. "Want me to make us some coffee?"

"How many questions are you going to ask and not answer?"

"As many as it takes to keep you talking to me."

Grace dropped into an armchair.

Beau sat on the coffee table in front of her. "I promise I won't tell anyone about your mother. That's why I asked Tariq to let me sleep here."

"Thank you."

"We also talked about Preston Carlisle. He said when someone with Alzheimer's is agitated the best thing is distract them and give in a little. Maybe we could have let him take you aside and talk for a few minutes. His wife should have known that."

"Poor Maura. For one evening, she wanted the social life she had before her husband got sick. When I looked around that room last night, I realized my mother probably trawled for wealthy prospects at places like The Discovery Ball. There may have been dozens of people there who had known her. Maybe even your stepmother."

"Don't worry about Marilyn."

Grace gave a weary shake of her head. "As someone who has no family, I don't ever want to come between you and yours."

He cupped her cheek and gave her a crooked smile. "Don't worry. That'll never happen."

Chapter 31

BY MONDAY MORNING, Grace hadn't heard or read anything about the police being called to The Breakers on Saturday night. After all, it was child's play for the enclave of excess, known as Palm Beach, to squash a story about a wealthy citizen going berserk at a charity event, but the Internet was harder to control. She found one video on YouTube called *Crazy Old Man at The Discovery Ball*. Only quick flashes of her were seen, and she was out of the film entirely after Preston Carlisle was wrestled to the ground.

After her morning class ended, Grace returned to the English Department.

Carolyn, her secretary, stopped her. "Dr. Black-Stone, please call Dr. Harter's office. She would like to speak with you."

A chunk of icy fear hit Grace. Why did the dean want to talk with her? "Thanks, I'll do it right away."

Did the university find out about the Discovery Ball skirmish? The police didn't ask where she was employed. She punched in the number for Dr. Harter's office and waited to be connected.

"Hel-lo." The female voice spoke between humming to orchestral music audible in the background.

"This is Dr. Black-Stone. I have a message to call you."

"Thank you for getting back to me. I wanted to speak to you about an issue recently brought to my attention."

Grace steeled herself like a gladiator about to enter the arena. "Yes, Dr. Harter?"

"I heard your car was badly damaged during finals week. I was wondering if the matter has been resolved to your satisfaction with the construction firm."

Grace stared at the phone in disbelief.

An uncertain voice came through the speaker. "Dr. Black-Stone? Are you there?"

"Yes, I'm here. The owner of the crane company has made sure I'm completely satisfied." Grace smacked her palm against her forehead.

"Good. Good. Bye now."

Chapter 32

THE FOLLOWING TUESDAY afternoon, Grace had office hours for student conferences, so her door was open. Engrossed in her work, she jumped when the desk phone rang. Almost no one ever called her on it. She received most messages from students and colleagues via email and personal calls on her cell phone. She raised the receiver to her ear like it was an alien object. "Dr. Black-Stone speaking."

"Hello, Grace. It's Marilyn Charvet. I hope you don't mind me calling you at work."

"No, not at all."

"I was wondering if we could get together for a chat."

"A chat? About what?" A momentary rush of panic pierced Grace's chest. Did Marilyn want to discuss what happened at The Discovery Ball?

"I wanted to talk to you about your mother, Juliette."

Grace swallowed hard as a kernel of wrath stiffened her body. Had Beau broken his promise? Did Marilyn want to prevent his further involvement with a woman of questionable parentage, one who was the twin image of a deceased prostitute? "Did Beau tell you who she was?"

"No. I looked you up on the FAU faculty website. When I saw your name was Black-Stone, I knew why you looked so familiar. Is Juliette still living in the area?"

"No." Grace's anger drained replaced by wariness. "My mother died almost nine years ago."

Marilyn's voice had a note of genuine regret in it. "Oh, I'm so sorry to hear she's gone. I first met Juliette years ago in Chicago."

Faintness washed over Grace. "You knew my mother before she moved here?"

"Yes. That's what I really wanted to talk to you about. When can we meet?"

Chapter 33

THE PLAN WAS for Marilyn to come to the campus when Grace's Wednesday evening class ended, so they could speak in private. At a quarter after eight, Grace walked downstairs from her second-floor classroom as several students trailed behind. Beau's stepmother waited outside the locked English Department. She was dressed in an elegant gray pencil skirt and a silk blouse.

Grace waved good-bye to her students as they headed to the exit. She closed the distance on shaky legs to where Beau's stepmother stood. "Hello, Marilyn. Thank you for coming here to meet." She unlocked the door to the reception area and relocked it behind them. "You can follow me." Once inside her cramped office, she opened a mini-fridge in the corner. "Would you like something to drink?"

"No, I'm fine."

Grace sat behind her desk. She opened a water bottle and sipped to moisten her dry mouth. "I was surprised when you said you knew my mother in Chicago. I had no idea she lived there. When did you meet her?"

Marilyn's eyes brightened. "It was in the spring of 1987. I was still married to my first husband. We were at a symphony concert and ran into my brother and your mother in the lobby during intermission. It was quite a surprise to see George with her."

Marilyn's brother was probably married. Grace didn't have to ask why the woman was surprised, but she did anyway.

Marilyn hesitated. "Well, my brother was much older than her, and he was married. He and his wife, Elsa, had been legally separated for about five years, I guess. I don't know why they never divorced. He lived and worked in Chicago. She had a high-powered job on Wall Street and lived in New York City. They never had children together."

A multitude of questions scrolled through Grace's brain. Perhaps it was best to let the woman reveal what she knew before questioning her further.

Two lines formed between Marilyn's eyes. "Let's see, the last time I saw your mother was at a charity luncheon in Boca about ten years ago. I recognized her immediately. When I told her George had died, she didn't seem surprised. I think she already knew. Anyway, I brought a photograph of him for you to see."

Before Grace could ask why she needed to see Marilyn's brother, the woman pulled a small picture out of her purse and slid it across the desk. It was a typical business-suited professional pose. The man in the headshot was fair-haired and wore metal-framed glasses. A white flash of shock reverberated through Grace's body. When she looked up, Marilyn's eyes were glued on her.

Grace licked her lips before she spoke. "I met him once. He told me his name was Mr. Mack."

"Most people did call him Mack." Marilyn looked past Grace as though she recalled a fond memory. "Since I was a child, I called him George or Georgie."

"Your brother's name is George Mack?"

"Actually, it's Makowsky."

A sudden revelation made Grace's breath hitched in her throat. The one time that she met Mr. Mack he asked her name. She had told him it was Grace Georgette Black. Was her my middle name a combination of George and Juliette? Oh my God. "Did you know …" Her voice came out husky, so she cleared her throat. "… my mother as Juliette Black when she was in Chicago?"

"I didn't know her last name at that time. George only introduced her as Juliette. At the luncheon where I last saw her, we all wore name tags and I saw the name Black. I thought maybe it was her married name. Grace?" Marilyn waited until their eyes met. "Am I your aunt?"

The air squeezed out of Grace's body. Her chest grew heavy, like a bag filling up with sand. She forced herself to inhale enough oxygen to speak. "Why would you think you're my aunt?"

"George doted on my son, Skip. I once asked him if he wouldn't like to have a child of his own someday. He said, 'What makes you think I don't?' He loved being cryptic and keeping people off balance. George was so brilliant. It's a shame he died in the prime of his life. He was a chemist and a prolific inventor. His patents made him very rich. I often wondered at what cost. Was his leukemia a result of exposure to all the dangerous chemicals he worked with?"

Sorrow and pain flashed through Grace. Her father was dead too. The threat of tears dampened her eyes. She blinked to hold them back as she stared at the photograph in her hand.

"Grace, when were you born?"

She waited several seconds, tamping down the rawness of new grief and loss before responding. "June, 1988."

Marilyn's eyes were raised toward the ceiling in a beatific expression. "The last time I saw Juliette and George together was at the country club's Thanksgiving dinner in 1987. I was very pregnant with my son, Skip, at the time and gave birth a week later. While my husband and George chatted, your mother asked me questions about my pregnancy, especially the first trimester. I thought it was just female talk at the time." Marilyn's gaze dropped, and she stared at Grace as if she wanted to convey some vital information telepathically. "If you were born seven months later, maybe Juliette knew or suspected she was pregnant."

"But that doesn't mean your brother is my father."

Marilyn gave her an indulgent smile. "Grace, you know you look like your mother. But I remember she had big, blue eyes. You're a brown-eyed blond like George and me. You also have the Makowsky mouth, the full lower lip and the thinner upper one."

Grace looked at Marilyn's mouth. There was a similarity. Juliette had full lips, upper and lower.

"Am I your aunt?" Marilyn repeated.

When she agreed to this meeting, Grace had prepared herself for an emotional mini-drama about her mother's earlier life but never anticipated finding out about her dead father and his living sister. "I don't know if we're related. On my birth certificate, the father is listed as unknown." Her brain worked at a feverish pace to filter her history into two categories: Things to

Tell Marilyn and Things to Keep Quiet. "When I was in high school, I badgered Juliette about my father's identity. Since Mr. Mack was the only man she had ever introduced to me, I asked if he was my father."

Marilyn looked like she held a possible multi-million-dollar lottery ticket and waited in breathless anticipation to hear the last number called. "What did she say?"

Grace glanced at the photograph of George Makowsky then at Beau's stepmother. "She said he was."

Marilyn's hands covered her open mouth. Her eyes filled with tears. "Oh, my God. Oh, my God."

"But that doesn't mean she told me the truth. I asked her other questions about Mr. Mack, but she refused to give me more information."

She and her mother had several angry confrontations about her father. Following one particularly contentious argument, Juliette banged her fist on the table. "I'm sorry I ever told you. Don't ask me about him again."

Marilyn dabbed at her damp lashes with a tissue. "I knew it. I just knew in my heart that you're my niece. When we met at The Discovery Ball, I had such a strong reaction to you. It was as if a long-lost relative had finally come home." Before Grace could rein Marilyn in, the woman sat up straight. "We should do DNA testing as soon as possible. That would confirm what I already know is true."

Marilyn had mentioned her brother died childless and rich. Maybe this emotional act was all staged. "Do you want the confirmation because your brother was wealthy, and I could be an heir?"

Marilyn sniffed as two fat tears slid snail paths on her pink cheeks. "This has nothing to do with money. I want to know that a part of my big brother lives on today. Georgie wasn't perfect, but I loved him with all my heart. It would be a dream comes true if you were his daughter. He'd be so proud of you. You're a college professor and the mother of a little girl. Oh my, that would make me a great-aunt, something I never thought I'd be."

A bloom of affection for this woman, relative or not, filled Grace's heart, but she had to keep her feet anchored in what was real and not get excited about what was possible. "You have to be concerned about someone with a claim to his estate."

"George knew he was dying for a long time and was meticulous about his will. Yes, his estate still receives money from the few remaining patents which have not yet expired, but it goes into an endowment he established here at FAU. In fact, it's paying for the construction of the building across the street; the one where you met Beau when your car was damaged."

A name pounded in Grace's head like a drumbeat. It was on the large sign posted next to the faculty parking lot where the accident occurred. "The G.G. Educational Endowment?"

"You've heard of it." Marilyn's face glowed. "The law firm of Sandberg Truman here in Boca set up the endowment as part of George's estate. I've been active on the committee which decides how the money is spent."

The fluorescent lights on Grace's office ceiling flickered in her eyes. Sandberg Truman oversaw the trust which paid for her and Juliette's living expenses and her education. One of their attorneys handled probate after her mother's death. John Truman, a founding partner, had been appointed to the FAU board of trustees two years ago. The trustees had the final say in tenure approval, such as when it was granted to her, a twenty-nine-year-old English professor, who had been employed for only three years. Another managing partner had been on the board when she was hired for her full-time position, even though she was ABD, all but dissertation, having passed her orals but not yet defended her research.

"Marilyn, do you know why it was called the G.G. Educational Fund?" Grace's voice sounded somewhat grainy to her.

"No. George was already gone by the time I learned about the endowment. I assumed he named it after our father, George Senior and himself." Marilyn canted her head to one side like a bird. "Grace, what's your middle name?"

There was a beat of silence before she responded. "Georgette."

Marilyn's lips tightened in an I-knew-it smile. "Our next step definitely should be DNA testing. I've already set up an account on the Ancestry.com website. You should do the same, so when we get our results back they can confirm our genetic match."

Grace did not tell Marilyn she had an Ancestry DNA kit at home in her office. Robert and Tariq gave it to her for her birthday. At the time, she did not say a word, just stared at the unwrapped box.

Robert had jumped up from his seat and sat next to her. "Honey, you need to find out about your family."

She bit her lip before responding. "But what if there's no one out there who's related to me." Or there was no one out there who wanted to be related to her.

He patted her back. "That's a possibility. What is more probable is that you'll discover a few relatives that might be able to provide you with some answers. At the very least, you'll find out what your ethnic origins are."

At home, she placed the kit at the back of her desk drawer and tried to forget about it. But every time she needed envelopes, the corner of the white box seemed to jump out at her, like a crouching snow leopard. For her sake and Lily's, it would be good to have a health history. Her chest bubbled with panic every time she had to complete a medical questionnaire at a new doctor's office.

No, I don't know what diseases my parents suffered from.

No, I don't know what age my father was when he died.

No, I don't know what health issues I'm passing on to my daughter.

She had researched adoptees who sought information about their biological parents. After all, she was as clueless about her family as they were. Grace learned that the search process was not for the fearful, for the eternal optimist, or for those who cannot withstand rejection. But like many of those adoptees, she craved a connection.

In the case of her unknown father's people, she was not expecting acceptance from them. After all, she was his secret bastard. To her surprise and delight, Marilyn seemed thrilled with the possibility they were related, but would the rest of the Charvets be prepared to welcome her into the family?

Chapter 34

GRACE CALLED ROBERT when she arrived home from her momentous meeting with Beau's stepmother.

"What's up?" His voice carried its usual chipper tone despite the lateness of the hour.

"Are the girls asleep?"

"Maxi and Lily are. I don't know about Erin, but I'm not about to open her door and find out."

"Can I come over and talk?"

"Sure. What's wrong?"

"Believe it or not, tonight I found out who my father was."

Robert paused. "Was? Not is?"

"Yes. Was."

"I'm sorry to hear that." Robert's voice held a tentative note. "How did you find out?"

Grace told him in a few words about the meeting with Marilyn.

He spoke in a soft, soothing, sympathetic tone. "How do you feel, Grace?"

"I guess happy and humiliated."

"Honey, the only similarity between those two emotions is they both start with the letter h."

Grace was unable to speak. Finally, her words tumbled out in a rush followed by a sob. "Personally, I'm happy I know who he is, or was, but professionally, I'm humiliated."

"Come on over. I'll open a bottle."

Following two glasses of wine and a long conversation with Robert, she walked home and, as soon as she entered her house, retrieved the Ancestry.com DNA kit. She opened it and read the instructions. After providing the test sample and preparing the kit for mailing, she heaved a sigh that seemed to come from her toes upward. Before the meeting with Marilyn ended, they agreed to keep the possibility of their familial connection private until the DNA confirmation was in hand. Marilyn had not shared with her husband that she suspected Grace was her brother's love child and, more importantly, she had not discussed her hunch with Beau.

Grace's trepidation wasn't just her possible relation to Marilyn. There would be a connection to the Charvets extending beyond dating one of the family's members. Both she and Lily would be blood relatives of Skip and his half-sister, Zoe. In a perfect world, she and Beau would fall in love, marry, and they would all live happily ever after as one big family. But no world was ever perfect. Heartache, rejection, and pain touched everyone's life. She could handle these obstacles as she had all her life, but Lily didn't deserve to have Grace's illegitimacy affect her as well.

Chapter 35

TWO WEEKS LATER, Alice blew through the open door of Grace's office. "Do you have time for lunch?" Then she stopped in her tracks. "Oh, I'm sorry. I didn't realize you were with someone." She stepped back to exit when the person seated in front of Grace turned around. Alice gazed at the man in the chair. "Hello, Beau." She rubbed her fingertips across her cleavage. In the presence of an attractive man, Alice tended to ignore the modesty lessons from twelve years of Catholic schooling.

Grace smiled. "This is my friend and colleague, Alice Crist. She went by the name Ali the night of speed dating."

Beau rose to his feet and towered over the petite woman. "It's nice to see you again." He held out his hand.

Alice extended her arm, palm down, in the way of a Victorian maiden. Beau laid her hand in his palm, bent low, and touched his lips to the back. She shot a smoldering stare at his bent head before he straightened.

Cradling her kissed hand, Alice took a step back towards the open doorway. "Sorry for the interruption. I'll leave you two alone."

Grace rolled her chair away from the desk. "Beau came to take me to lunch. Why don't you join us?"

"No, I couldn't." She tilted her head back and batted her eyelashes at Beau. "Well, if you're sure *you* don't mind."

"What man wouldn't want to escort two beautiful women to lunch?"

"I'll …" Alice pointed over her shoulder. "… get my purse." She backed out of the office and bumped against the door frame, turned, and scurried away.

Beau chuckled. "What does she do here?"

"Alice teaches English literature and works on rare books from all over the world."

"She's a professor like you?"

Grace opened her desk drawer and retrieved her cell phone and keys. "Actually, she's a full professor. Alice was my mentor when I started working here. Now we're good friends."

The three of them trooped out of the building to where Beau's BMW was parked at the construction site. They drove to the P.F. Chang restaurant, across from the campus' main entrance. After their orders were placed, Beau asked Alice about her work.

She described her current restoration assignment on a seventeenth century book. "This summer I'm scheduled for an authentication project for the Bodleian Libraries at Oxford. I'll be spending six weeks during June and July in a sterile room." As Alice talked about the painstaking research and workmanship involved, Beau's perception of her seemed to change by the questions he asked. The conversation was abandoned with the arrival of their lunches.

Alice speared a forkful of her sesame chicken. "I have a question for you, Beau. Did you write Grace's name down at speed dating?"

Beau swallowed his mouthful of food. "I did."

"How many other women's names did you put down?"

"All of them."

"You did?"

Grace turned in her seat. "You did?"

A slow grin creased his face. "I thought it might increase my chances to get at least one date."

Grace frowned. "Did anyone match with you?"

"A couple of them. I was going to get in touch, but then you and I met again. Now I have a question for you, Alice. Why didn't *you* write *my* name down?"

Grace smirked at her friend.

Alice laid her fork next to her plate and wiped her mouth with the napkin. "Well, Beau, I could never date anyone who isn't a registered Democrat. You said you voted for Obama's reelection, but that just wasn't enough."

Wasn't she going to mention his shirttail hanging out?

Beau nodded. "I'm glad it wasn't that you didn't like my hair or the way I was dressed."

Alice shot an accusing glare at Grace. "No, it wasn't anything trivial like that."

"It's funny the two of you went speed dating together. I also went with my stepbrother."

Once again, Alice glowered at her friend. "Really? Grace never told me. Who's your stepbrother?"

"His name is Scott."

"The blond lawyer?"

"You remember him?"

"I certainly do. I thought he'd be perfect for ..." Alice's gaze shifted to Grace who held her breath. "... me. But, unlike you, he didn't write every woman's name down."

"You're lucky he didn't."

"Why? What's wrong with him?"

Beau laughed. He told Alice about Scott's transfer to Dubai just weeks after the night of speed dating. "As far as I know, he didn't have time to go out with anyone before he had to leave the country."

They finished their lunch. When the bill arrived, Alice reached for her purse. Beau laid his credit card on the server's tray. "My treat."

Alice smiled at him. "Thank you." She propped her chin in her hand and spoke in a breezy tone which belied her curiosity. "Do you two have plans for Spring Break?"

The university's week-long vacation was scheduled to start the following Monday.

Beau said, "I'm taking Grace and Lily to my family's vacation home on Big Pine Key. I can't take off work until Thursday, but we'll have a long weekend."

"Does Lily know about the trip?"

Grace answered first. "She's been driving me crazy. I finally put a calendar on the refrigerator, so she could count down the days."

"Won't she put a crimp in your time alone together?"

Beau's smile sent shivers to Grace's toes. "I've come up with a couple of ideas."

Chapter 36

THE SATURDAY BEFORE their vacation, Grace and Beau ordered takeout at a Vietnamese restaurant and waited at the bar for it to be readied. She turned to him. "Speaking of food, what should I bring to the Keys?"

"The kitchen is kept stocked. If you need anything special, bring it or we can pick it up in town."

"What clothes I should pack?"

"We'll go to the beach at least one day, more if we can. I'm planning a romantic dinner out on Saturday night, so you should bring a nice dress. I've made arrangements for Marta, the housekeeper, to babysit Lily."

"The place has a housekeeper?"

"She gets houses ready before the owners come and cleans them after they leave. She'll watch Lily on Saturday night."

Beau's amused expression warmed Grace. "So that's what you were referring to at lunch last week. The babysitter will give us some alone time."

"And I have another trick up my sleeve." He flashed an enigmatic smile. "Just wait and see."

Chapter 37

ON THE DAY of their trip to the Keys, Grace placed the last bag on the living room floor when Lily called out from the dining room window. "He's here." The little girl raced into the foyer and flung open the unlocked door.

When Beau exited his car, he was dressed in sandals, cargo shorts, and a tropical print shirt. Grace waved hello.

Lily bounced in place. "Today we go to the Keys, Mr. Beau."

"I know. Are you ready?"

She nodded so vigorously she had to swipe hair out of her eyes with both hands. "Let's go."

He kissed Grace and pointed to the two piles. "Is this everything?"

"First, put in Lily's booster seat. These things go in the back with her. The rest can go in the trunk." Between the two of them they had everything loaded ten minutes later.

Beau started the engine then twisted in his seat to face Grace. "It's two o'clock. Can you and Lily wait until five to eat?"

"We're fine with whatever you've planned."

At the first stop sign, Beau let the car idle as his eyes lingered on her. She wore flip-flops, tiny white boy shorts, and a tube top covered by a gauzy sleeveless blouse. He scanned her from head to toe. Her skin prickled with the awareness of what his look meant.

A little more than three hours later, they arrived at a restaurant near the airport on the island of Marathon. The place was a nondescript but typical Keys joint which consisted of unpainted wood and screened windows. There were a number of available seats at wooden tables with benches. The saltiness of the Gulf of Mexico on one side of the island and the Atlantic Ocean on the other seemed to permeate the strong breeze which blew rustling palm fronds and kicked up dusty sand.

Once they were seated, a young waitress brought menus and took their drink orders. "Do you have any questions?"

Lily raised her hand like she did in preschool. Grace's breath hitched. Her daughter stared at the waitress's numerous piercings and tattoos with frank curiosity. "Who took your tables?"

"Huh?"

"You got pic-a-nick tables."

"Yeah, we do."

"Where are the other tables?"

Grace closed her menu. "I'll explain the seating to her."

The inked girl gave a weak smile, clearly confused, and left.

"Mommy—"

"I know you usually see picnic tables outside, but here in the Keys they do things differently."

When their appetizer of conch fritters arrived, Lily eyed the fried food with the intensity of a scientist studying a rare life form. She poked the one placed on her plate. "Is this a Keys meatball?"

Beau pointed to his fritter. "It's made with—"

Grace jumped in. "Special meat and bread from the Keys." She shot Beau a hard stare. He nodded his understanding. An explanation about a conch and how it ended up on her plate was more than Lily needed to know.

The little girl took a tiny, tentative bite. "I like it."

After dinner, they drove almost another hour to the Charvet's vacation home. It was nestled in a residential area on the Gulf side of the island. Beau pulled into a carport next to a one-story concrete block house with a metal roof. A seawall ran the length of the backyard with a boat ramp sloped to a canal. Grace took her daughter's hand when she was out of the car.

Lily squirmed for release. "I wanna see."

"This is Mr. Beau's house. I'm sure there are rules here for little kids."

They met him at the front of the car and surveyed the tropical oasis.

Lily put her hand in Beau's. "Mommy says you have rules."

"She's right."

Lily pointed to a small concrete block structure with a flat roof. "Is that the house for Mommy and me?"

"No, it's a storage shed, but you can't go any closer to the water than that building." He walked the child to the corner of the structure then on a parallel path along the canal to the other side of the backyard.

As Beau and Lily continued to pace the child's boundary limits, Grace turned in a circle to study the property. There were no neighbors directly across the canal or on either side of the lot. The only other houses were across the street.

Lily and Beau rejoined Grace. He unlocked a door which opened onto the carport. An updated, eat-in kitchen was on the left and a family room on the right. They followed him down the hall to the three bedrooms.

He entered the smallest one on the left. "This is yours, Lily."

The double bed had an arched rattan headboard and a window which looked out to the front yard. Next to Lily's room there was a bathroom with an acrylic shower tub. At the end of the hall was the master bedroom with an ensuite bathroom. On the far wall of the bedroom, Grace pulled the curtains aside and peered out a sliding glass door. A screened porch extended across the back of the house.

Lily patted the bed. "Who sleeps here?"

"Your mommy."

Grace turned around. "No, Beau. I'll take the bedroom across the hall from Lily. We'll share the bath out there."

The third room contained a queen-sized bed and also had a sliding glass door. Grace opened it and stepped out to the porch. Beau stood in the doorway. The slider to the master bedroom was separated from this one by only a few feet.

Grace tilted her head and gave Beau a meaningful look. "Is this one of those tricks you were talking about?"

He grinned. "That and a baby monitor for Lily's room."

By the time they unloaded the car, unpacked, and explored more of the property, it was almost eight o'clock. When Grace said it was time to get ready for bed, Lily stamped her foot. "I don't wanna go to sleep, Mommy. We just got here."

Before Grace could respond, Beau knelt in front of the little girl. "We're going to the beach tomorrow. If you get tired, we'll have to leave early."

Lily raced to the bedroom with Grace in her wake. While she bathed her daughter, the sound of the shower in the master bath rattled the pipes for several minutes.

After Lily was dressed in her pajamas, Grace tidied the room. "Okay, let's find Mr. Beau, so you can tell him goodnight." They checked the master bedroom and family room, but he wasn't there.

Lily put her hands on either side of her mouth. "Where are you, Mr. Beau?"

"I'm on the porch. Come and sit with me for a few minutes."

Lily ran to the doorway of Grace's bedroom slider. Beau was seated on an outdoor sofa inside the screened patio. She stepped down onto the concrete floor, and he lifted her onto his lap. Grace curled against his other side. Soft music played somewhere in the house. Candles flickered on the end tables. Water currents slapped the seawall and night insects sang harmony. Lily was asleep five minutes later.

Grace sat up. "Let me put her in bed."

Beau pulled her back into the crook of his arm. "Relax. We're in the Keys."

They cuddled as the night slipped closer to the next day. When Beau yawned, Grace blew out the candles then followed him inside with Lily draped over his shoulder. He tucked her into bed.

In the hallway, Grace walked into Beau's embrace. "Let me clean up, and I'll join you in your room for a while."

"I'll turn on the baby monitor."

She took a quick shower and tiptoed into the master bedroom with only a bath towel wrapped around her. Beau snored softly. It appeared he had sat on the edge of the mattress, lay back, and fallen asleep with his feet on the floor.

"Beau." She touched his knee. "Beau."

When he didn't respond to her gentle attempts to wake him, she switched off the baby monitor and table lamp. He had been working hard the past several days to be able to take off for this long weekend. Grace returned to her own bedroom and, within minutes, she was also asleep.

Chapter 38

FRIDAY WAS A breezy, warm day in paradise. They arrived at Bahia Honda State Park after a ten-minute drive. Beau showed his family's annual pass at the guard shack then drove toward the parking lot straight ahead. The long, narrow strip of powdery beach was dotted with seaweed washed ashore and clumps of sea grass.

Grace studied the sandy shore then turned to Beau. "There seems to be more sea grass here than on the mainland beaches."

"It's allowed to grow unchecked to help stop erosion. How's this spot to set up?"

While Grace cleared an area of loose ocean debris, Beau secured the wide umbrella deep into the sand. He arranged low-slung chairs in its shade and laid down a mover's blanket.

Grace slathered Lily with sunscreen as she wiggled in place. "Hold still. I don't want you to burn."

"Hurry, Mommy." When coated to her mother's satisfaction, Lily rummaged through a mesh bag for beach toys.

Beau removed his sandals and shirt. Long-legged board shorts were tied low on his flat, ripped abdomen. He watched the little girl run toward the water's edge. "Stay on the sand, Lily, until I get there."

Squatting with her back to him, she waved the toy shovel in acknowledgement.

Beau turned to Grace who fussed with the angle of the umbrella and the placement of the chairs for optimum shade and ocean viewing. "C'mon, Grace. Take off your top. I want to see your swimsuit." His eyes pleaded then leered.

She grabbed the shirt's hem and pulled it over her head. Her newly purchased one-piece maillot had high leg openings which required a bikini wax at a local spa. Its V-necked bodice plunged below her breasts and suited her slender and not-too-curvy figure. He ogled her from neck to thigh.

When their beach spot was situated to Grace's satisfaction, she relaxed in the shallow water near the shoreline while Beau and Lily frolicked in the gentle waves. The tall man and little girl walked hand-in-hand into the ocean on the shallow sandbar. It wasn't until they were many yards from shore that Beau had to pick her up to keep her head above water. Soon they returned to the beach where he provided construction advice for building a sandcastle.

With her princess house complete, Lily stood and brushed off her legs. "I'm hungry."

Under swaying palms in the picnic area, they ate the food Grace packed in a cooler.

Lily tapped the table top with the emphasis of a monarch issuing an edict. "*This* is where a pic-a-nick table goes. Not in a rest-rant."

After the meal, they walked the water-packed shoreline as sea birds swooped and rode the currents of air. Lily gathered shells in her bucket. They passed an elderly man who wore a pith helmet, no shirt on his droopy brown chest, and sagging cargo shorts. Headphones covered his ears, and he waved a metal detector above the sand. As they drew near, he looked up. His eyes went from Grace to Lily to Beau.

He nodded. "You're a nice-looking family."

Then the man returned to his detection again. Beau kept walking, focused straight ahead as if he did not hear what the treasure hunter said.

An hour later, they prepared to leave. Grace rinsed sand off Lily and dressed her in clean clothes while Beau loaded the car. At the house, the sleeping child was put in bed. Grace and Beau hosed off the beach gear and shook out the towels and blanket.

When the cleanup was done, she wrapped her arms around his waist. "Thank you for a fun day at the beach. I'm going to take a shower. Would you like to join me?"

"If I ever say no, call 9-1-1. Let's use my bathroom."

Chapter 39

AT DINNERTIME, WHILE Grace prepared a salad in the kitchen, Lily emerged from her bedroom and knuckled sleep from her eyes. "Where's Mr. Beau?"

"He's outside at the grill."

His voice called out. "Steaks are ready."

"Here, you carry the silverware and napkins." Grace handed Lily the items and picked up the wooden salad bowl.

They ate at a teak table with folding chairs set up on the concrete patio. When Beau cut into his rare T-bone and the red juices ran out, Lily wrinkled her nose. "I don't wanna eat *that.*"

"Don't worry. I cooked yours more."

Rather than give Lily an entire steak, Grace had instructed him to cut off a section from her piece of meat. He grilled the bigger piece of beef to medium and Lily's fillet to almost well done.

With her fork, Grace pointed to the empty land across the canal and next to the Charvets' property. "I'm surprised there aren't more houses here."

"Dad owns the lots on either side. He's talked about constructing two new houses or expanding this one, but it can take years to get one of the few permits available from the county building department."

They continued to discuss aspects of life in the Keys which made it different from the mainland, like higher real estate values, almost no shopping malls, and storm evacuations. Grace stacked Lily's empty plate under hers.

The little girl opened her mouth to speak, but was stopped when Beau told about a recent accident with a fuel tanker. "The fire melted the asphalt road and shut down the highway in and out of the Keys for more than a day. Luckily, Dad and Marilyn were staying for the week."

During Beau's story, Lily wiggled in her seat, sighed audibly, and propped her head in her hand. Grace shot her a warning look to wait her turn to speak. As soon as he finished, she jumped in. "Mr. Beau, you can't touch a boy's pee-pee, right?"

An image flashed through Grace's mind of their shower together a few hours earlier. She slid a quick glance at Beau who stared back, speechless. Grace affected a casual maternal interest. "How do you know that, Lily?"

"My teacher told us." Lily's preschool had sent a letter home about the initiation of a program called Safe Child which teaches personal safety. Parents were instructed to contact the classroom teacher if they had questions or concerns about their child's participation. Lily laid her hand on top of her head. "Does my hair belong to me?"

Grace was unsure where this was going. "Yes."

"I told Drew he couldn't touch my hair, or I would tell." She crossed her arms over her chest with a no-nonsense expression. "My body belongs to me."

Grace tightened her lips, so she wouldn't smile. "You're right."

"Drew said Mrs. Connor didn't mean hair. He said she means his pee-pee."

Grace explained that body parts always covered by clothes are off limits. "But if you don't want to be touched anywhere, it's okay to say no and tell me or your teacher."

Lily looked at Beau who had visibly relaxed after her first question. "Do you tell people not to touch your pee-pee, Mr. Beau?"

His head jerked toward Grace who smirked. His Adam's apple bobbed as he swallowed. "Not anymore."

"Why not?"

"Because I'm not a little kid."

She nodded as if his response confirmed her suspicion. "Can we have ice cream now?"

After the dinner cleanup, they sat in the family room with Bingo and Uno. Lily knew how to play these games with no assistance. It was almost ten PM when Grace got her daughter ready for bed. Beau entered the room. Lily lay with the sheet pulled up to her chest. After goodnight kisses, she rolled over and dropped off to sleep. Grace closed the door part way and turned to find Beau had already moved down the hall toward the family room.

He motioned her to follow him. "We need to talk."

She stood until he settled on the wicker sofa. He didn't look at her, but leaned forward with his elbows on his knees.

Grace tucked her leg under and lowered the rest of her body to the cushion. She faced his profile. "What's the matter?"

He didn't answer for several seconds. "You said I love you. "

Panic bubbled in her like when an alarm sounds, but no one dares move until they know more. "When did I say that?"

"In the shower."

Grace relaxed and sank against the back cushion. "I was in the O-Zone. You know anything can come out of your mouth then. I'm surprised I haven't called you Michael yet."

He looked at her. "So, you didn't mean it?"

"I probably did at the time. I care about you a great deal. Is that a problem?"

"I wasn't expecting you to say it."

"Neither was I. Beau, my mother made love to men with money *for money* but never said she loved me. I had a husband who told me he loved me then walked out the door to spend Christmas with his mistress." Grace paused and stroked her finger under her nose. "So, those three words carry a mixed message for me."

Except she was falling in love with him.

Beau rubbed his palms together between his knees. "Today at the beach, it hit me how much you and Lily mean to me. Especially after the old guy said we made a nice family. I ... you should know ... I'm not looking for a permanent relationship right now. I don't want to hurt you or Lily, but after you said I love you I ..." His head dropped lower. "I just don't know if I can say it back."

Grace waited to hear the word *yet* tacked onto his statement or a request for more time. His sister's words echoed in her head. *I don't think he can love another woman again.*

She sighed. "I wasn't expecting you to say it back. I didn't even know *I* had said it."

He sat back and twisted to face her with one bent knee on the cushion. "I feel like I have to be careful. I don't only blame Megan for what happened to end our marriage. I take responsibility too."

"I know what you mean. I felt the same way for a long time after Michael's death. It wasn't until Alice pushed me to try speed dating that I knew his actions had turned me into a love cripple. I think we're both more recovered and resilient than we realize."

A tiny smile lifted the corners of his mouth. "You're okay with me not saying I love you?"

She gave him a snarky smile. "You know, that's the third time you've said it since we sat down."

He shook his head back and forth as a grin spread across his face. Without warning, Beau jumped to his feet, grabbed her around the waist, and slung her over his shoulder. "You professor, me caveman."

She squealed. "Fred Flintstone, what are you doing?"

He smacked her bottom as he headed down the hallway to the master bedroom. "Quiet, Wilma, you'll wake up Pebbles."

Chapter 40

THE NEXT DAY, Lily frowned when an umbrella stroller was placed in the car trunk for their visit to Key West. "We don't need that. I'm not a baby."

Grace lifted an insulated bag with drinks and snacks. "I know. But we'll be doing a lot of walking today. If you want, you can ride in it, or we'll use it to carry the cooler."

When they had planned their Saturday, Beau proposed a tour of the Ernest Hemingway house. Grace vetoed the idea since six-toed cats roamed inside and out. "Lily is allergic to feline dander. I don't want her to have a reaction and cut our vacation short."

They were in the first tour group of the Little White House, where several presidents after World War Two had visited. Grace found it charming with its unpretentious furnishings from the fifties and sixties.

In the office used by President Harry Truman, Lily pointed to a black, manual typewriter on the desk. "What's that, Mr. Beau?"

"A typewriter."

"What does it do?"

"You write with it."

"Like a computer?"

"No." Beau cocked his head at Grace as if to say: *Help me out here.* "You press the keys and it types on paper."

"Like a printer?"

"Except you write and print at the same time."

"Then you send it?"

"Yeah, then you can send it."

An older couple with the group observed this generational exchange and laughed. The man clapped Beau's shoulder. "Your kids are the ones who really make you feel your age."

Beau did not correct the misconception that Lily was his. He nodded and flashed a quick, false smile at the couple. By the end of the tour, he seemed to have forgotten the remark. Grace breathed a sigh of relief. She did not want another conversation where he reminded her he had no interest in marriage and a family right now.

Lily loved their next stop, The Key West Aquarium. Her eyes were wide during the shark and turtle feedings. She petted or held every prickly or slimy creature in the Touch Tank while other small children squealed or shied away. When the tour ended, she hung onto Beau's hand. "Let's do it again."

He patted his stomach. "Aren't you hungry? I am."

"Okay, but no fish friends for lunch."

They went to an Italian restaurant near Duval Street for pizza and gelato. Afterward, they strolled past kitschy tourist shops on their way back to the car. Beau bought Lily an overpriced pink T-shirt with the imprint of a sailfish on it. They stopped at Kino Sandals, a Key West landmark. Grace still wore a pair of handmade leather thongs she bought there when she was in college. Beau sat in a wooden chair by the entrance with other men who waited for women to finish shopping.

Lily sat on his lap, her hands covering her nose to ward off the pungent smell of just-cut leather. "It stinks in here, Mr. Beau."

"That's what leather smells like."

"What's leather?"

"It comes from cows. It's their—"

"Stinky poop?" She giggled.

Grace smiled as she handed the clerk eleven dollars for a pair of shoes which would last her another decade. She motioned them out the door. "C'mon. It's time to go."

Lily hopped off Beau's lap and ran out into the sunlit tiled courtyard. His shoulders sagged. "She's been throwing me with her questions on this trip."

"It won't get any easier as she grows up."

Lily slept on the ride home. She staggered into the house and lay on the family room sofa while the adults unloaded the car. The babysitter arrived an hour later. Marta was a tiny, spry woman with a wide grin. Within minutes, Lily's shyness disappeared under her effusive compliments.

The Cuban housekeeper clasped her hands in front of her chest. "*Lee-Lee* ees so pretty, *que linda*." When the little girl showed the woman how to play *The Human Body* app on her LeapPad, Marta's dark eyes flashed. "You so smart, *Lee-Lee*."

After Beau showered, Grace went into her bathroom to get ready. She donned a floor-length, navy blue halter dress and jeweled sandals. In the family room, Marta, Beau, and Lily were playing Bingo around the coffee table. He looked island-casual in a white dress shirt with the cuffs rolled up and a pair of tan linen pants.

Grace kissed the top of her daughter's head. "You be good and listen to Marta."

"I will, Mommy." Lily's eyes never left the game on the coffee table. She pointed to a card. "Marta, you have Bingo right there."

Chapter 41

THE DRIVE TO the Little Torch Key welcome station took minutes. Within the half hour, Grace and Beau disembarked from the wooden motor launch which shuttled them to the island. On the ride, the sun had begun its descent in the west and striped the sky with purple and pink bands of clouds. As soon as they stepped onto the dock, a blond hostess greeted and escorted them to their table inside the dining room. People were also eating outside on the veranda.

Beau pointed out the large glass window to tables on a beachside patio area. "We don't want to be seated out there. At dusk, the wait staff has to pass out bug spray. Also, the little Key deer can be pesky. One time when we ate here, a deer tried to grab the bread basket off the table. Megan screamed and hit it with her purse."

Sharing what he considered a humorous anecdote obliterated Grace's good humor like a numbing dart to the chest. Was this island restaurant his go-to place for romantic dates with his ex-wife?

A uniformed young man with slicked-back hair, a deep tan, and the lean physique of a surfer stood next to them. "Good evening. I'm Patrick, and I'll be your server tonight. May I start you with wine or a cocktail?"

Beau discussed the wine list with the waiter while Grace gazed out the window at the perfect tropical evening. Soon the movie-like setting restored her spirits. On both the veranda and in the dining room, tables were laid with snowy linens, crystal stemware, and white china. A small votive candle nestled in a wooden holder next to a tropical flower in a bud vase.

Her enjoyment of the romantic ambiance lasted until she opened the dinner menu. Beau had told her the entrees varied each night, so he couldn't recommend a dish he'd eaten there before. What he neglected to mention were the prices. A bowl of mushroom soup was sixteen dollars. Each appetizer was over twenty. The least expensive entrée was forty-five dollars. Either she was in for a fantastic culinary experience, or people paid big bucks for the delight of dining in such sublime beauty.

Patrick returned, decanted the wine, and poured out a sample for Beau to taste and approve. "Have you decided on your selections for tonight?"

Grace studied the list of food options with a falsely confident air. She could order the yellowtail snapper now or wait until later and get fifty-two junior cheeseburgers at Wendy's.

Beau peered at her over his menu. "Are you interested in the Dinner for Two?"

"That's fine with me."

Each course when it arrived was a plate of gastronomic artistry. Grace's cup of coconut lobster bisque was dotted with ginger oil and topped with taro root crisps. The silky soup was a mouthful of delight. She could have easily devoured another bowl. Beau consumed six colossal Key West pink shrimp nestled in a Willi glass of crushed ice accompanied by spicy cocktail sauce. When their dinners of sliced Chateaubriand with a Caribbean spiny lobster and grilled asparagus were finished, her appetite was satisfied. The portions were perfect for her, but hardly man-sized for Beau who stared with hungry, vampire-like longing at food delivered to nearby tables. He lifted the napkin on the empty bread basket twice.

Grace laughed to herself. Was he expecting the miracle of loaves and fishes?

At different times during their meal, several women climbed the steps from the beach and entered the restaurant. They all wore the same white, one-shouldered Grecian-like gown with a gold belt. After several minutes, they returned outside.

When Patrick brought them coffee, Grace pointed to the double doors. "Is there a party on the beach?"

He craned his neck and peered. "It's a wedding reception. A couple got married out there at sunset."

"That's why I saw several women in the same dress. Is that the way to the ladies' room?" Grace motioned in the direction the women had gone.

"Around the corner and down the hall."

Grace laid her napkin on the table. "I'll be just a moment."

Beau caught her hand as she passed, raised it to his lips, and kissed the back. She smiled at his courtly gesture. Liquid warmth ran up her arm and she carried the pleasant feeling with her into the ladies' room. Staring at her reflection in an ornate rococo mirror, she chided herself for her initial moodiness. Of course, Beau would have brought Megan here. His parents owned a nearby vacation home, and there weren't that many upscale places like this in the Keys.

Upon her return to the dining room, Grace rounded the corner and found Beau was no longer seated in his chair. He stood next to it and faced a woman who was almost his height. The statuesque, auburn-haired beauty was the stuff of men's wet dreams. She had one hand on his upper bicep, the other lay over his heart. She was dressed in a gown worn by the bridal party.

Grace stopped. Something seemed off balance about the scene. The woman spoke close to Beau's ear. His eyes widened. She took a small step back, eyed him up and down then talked more. At that moment, Beau's eyes shifted and collided with Grace's. He looked at her as if he had just exited an adult bookstore with an armload of porn and ran into his priest. The tall woman cocked her head at his open-mouthed expression. She turned and followed his gaze. Grace strode forward, a neutral expression plastered on her face.

The first one to speak was the redhead. "You must be the girlfriend, Grace."

Summoning her professionalism and a bit of her mother's *chutzpah,* she held out her hand. "Dr. Grace Black-Stone. And you are?"

The other woman held out her hand with limp reluctance, like Grace had neglected to wash hers after using the toilet. "Megan Donnelly ... Charvet."

Grace raised her eyebrows, unable to disguise her shock. Megan grinned, as if pleased with the reaction. To give herself a moment to recover, Grace looked from the neckline of the Grecian gown which ballooned over impressive breasts, down to the flat sandals, and up again. In heels, this Amazon would be as tall as Beau. "You're wearing the same dress as the wedding party. Did you get married today, Megan?"

The ex-wife gave a tinny laugh. "No. A friend of mine did." From under her thick false lashes, she looked up at Beau and placed her palm over his heart. "I was reminded of how happy we were on our wedding day. Do you remember?"

The words seemed to snap him out of his state of suspended animation. Taking a deep breath, he squared his shoulders and removed Megan's hand from his body. His voice sounded thoughtful, but a hint of intentional cruelness seeped through. "Too bad that happiness couldn't have lasted longer than two years."

Megan's lips pursed as she took a half-step away from him. "Yes, too bad. Well, I should get back to my friends." She turned to Grace. "Nice meeting you." The words were uttered in a polite social tone with no sincerity behind them. To Beau, she said, "I'll send you the information about those state bridge projects. Have a nice evening."

Beau took his seat and met Grace's gaze after she sat and faced him. "Wow. That was a shock. We haven't seen or talked to each other in three years."

Somewhat annoyed, her words came out harsher than she intended. "Was it so shocking you couldn't stop her from touching you?"

His lips puckered, and he sported a sheepish expression. "I'd forgotten the impact she has on men. On me."

"Had you told Megan my name?"

Beau fixed his eyes on the linen tablecloth between them. "She already knew it."

"How?"

"She and Gen are friends. I assume my sister said I was dating a woman called Grace."

"Why did you look so surprised when you saw me come back from the ladies room?"

He winced and remained focused on the tabletop, like he would rather have his fingernails chipped out with a rusty ice pick than answer the question. "Megan had just asked if you would be interested in a *ménage à trois*." Beau voiced the words with a strong French pronunciation.

"Oh." Grace was thrown and swallowed hard before she spoke. "Was that something you and she—"

"No. Never." Beau looked aghast before his eyes flicked away from hers. "But that's what I found when I came home from work one day."

Now Gen's comment about Beau being unable to love again made more sense. The breakup of his marriage involved more than two people who no longer loved each other or could not get along. In the Suffering Sweepstakes of Marital Infidelity, which was worse: having your husband die with his mistress on the other side of the world or watching your wife cavort with more than one partner in your bed?

Beau interrupted her reverie. "I'm sorry if Megan ruined our date."

Grace gave him a weak smile. "Well, she didn't ruin it, but certainly affected it." The leather bill holder sat on the table. "Have you paid already?"

He nodded.

Grace scooted her chair away from the table. "I think we should leave then."

Beau was quiet on the boat ride home. Grace attributed it to the noise of the outboard engine and the other passengers who filled the vessel on this return trip. He drove back to the house without a word. After Marta left, he sat on the sofa, his face dragged down with some unidentifiable emotion.

Grace stood across from him. "What's wrong?"

His posture and expression were similar to the previous night when he was upset by her inadvertent declaration of *I love you*. When he spoke, he sounded self-conscious, as if he were talking to her in front of people he didn't know. "I'm just thinking about what Megan said at the restaurant."

Grace's breath caught. "The threesome?"

Beau's head jerked up. "No! Not that. She's working for a firm that designs bridges and highways. They're scheduled to bid on some big upcoming projects for the Florida Department of Transportation. Charvet Crane would really benefit if we could get hired for some of them, but I hate the thought of owing Megan."

Grace sat on the cushion of a wicker chair across from him. "If your company won the bid, would you have much contact with her?"

Beau shook his head. "None at all."

"Then what's to think about?" Grace stared at him, frustrated with his obvious distress. "Beau, she cheated on you. You're divorced. Why should seeing her again affect you or your business? It's not as if Michael intruded on our date. Now *that* would be a shock."

"It's just —"

An icy chill slid down Grace's spine, formed into a glacier, and froze the blood pumping through her heart. "You still have feelings for her?"

Beau's hand sliced sideways across his body. "Definitely not."

"Then what?"

"I thought after … I thought she could never—"

"Turn you on?"

His face looked bleak. "That's what she whispered to me. 'I can still make you hard.' I'm sorry." His sincerity was apparent even though his words hurt. Without warning, he stood up. "Excuse me." He hurried down the hall, into his bedroom, and shut the door.

She stared after him then rose to her feet and entered Lily's bedroom. Her daughter was curled in the middle of the bed, peaceful in slumber. In the hallway, Grace moved to Beau's closed door and listened.

"Beau? Are you okay?"

"I'll be fine, Grace. I just need some time alone."

"Let me know if I can get you anything."

"I will."

She went into the kitchen, emptied the used grounds from the coffee maker, inserted a new filter, fresh coffee, and set the timer for seven in the morning. After preparing for bed, Grace covered herself with a sheet, turned off the light, and stared into the darkness.

Chapter 42

THE NEXT MORNING she and Lily ate alone at the kitchen table. "Why is Mr. Beau still sleeping?"

"He's sick."

"Does his tummy hurt?"

Grace gathered their cereal bowls. She walked to the sink to hide any errant expression of disgust. "And his head."

She had found an empty fifth of bourbon in the kitchen trashcan. The bottle had not been there the night before. After breakfast, she and Lily were outside feeding ducks in the canal with pieces of bread when the screen door squeaked open. Beau gripped a cup of coffee and squinted at the bright sunlight. He walked like he was barefoot on gravel.

"Mr. Beau." Lily squealed and ran toward him.

He closed his eyes and rubbed his forehead. Grace grabbed her daughter by the arm. "Settle down. Remember, he doesn't feel well."

Lily approached with caution, her face creased with concern. "Does your head hurt?"

Beau gave her a weak smile. "I'll be okay, but I'm afraid we'll need to leave early. I'm not up for another day at the beach."

They packed after Grace insisted Beau drink a bottle of water and eat a piece of buttered toast. She offered to drive, and he let her. Lily was quiet in the backseat with her LeapPad and a headset. Despite his long shower and the additional fluids he consumed, a fermented odor leached from his skin within the closed confines of the car. He sat with his eyes shut and leaned against the headrest for most of the trip. By the time they reached Grace's house three hours later, some color had returned to his face.

He helped carry their belongings inside then squatted in front of Lily. "I'm sorry we couldn't stay longer."

"That's okay." She touched his cheek. "Do you feel better?"

He nodded and rose to his feet. His smile faded when he faced Grace. "I'll be out of town all week."

"I need to ask you—"

He kissed her cheek and got behind the wheel. "I'll call you in a couple days." He closed the car door and drove away.

Chapter 43

AT WORK, ALICE asked about her weekend in the Keys. Grace forced a smile and spoke in a post-vacation-with-coitus tone of voice. It sounded false, but Alice gazed at her with eager hope. It was as if her friend needed the validation of a true love story for one of them. Grace didn't have the heart to tell her *The Bachelorette* relationships had a longer shelf-life than hers and Beau's.

Grace called him on Wednesday since he hadn't contacted her. She left a message. By Friday, he had not called back. When she dialed his cell and was again routed to voice mail, she dialed his office number.

"Hello, Charvet Crane. How may I help you?" The voice had Cathy's southern drawl.

Grace breathed a prayer of thanks that Gen had not answered the phone. "Cathy, this is Grace Stone."

"Hi, there. Did you and your daughter enjoy your weekend in the Keys?"

"Lily had a wonderful time. I was wondering when Beau will be back."

"Well, he was here this morning. I don't know if he'll return to the office before I leave today."

A horrible thickening in Grace's chest made it difficult to speak. She cleared her throat. "Was he out of the office much this week?"

"Well, he's got a big job up in Delray and another one in North Miami. He's been bouncing between the two. Try his cell. He'll answer it as soon as he can."

Three hours later, Beau called her as she dished macaroni and cheese onto two plates for supper. She had set her phone to vibrate. She checked the screen, slipped it back into her pocket, and laid a plate in front of Lily.

"Mommy, your phone's buzzing."

"I'll call them back later."

After she put Lily in bed for the night, she checked and found three missed calls from Beau. Her phone vibrated in her hand.

It was the guard at the front gate. "There's a Beau Charvet here."

She had requested security remove his name from her approved entry list. "Please don't allow him to enter."

Less than a minute later, her phone hummed. "Hello, Beau."

"Why can't I come in? What's going on? Cathy told me you called the office today. I'm sorry I didn't get in touch with you earlier."

"You lied to me about being out of town." She blinked back hot tears. Her dead husband had taken dozens of so-called business trips. How many of those had been legitimate, and how many were overnight stays at his mistress' place? "We left early on Sunday because you were hungover, not sick. As far as I'm concerned, there's nothing more to talk about on the phone or in person. Please don't contact me again."

She ended the call and shut off her phone. Lily would be saddened by the loss of Mr. Beau. Her daughter already foresaw a future with him. The week before they went to the Keys, Lily had dropped a pencil and pad of paper in her mother's lap. "Write Mr. Beau's last name, Mommy." She did, and Lily went off to her room. The next day, Grace found the tablet with *LILY CHARVET* written several times in childish block letters.

This was an important lesson for a single mother to learn. Despite having sexual needs, she must first protect her child's physical and emotional well-being. When she was Lily's age, she had wished for two parents like other children, but never developed a misplaced expectation of a father figure with one of Juliette's boyfriends. Her mother wasn't a nurturer, but she always kept Grace separate from the men in her life.

When Juliette spent hours preparing for her dates, Grace would watch her mother transform into an achingly beautiful creature with smooth hair, perfect makeup, a beautiful gown, and sparkling jewels. As a child, she had asked her mother several times if she could meet the man whisking her away to a fancy restaurant, a charity ball, or a symphony concert. Since Juliette looked like a Disney princess, surely the man had to be the prince of a fantastical kingdom. Of course, her mother's answer was always a firm: "No". She also learned to never ask if she could go with them. Juliette would give a tinkling lilt of a laugh and respond with a flip, almost cruel, denial. After several rebuffs she stopped asking, followed by avoiding her mother's bedroom altogether while she readied herself for a *date*.

Maybe Grace would have to wait until Lily is of age before she could allow another man to share her bed and life. A tear slipped down her cheek as fourteen lonely, loveless years stretched out in front of her.

Chapter 44

ON SUNDAY AFTERNOON Grace swept out the garage while Lily napped. She jumped and dropped the broom when a tall figure stood outside the open door, backlit by the sun. It was Tariq.

Grace put a hand over her thudding heart. "You scared me."

"Sorry. We need to talk."

She gave him a hard-eyed look. "He called you guys, didn't he?"

"I think you should hear Beau out. The man cares for you, and he's a good guy." Tariq's voice took on an ER doctor's firmness. "Meet with him then decide whether or not to go your separate ways."

She picked up the broom. "Fine. I'll call him."

"He's waiting at our house."

She stopped sweeping. "Of course, he is. And Robert is probably serving him tea and sympathy."

"Don't go bitchy on me, Grace. Freshen up and I'll stay here with Lily. He's waiting for you on our patio."

Grace washed up and brushed her hair. She walked across the backyard and approached the door of her neighbors' pool enclosure. Beau sat in a wicker chair, bent forward with his elbows on both knees. She pulled on the screen door's latch. His head jerked toward the sound as she blew through the opening. He rose to his feet. She stopped and faced him across the small wicker bench used as a coffee table.

Beau nodded at her. "I appreciate you agreeing to talk."

Grace took a chair across from him and waited, her eyebrows arched and lips pursed. Over the past week, she had deliberated on the possibility of being related to Marilyn and how that connection impacted her newly-ended relationship with Beau. The situation was complicated and tainted her dreams of welcoming family get-togethers. The likelihood she and Lily could spend time with Marilyn, Skip, and Zoe to the exclusion of the other Charvets, especially Beau, seemed impossible at best.

He sat and met her gaze. "I'm really sorry. I don't know why I acted so stupid when I saw Megan again. I would have bet everything I own that nothing she could say or do would bother me." He dropped his head as if no longer unable to tolerate a face-to-face conversation. "More than anything else, I'm embarrassed. After the divorce, I acted like this tough guy with no regrets, but it took badgering from Skip to get me to try dating again. Then the first time I see my ex-wife, I make a damn fool of myself ... in front of you, someone I really care about and respect." Grace relaxed her stiff posture, and Beau lifted his head. "I have no right to ask for a second chance, but I'd like to prove I'm still the good guy I promised you I was. What do you say? Can we try again?"

Grace gave him a steady stare then inhaled and plunged ahead. "If you haven't figured it out already, Lily has decided you would make a good father for her."

He smiled. "Yeah, I know."

"Well, she'll be heartbroken when that doesn't happen."

Her brusque words caused Beau's smile to disappear.

In a clipped toneless voice, Grace said, "Since Michael died when Lily was just an infant, she never experienced the loss of a flesh-and-blood father. I worry about her attachment to you. She's not going to understand that you're not looking for marriage and a family. Why should we continue in a dead-end relationship which will eventually hurt my daughter and me?"

Beau looked as though he'd been slapped. He took a moment then cleared his throat. "Since we went to the Keys, I've thought about how you called yourself a love cripple and realized I'm one too. Maybe I don't know what real love feels like, but my best chance of finding out is with a woman like you."

His words gave Grace a glimmer of hope, but she was still concerned about protecting a four-year-old who didn't understand that choosing a would-be daddy didn't guarantee one.

Before she could respond, Beau spoke again. "For me, you and Lily are a package deal. I care more about the two of you than I ever thought I could. I can't make you a definite promise about the future, but I'd sure like to keep trying."

Options and their outcomes raced through Grace's brain. Since she had become a single parent, every choice she made carried a modicum of risk affecting Lily. Beau studied her with an expression of unease as her silence continued.

At last, she opened her mouth, but her voice sounded unsure and scared. "You're the first man I've wanted to get involved with in four years. I know there are a lot of single women are out there looking for Mr. Right. I once thought that person was Michael, which is why I married him. But he turned out to be no different than the men my mother *dated*. When we started our relationship, I made a major mistake."

From day one, her daughter had been doing her best to win Beau over and push Grace into his arms. After all, she had told him that her mommy really needed a kiss. She was a big part of their relationship. On Christmas, their attraction to each other had been confirmed when Lily saw them kissing in the kitchen. At that time, Grace should have prepared her daughter for the possibility that Beau may be not want to be their husband and father.

Beau's voice was formal and restrained as if he were on the witness stand about to be accused of something for which he had no control. "What was your mistake?"

"I didn't realize that we're not just a couple. With Lily, we've formed a kind of family, but a dating family."

"That's what that old guy at the beach thought we were."

"And so does Lily. The problem is she doesn't know that our quasi-family isn't necessarily going to be legal or permanent. I should have talked with her long before this. She needs to understand that the possibility of a father is very different than the reality."

Beau licked his bottom lip. "Grace, I—"

She closed her eyes for a silent prayer. "But I'm willing to give you another chance."

"You are?"

Grace opened her eyes and nodded. "I don't know if you're our Mr. Right, but you can be Mr. Right Now. However, I'm giving you fair warning."

He stared at her with starry-eyed enthusiasm. "About what?"

Grace was determined to add a caveat to this reconciliation. "Life is too short and my daughter is too precious for me to remain in a relationship where neither of us is treated right."

"I'll do my best to not hurt either of you." Both were silent then Beau gave her a bashful smile. He held his arms wide, like a politician at a podium. "Mr. Right Now could really use a hug right now."

They stood and came together at one end of the low table which had separated them. Once Grace was enfolded in Beau's arms again, a sense of peace flowed over her, and she squeezed him tighter as a little flip of apprehension intruded, like the foreshadowing of a possible unfortunate outcome.

Chapter 45

A MONTH LATER, Grace received the email which changed her life. She was glad to be on her home computer and not at work. Her heart skipped a beat when she read the subject line: *Your AncestryDNA results are in.*

With a trembling finger, she clicked on the message. A green *See my results* button was in the middle of the screen. She signed into her Ancestry account and up popped *Hello Grace!* Below the greeting were three columns. One said *DNA Story* and listed her ethnicity as forty-three percent Europe West, twenty-eight percent Ireland, Scotland, Wales, and thirteen percent Europe East. Migrations showed Ohio River Valley, Indiana, and Illinois settlers. No surprise there based on what Marilyn had told her.

The next two columns made her heart beat faster. The middle column was called *DNA Matches.* Listed were the names of people who were fourth cousins or closer. Within the photos of these relatives, Grace spotted Marilyn before her eyes flooded, and she was blinded by tears. In addition to Beau's stepmother, there were four hundred and thirty-seven people on Ancestry related to her.

She clicked on *View All DNA Matches.* The first name was Marilyn Charvet and she was identified as a possible aunt. The third column was *DNA Circles.* She had only one showing a great-grandfather named D.J. Makowsky. For the next three hours, Grace studied all the people who were closely and distantly related to her. The ones who had an eastern or western European lineage were Marilyn and several first and second cousins. The relatives with ethnic origins from Ireland, Scotland and Wales were third and fourth cousins. Those people were likely from Juliette's side of the family.

Grace sat back in her chair and laughed aloud, almost giddy with excitement. She reached for her phone to call Marilyn but halted. The time on the screen said it was almost midnight. She would call her *aunt* tomorrow with the news.

Chapter 46

THE NEXT DAY Grace called Marilyn. "Guess what?"

In a cheery voice, Marilyn said, "You're my niece."

"You know already?"

"I received my results last week. I've been dying to call. I hoped you sent your DNA kit in about the same time as me. How do you feel knowing George is your father?"

She hesitated. Despite years of yearning to know who sired her, all she thought about was her living family members. "To tell you the truth, I've been mostly concerned with how this confirmation will affect my relationship with Beau."

"Why? You're not related by blood." Before Grace could respond, Marilyn gave a sharp inhale that was audible over the phone. "Oh, right. You're worried what will happen if you two are no longer a couple?"

"Of course. After years of being alone, I've finally found a family, but you have to admit it could be awkward. I'm ..." She almost said *sleeping*. "... dating one member and should that relationship end, it will make things difficult. Also, I'm the result of an illicit affair, not some long-lost child."

Marilyn sought to alleviate Grace's concerns with platitudes about acceptance and open-mindedness on behalf of all the Charvets. "We'll just take it one day at a time. How should we share this information with everyone?"

They decided Marilyn would inform the family at a dinner the next evening for her husband's birthday. She was confident everyone would be thrilled with the revelation. "Do you and Lily want to come?"

"I think it best you tell them without us there."

Meanwhile, she would deal with Lily. Any additional connection with Mr. Beau was sure to please the little girl. The challenge was going to be explaining the intricacies of aunts, uncles, cousins, and relatives by marriage.

After the call with her new-found aunt ended, Grace found Lily in her bedroom and sat on the child-sized bed, patting the mattress beside her. "Come sit here with me. I have something I need to tell you."

A frightened expression creased the little girl's features. "Is it about Mr. Beau?" The seriousness of her mother's expression must have conveyed Lily's worst fear.

"Remember the party Robert helped me get ready for?"

"You wore Grandma Juliette's dress."

"That's right. I met Mr. Beau's mother that night." Later, she would explain what a stepmother was.

"What's her name?"

"It's Marilyn, and she knew your Grandma Juliette." Grace leaned in close and lowered her voice to reveal a big secret. "And her brother is my father and your grandfather."

Lily's hands covered her mouth in childish surprise. "What's his name?"

"George Makowsky."

"Is he gonna come see me?"

After the initial meeting with Marilyn, Grace had researched her probable father's obituary and lifetime achievements online. Dr. Makowsky had passed away when she was only a few years older than Lily. "No, sweetie. He died when I was just a little girl. But now I know his sister is my aunt."

"Mine too?"

"Yes, she is."

On Saturday evening, Grace waited in nervous anticipation to hear the results of the big reveal at the Charvet household. Marilyn was the first one to contact her.

Her aunt spoke in a hushed tone. "Hi, Grace. I wanted to let you know I told Beau, Bojo, and Gen about you."

A feeling of dread raised the hairs on her arms. "Why are you whispering?"

"I'm in the kitchen. I couldn't wait to call you. I can hear them talking in the dining room."

"How did Beau, I mean Bojo, take the news?"

"He was very surprised." Marilyn giggled. "Once Bojo realized there was nothing inappropriate about your relationship, he was excited and talked about how nice it will be to have you and Lily at family gatherings."

"And your husband?"

"Beau was flabbergasted at first then he saw how happy I was. He knows how much I miss George and regretted not having a living link to him. Well, I better go. I just wanted you to know they all know."

"Wait a minute, what about Gen?" The beats of silence echoed across the line.

"Don't you worry about Gen. She'll come around. I'll call you tomorrow, and we'll talk more. Bye, now."

The second call was from Beau. From the background sounds, he was in his car. "Hey, Cuz."

Grace smiled. "Hey, yourself. Are you upset I hadn't told you about this?"

"No, it's fine. Marilyn let us know about meeting with you and how this was all her idea. I think it was smart to not go around telling people until you knew for sure. It's great you finally found the family you've been hoping for, and even better, your part of my family."

"Um ... what about Gen?"

Beau cleared his throat. "She was surprised and thinks we should take it slow."

"Slow?"

"She's okay with you being related to Marilyn and Skip. Oh, and Zoe too. We just need to give her more time. I've pulled into my garage, so I'll talk with you later. Okay?"

"Are we still on for dinner with Robert tomorrow night?" They had made the arrangements a week ago after learning his father's birthday dinner fell on their usual Saturday date night.

"I'll be at your place at six. Good night, Grace."

Chapter 47

ON SUNDAY EVENING when the Chan-Stone-Charvet group had finished dinner at Pizza Time and waited for the check, Lily stood on the seat of her chair. "Guess what? We have aunts."

Robert laughed. "Got a little pest problem next door?"

Beau pulled out his phone. "I know a good exterminator if you don't have one. I can give you his number."

Grace's voice verged on good-humored annoyance. "We don't have *ants*."

"We do, Mommy, and I know her name."

Grace had her *aha* moment. "I told her about my father and that Beau's stepmother is my aunt and hers also." She and Lily had breakfast with the neighbors that morning and shared the results of the DNA report. "Therefore, we have *aunts*."

Beau laughed and hugged Lily. "Mom and Dad are going to love you."

After they returned home and Grace put Lily to bed, she and Beau moved to the sofa in the living room to talk. "Had you ever met Marilyn's brother, George?"

He put his arm around her shoulders. "No. When she and Dad got married, he was too sick to attend the wedding and died a few months later." Beau's voice became low and gentle. "How do you feel knowing he's your father?"

"Robert asked me the same thing. It's a relief to know I'm not alone in the world, except for Lily. I can't wait to find out more about the Makowsky history and try to find someone from Juliette's side of the family." Grace hesitated. "Beau, there is something we need to discuss. We—"

He interrupted her. "You're worried about what will happen if you and I break up."

"I am. Having a family is so new and precious to me. I don't want to lose it. That would be harder to bear than not having one in the first place."

He pulled her close and rested his cheek against her hair. "We can make this work whether we're together or not. You have a right to share Marilyn, Skip, and Zoe with the Charvets."

Grace prayed she could honor what she was about to say. "I appreciate your understanding and I promise, regardless of what happens between us, I will always respect you as a step cousin."

"I promise as well." He kissed her forehead. They sat in companionable silence until Beau said, "What are your plans are for next weekend?"

"What did you have in mind?"

"Marilyn wanted me to ask if you would like to come for dinner next Sunday. She and Dad are dying to meet Lily."

"Why don't we invite them here, and I'll cook."

Beau's brow was furrowed. It was like his thought came out in a dialogue bubble: *Will we be eating beans and weenies again?* She had never prepared an entire meal from scratch for him. Dinners with Lily consisted of foods which required little or no preparation. When she was with Beau they usually ate out, but next weekend she would surprise him.

Chapter 48

ON THE FOLLOWING Sunday, Lily kept vigil at the dining room window. "Our aunts are here."

Grace wiped her hands, took off her apron, and opened the front door. "Come in."

Marilyn entered first with a smile for Grace. A softening look crossed her face when she spotted Lily. She carried a plate covered with foil. Mr. Charvet followed her inside. He toted a large, cellophane-wrapped basket. Lily looked up, silent and wide-eyed. Beau stepped forward and pulled the door closed behind him.

Marilyn kissed Grace's cheek. "Thank you for the invitation. I didn't know what to do with myself, so I baked some cinnamon buns."

Mr. Charvet bent toward Lily. "Are you the good little girl Bojo's been talking about?"

Lily eyed the basket. "Who's Bojo?"

Beau Sr. nodded at his son. "Him."

"He's my Mr. Beau." She put her hand in his. "And I'm his good girl."

Mr. Charvet lowered the large gift. "Then I guess you get this basket because it's especially for good little girls."

Lily smiled and held out her arms, but the gift was too large for her to carry.

Grace motioned toward the living room. "Let's put it on the coffee table."

Beau relieved Marilyn of her plate before she sat on the sofa. Her husband placed the tall basket on the low table. Grace followed Beau into the kitchen where he laid the plate on the counter and eyed her head-to-toe. She wore a pale pink sleeveless sheath with a long pearl necklace. Her hair was twisted into a bun on the back of her head.

He murmured against her lips. "My lady."

They returned to the living room where Lily lifted a stuffed, white rabbit with a pink neck ribbon and skirt from the basket. "Look, Mommy, a girl bunny." As she dug through more of the contents, a Barbie Doll outfit emerged, along with books, nail polish, candy, and an assortment of stickers. Before Grace could remind her daughter to say thank you, Lily ran to her. She motioned for her mother to bend down. With her hands cupped around her mouth, she spoke in an audible whisper. "What are their names?"

Grace placed her hand on the back of her daughter's head and walked to their newfound relative. "This is your Aunt Marilyn and mine too. You need to ask what she wants you to call her."

Lily tilted her head to the side with a hint of shyness. "What's your name for me to say?"

"Why don't you call me Mémé?" Marilyn looked at Grace from her seat on the sofa. "It's what Gen's little girl and boy use."

Lily put her hands on Marilyn's knees. "Thank you, Mémé, for the basket."

The woman's eyes moistened as she smiled at her brother's grand-daughter. "May I give you a hug?"

After Lily nodded, Marilyn wrapped her arms around the little girl and blinked back tears. In a quiet voice, she said, "George would have loved her."

Lily moved to stand beside Beau's father who sat on a side chair. "My name is Lily Anne Stone. What's yours?"

"Call me Pépé."

"Thank you, Pépé."

He pointed to his cheek and Lily leaned forward to kiss him. She returned to her new toys as a timer sounded in the kitchen. Grace excused herself.

She pulled out the oven rack as Beau entered. He took the potholders from her and lifted the tangerine glazed ham from the upper oven and placed it on the stovetop. Then he removed roasted potatoes, green beans Provencal, and honey carrots from the lower oven. Grace put on oven mitts and carried the serving dishes to the dining room table. Beau sliced off a dozen pieces of ham and fanned them out on the platter.

He slipped a sliver of meat into his mouth and chewed. "I guess I didn't have to worry about eating beans and weenies."

Dinner was a pleasant affair with conversation flowing around the table with ease, despite the occasional intrusion from a preschooler. Lily's current interest, or obsession, was her upcoming enrollment in kindergarten. Her almost insatiable demand for information about the public school program required Grace to cull her memory for her own experience decades ago. Lily drew pictures of the activities she would do in class, played teacher with Maxi and Erin, studied magazines and catalogs for clothes and supplies she would need. Every bedtime story was a book about school.

Despite the dinner topic under discussion by the adults, Lily would quiz Beau's parents about their kindergarten knowledge. "What did you learn, Pépé?

"I learned that I had a lot to learn."

"Is that when you got your super powers?"

To Marilyn, she asked, "Do kids in kindergarten eat snacks?"

"Um, I'm not sure."

"We have snack time in preschool after learning centers."

"What do you learn in a learning center?"

"I learn I like snacks."

After everyone ate the made-from-scratch carrot cake for dessert, Grace talked with Marilyn and her husband while Beau commandeered Lily into clearing the table with him. While he and Grace put away the food and loaded the dishwasher, Lily carried out her baby album to show Marilyn and her husband. Grace and Beau joined them when the last photograph had been viewed.

Lily closed the album with a snap. "That's the end of me."

Marilyn lifted her great-niece onto her lap. "Thank you for showing us those pictures. You know, in addition to me and Pépé, you also have two cousins, Skip and Zoe."

"What's a cousin?"

"A cousin is your aunt or uncle's child. Skip is my son, and Zoe is the daughter Pépé and I have."

"Where are my cousins?"

"Zoe is away at college and will be home for the summer. Skip is a long way from here right now because of his job, but he'll back soon."

"Has Mommy seen my cousins?"

"Not yet."

Beau cleared his throat. "Actually, she's already met Skip."

Mr. Charvet frowned. "How could she? The accident with the car happened after he left for Dubai."

"Back in October, Skip and I went speed dating together."

Beau's father gaped like his son had pulled out a crack pipe and started smoking. "What do you mean you and Skip dated?"

"We didn't date each other. We signed up for a speed dating event."

Mr. Charvet still looked perturbed. "Let me get this straight. You and Skip paid to meet women?"

"Yeah, and one of them was Grace."

Mr. Charvet swiveled toward her, his eyebrows arched. Before she could clarify speed dating to him, Marilyn lightly smacked her husband's arm. "It's the way things are done nowadays. Tell him, Grace."

"It's true." She nodded. "Speed dating has several benefits."

Mr. Charvet crossed his arms over his chest. "Like what?"

"There's no pressure. You can match with someone or not. No one will ever know."

"Did you match Bojo or Skip?"

"I didn't write anyone's name down."

"Why not?"

She shrugged. "I didn't think I was ready to date again."

Beau Sr. turned to his son. "What about you? Did you write her name down?"

Beau gave Grace a warm smile. "I did. I was disappointed she didn't match me. But, in the end, it didn't matter. We met again."

Mr. Charvet uncrossed his arms but sat with his hands laced together in his lap. He squinted at Grace. "What are some of the other *benefits* you mentioned?"

"Unlike other first-time dates, the five-minute time limit means you're not forced to make conversation all evening with someone who doesn't interest you. The event happens in a public place with lots of people and security around. In fact, the speed dates only know each other's first names, so there's a degree of anonymity."

Lily, who had been ignored, climbed off the sofa. "When I'm in first grade, I'm gonna have a boyfriend."

Mr. Charvet relaxed his stiff posture and chuckled. "You don't have one now?"

Lily picked up her stuffed bunny and hugged it to her chest. "Not till after kindergarten. Boys have to grow up."

An hour later, Lily was in bed. Beau and Grace walked his parents to the front door. They thanked her for a lovely meal.

Marilyn hugged her niece and followed her husband outside. "I'll be in touch."

Grace shut the door and headed to the kitchen. "I'll pack you some food to take home. I've got more than we can possibly eat."

"I need to talk to you." His voice was principal-stern. "Why didn't you tell me you could cook like that?"

She smirked as he pulled her into his arms. "I haven't done much cooking for just Lily and me. I forgot how much I enjoyed it. From now on I promise to feed you more than beans and weenies."

Chapter 49

GRACE WAS TRUE to her word. One evening when she didn't have a late class, she prepared a pot roast for dinner and invited Beau for an adult meal with a child, rather than a child-preferred meal with grownups.

When they finished, Lily skipped off to her bedroom to find a much-repeated and favorite bedtime story book. "I'll read it to you, Mr. Beau."

Her new trick was to flip through pages, using her mother's inflected voice in perfect imitation, even if she could only sight-read some of the words. She would sneak sidelong glances to make sure her listener was paying attention and impressed with her *reading* ability.

Beau leaned back in his chair and addressed Grace. "Do you have any plans for Saturday afternoon?"

"I'll have Maxi and Erin until about noon. Then it's errands and housework. Why?"

"My sister's having a party for her son. He'll be four. Three days later, I'll be thirty-four. Will you and Lily go with me?"

"Is this an invitation from your sister or just you? I don't want to horn in on your nephew's party."

"It's okay. I told Gen I was bringing you and Lily."

After Beau left, Grace added the date on a calendar posted on the kitchen wall. Lily entered the room. "What are you writing?"

"We're going with Mr. Beau to his nephew's birthday party on Saturday."

"What's a nephew?"

"You know Hana, Tariq's sister?"

"Nour and Amal's mommy."

"Yes. Tariq is their uncle, and they are his nieces. If they had been boys, then they would be his nephews."

"Will I have a nephew?"

Grace rubbed her forehead. How do you make a four-year-old understand the intricacies of family relations? "If you someday have a brother or sister—"

"I want one."

"A brother or sister?"

Lily nodded. "That too. But I want a nephew."

"Okay, but to have a nephew, you first need a brother or sister. When that brother or sister grows up and has a baby boy, then you'll have a nephew."

"Can I get a nephew now?"

"No. You don't have a grown-up brother or sister," Grace explained with painful patience.

"Can I have Mr. Beau's nephew?"

"No. You have to wait until your own brother or sister has a boy."

"Okay." With that said, Lily skipped out of the room.

Grace closed her eyes and sighed.

Chapter 50

WHEN BEAU CAME to Grace's house on Saturday afternoon, he opened the birthday presents they gave him. Lily drew a picture of them at the beach in the Keys and Grace mounted it into a frame. In the drawing, a boxy figure in short pants held hands with a much smaller one in a pink two-piece swimsuit. They wore big smiles as Grace's body lay on the brown sand in front of them.

Once again, Beau struggled to keep a straight face while he praised the artwork. He held the picture in one hand and hugged Lily with the other. He turned the drawing around to face Grace. "You look like a corpse."

She smiled. "And in the picture, the two of you are so happy about it."

Grace gave Beau a selfie of the three of them from their Keys trip. She enlarged it to a five by eight and put it into a shell-embossed frame. He also received a new pair of cargo shorts and a Tommy Bahama shirt. After he thanked them for his gifts, they left for the birthday party and Grace's first family gathering.

Tom and Gen lived in a West Boca McMansion, an oversized house on a small lot. All the houses in the neighborhood were almost identical with front doors tall enough a man on stilts could pass under the lintels. The landscaping was well-maintained, clean and regimental. Beau parked in front of one of the three garages on a brick paver driveway that would accommodate only one car between the closed overhead door and the street.

He opened the unlocked front door and stepped aside to let Lily and Grace enter. "Hello, anybody home?"

White marble floors glinted in the afternoon sun streaming through high windows. A staircase curved upward to the right of a two-story living room.

The sofas and chairs looked comfy and squishy. Shelves were crammed with books and family photos in a variety of frames. The evidence of children was everywhere with a scattering of toys, kid-sized shoes, and electronic games.

Tom Lundquist descended the steps and came forward. "Hey, Beau, happy birthday." The two men shook hands then Tom turned to Grace. "It's good to see you again. How do you like your Highlander?"

"It's wonderful. I love it."

The tall man bent low and put out his palm. "And you must be Lily." She put her hand in his, and he gave it a gentle shake. "How old are you?"

"Four." She held up her fingers. "It's this many."

Tom chuckled. "You're right. Come on, everybody's out on the patio."

They walked down a hall, through a family room, and out another set of over-sized French doors to an enclosed pool area. The aroma of sizzling meat drifted on the still air. Beau's sister stood with two other women who were sleek-haired and wore expensive clothes. Despite the strangers' resemblance to life-sized dolls, they smiled with genuine warmth at the newcomers, unlike Gen who wore her usual scowl.

A red-headed little boy hurtled himself at Beau's legs. "Uncle Bojo!"

Three other boys continued to chase each other around the pool with blood-curdling yells and verbal gunfire. A golf-tanned man in a patio chair reached out and snagged one of the children by the arm. The other father looked like he would be more at ease in a boardroom or a courtroom than a poolside kiddie party.

Gen came forward. She was makeup-free and wore flip-flops, yoga pants, and an oversized T-shirt. She grimaced with an insincere smile. "Nice to see you again, Grace."

Tom moved to stand beside his wife who took an almost imperceptible step away. He towered over her, slim, pale, and jovial.

Gen shifted her gaze to Lily and her voice warmed. "You must be Lily. The red-headed boy over there is Ben. He's four years old today."

"I'm four too." Lily's eyes shifted to the boys who threw Nerf balls into a child-sized basketball hoop.

"When will you be five?"

"When I'm tired of being four."

Tom and Beau laughed. Gen turned to her husband but stared beyond him. "The cooler needs more ice."

Without a word, Tom walked back through the open door into the house.

Beau spread his arms wide. "Don't I get a greeting? I'm a birthday boy too."

Gen hugged her big brother. "Happy birthday, Bojo." She pointed to the gift bags he held. "Are those for Ben?"

"Where do you want them?"

"Put them in the office with the rest of the presents." Beau turned and disappeared through the patio door.

Marilyn arrived and put a hand on Lily's head. "Let's go say hi to Pépé." She pointed to where Beau's father stood at a grill.

After she took her great-niece by the hand and led her away, Gen turned cool eyes on Grace. "There are sodas and beer in the cooler. Help yourself." She returned to the other two women who cast surreptitious glances in her direction.

The boys ran past into the house. To avoid a collision, Grace stepped aside and her arm bumped against someone.

"Hey." A small, auburn-haired girl stood close. The child had a heart-shaped face and stunning green eyes. She had the long, lean arms and legs of her father but the same blank expression her mother often sported.

Grace smiled. "I'm sorry. I didn't see you. Are you Sara?"

The girl eyed her more like a seventeen-year-old than a seven-year-old. "Are you my Uncle Bojo's girlfriend?"

"I'm Grace. Your uncle didn't tell me how pretty you are."

Sara pointed to where her grandparents fussed over Grace's daughter. With an aloof air, her voice went flat. "What's her name?"

"Lily. She's four years old, the same age as your little brother."

Beau and Tom stepped out of the dark rectangle of the doorway. They raised the lid on the cooler and tore open the bags they held. The crunch of ice being dumped sounded like broken glass.

Mr. Charvet waved his grill spatula in the air. "Gen, the meats are ready."

Children were rounded up and led to two long tables pushed together with eight, molded plastic chairs on each side. At each place setting was a white, helium-filled balloon imprinted with the Toyota logo and weighted with a die cast toy Prius or Camry. The paper products featured characters from the Disney movie, *Cars*. Gen herded people into seats like there were invisible place cards only she could read. All the Charvets ended up together at one end. Grace and Lily sat with the neighbors and their children. Prayers were said in both French and English before everyone ate.

A neighbor named Beth wiped catsup off her son's face and smiled at Grace across the table. "Gen told us you're a teacher here in Palm Beach County. What school?"

"FAU."

Beth glanced at Kelly; the other neighbor who sat to Grace's left. "What do you teach?"

"American literature."

The Lundquist's neighbors were pleasant dinner companions. Even Lily giggled with their little boys. After the plates were cleared, Tom and Beau hauled the presents to the table. Ben stood on a chair and tore into the wrapping paper and gift bags. The last two were the ones she and Beau brought.

Ben pulled a Stomp Rocket Junior from the bag Grace gave Beau for his present which matched the one from her and Lily. The toy included a stomp pad, hose, and four foam rockets. The birthday boy held the box above his head. "I got rockets."

"Let me see that." Gen snatched the box from her son. "This can't be appropriate for a four-year-old." She turned toward Grace. "You should know since you have one."

Beau called out. "Gen, that's from me. The box said it's for three-year-olds and up. There's also a card in there. Don't throw it away."

Gen picked up the gift, removed the envelope, and handed Grace's bag to Ben. "Here's the last one. Hurry up, so Uncle Bojo can open his presents."

Lily tugged on Grace's hand. "I need to pee."

Grace stood and walked her daughter into the house. They didn't wait to see Ben open their present of three *Cars* books, which inadvertently matched the table décor. They also missed Beau opening presents from his family. Upon their return, a car-shaped cake was on the table. Everyone sang

Happy Birthday, and Ben blew out four candles. Gen cut slices of cake while Tom scooped out ice cream.

As soon as the kids finished dessert, they began a game of chase. At first, Sara ran after the little boys and Lily. They circled the patio and disappeared into the house. When the runners returned, the little kids were in pursuit of the older girl. Lily laughed and ran with abandon among the pack. After racing around the pool, they entered the kitchen again.

Gen picked up the remains of the cake and called out. "No running in the house."

The other two women stacked towers of paper plates and cups. Grace caught Gen's eye. "What can I do?"

Beau's sister hesitated. Her lips moved but no sound came out, as if she stopped herself from saying aloud something she shouldn't. "Nothing." She lifted her chin and sailed into the kitchen.

The rebuff of her help was not because Gen was the perfect hostess, but rather to keep Grace separate and let her know she wasn't a friend or family member. Not only didn't Gen want Grace in her kitchen, she didn't want her anywhere near. The seating arrangement had been the first clue.

The men carried the chairs into the garage. At one point, Grace was alone with the neighbor. She held open a trash bag as Beth threw table debris into it.

The neighbor stopped and looked her in the eye. "I hope you weren't offended by what Gen said to you. She and Tom are going through a rough patch right now, and she's pretty much on edge."

After Grace put the bag into a large wheeled receptacle in the driveway, she followed the sounds of children's voices to the living room. She stood beside the boys who played with toy cars on the rug. "Where's Lily?"

The boys shrugged in unison.

Sara was sitting on the bottom step of the staircase. "She's with *my* Uncle Bojo." The girl jumped to her feet and stalked to the kitchen.

Grace followed the low rumble of men's voices. Tom was seated in front of a computer in his home office. His father-in-law and the two neighbor husbands were gathered around him.

Beau sat in a leather armchair with Lily in his lap, reading one of Ben's new birthday books. He looked up when Grace entered the room. "Ready to leave?"

She nodded.

Lily slid off his lap. She put the book on a low shelf stacked with other similar picture stories. When she turned around, a perplexed expression drew her brows down. "Mommy, what's a *bass-turd*?"

Chapter 51

THE QUESTION ECHOED through the room. Grace kept her expression neutral. "Where did you hear that?"

"Sara said a *bass-turd* doesn't belong in her family."

Tom slid his desk chair back and stomped out of the room. "Sara Jane! Where are you?"

Lily's lower lip trembled and her eyes darted to Grace who stepped forward and hugged the little girl against her. "It's okay, sweetie."

Beau and his father joined Tom in the front foyer while the other two husbands stared in false concentration at the computer monitor. Grace hung back with Lily just inside the office doorway. Gen, Marilyn, and Sara emerged from the kitchen.

Tom loomed over his daughter. Angry patches of color stained his pale cheeks. "Explain yourself, Sara. Why did you tell Lily she's a bastard?"

Marilyn gasped and covered her mouth. Sara crossed her arms, pinched her lips together, and remained mute. She swiveled her eyes up to her mother.

Gen glared at her husband with a cold stare, nostrils flared like a dragon about to breathe fire. "Sara didn't call her that. Lily is lying."

"I didn't lie." The little girl whispered the words then buried her face against Grace's thigh.

Beau joined the fray. "She didn't tell a lie. Lily doesn't even know what the word means. Sara said she didn't belong in this family."

His niece's arm shot out. She pointed at Grace. "*She's* the one that doesn't belong."

All eyes turned to Grace like a spotlight had caught her in its beam. Marilyn bit her lip, clearly upset.

Grace took Lily's hand in hers. "We'll wait outside."

A cacophony of voices began. Lily's body stiffened with the loud words being exchanged in French and English as they exited the front door. The late afternoon sun beat down. They stepped off the walkway and stood in the shade of a palm tree cluster. The neighbors and their children soon emerged from the house.

Kelly's husband stopped. "What about our cooler?"

His wife continued walking. "We'll get it later."

Beth approached Grace. "It was nice meeting you."

The door opened again. Raised voices were audible until Beau closed it behind him. His eyes shot daggers then softened when he caught sight of Grace and Lily. He joined the group. His voice was gentle, which was at odds with the tension radiating from him like waves. "We're going now too."

The two couples with their three boys headed to their respective houses. Grace walked Lily to the car. After the little girl was secured into her seat, they drove home in silence.

Grace would need to talk with her daughter about arguments among relatives. Being dropped into the Charvet family, like she and Lily had been, was like parachuting into unknown territory with unfamiliar obstacles and people with agendas different than yours.

When Beau parked in her driveway, they both twisted around to check on the little girl. Her head lolled, and she was fast asleep. Beau went to the passenger side and lifted her out.

Grace unlocked the front door. "Lay her on the sofa in the family room. She'll need a bath when she wakes up."

Once Lily was settled, Beau turned to Grace. "We need to talk."

"Let me get us something to drink."

He sat on the opposite end of the sofa from Lily. Grace handed him a bottle of beer. She lowered herself into a nearby chair with an icy rum and Coke.

Beau sighed. "I'm sorry. What my sister said about you was wrong."

"Your sister isn't wrong. I am a bastard." How would Gen's response differ if she also knew Grace's mother was, not only unmarried, but paid to be her father's mistress?

He winced.

The neighbor's words came to mind. "Is there something else going on with Gen? She seemed very ..." Grace stopped herself from saying *hostile*. "... upset."

Beau rubbed the back of his neck. "She's accused Tom of fooling around."

Gen's husband was an attractive, well-to-do businessman in the prime of his life. In Grace's own marriage, Michael had not resisted the on-the-job temptation of his personal assistant. Even though she was clueless about Michael's extramarital affair, most spouses suspected infidelity long before they confronted the cheater. "Is he?"

"I don't know. But I'd be surprised if he was. He's one of the most honest, trustworthy men I know. Infidelity is not an option for him."

Grace's mouth dropped open. How could Beau be so naive, especially after his own experience? "Are you kidding me? Any man is susceptible to testosterone-induced stupidity. It just takes the right woman to make him forget his morals. Depending on the circumstances, infidelity is always an option. You should know that. If Michael hadn't died the way he did, I have no doubt I would have eventually discovered his affair. Cheaters always think they can get away with cheating. What they fail to understand is they're married to someone who knows them better than anyone else."

Beau wiped a hand across his mouth. "You're right. I just hope he hasn't done something stupid, both for his sake and my sister's."

Chapter 52

THE WEEK AFTER the Ben/Beau birthday party, the spring semester ended with commencement ceremonies. Beau's half-sister, Zoe, came home from college and started a summer job with her father's construction company.

Marilyn called with an invitation to attend a welcome home dinner on Sunday. "Gen's not coming. She's taking the kids to the Keys."

"Just her and the kids?"

"Tom's in California for a Toyota conference and won't be home until Sunday afternoon."

Whenever Grace heard about a husband away on a business trip, she had to stop herself from blurting out: *Are you sure it's strictly business?* Many philanderers used company travel as a cover for an extramarital affair. The out-of-town trip provided a distant location far from prying eyes. In Michael's case, his employer likely picked up the tab for many of his indiscretions with Deirdre. During the time she was pregnant and after Lily's birth, he used a limo service to take him to the airport and bring him home. His reason was he didn't want her to get up early in the morning to take him or drive late at night to pick him up. In hindsight, he probably didn't want her to see who traveled with him.

Grace looked at the calendar. "Sunday is Mother's Day. You shouldn't be cooking." She did not ask why Gen was not going to celebrate the holiday with the woman who helped raise her.

"I'm not doing anything. Beau is grilling, Zoe is making a salad, and Bojo's bringing dessert. They've planned the whole menu. Just like me, you and Lily only need to show up."

Chapter 53

BEAU CALLED GRACE after Marilyn's invitation. "How about I pick you and Lily up on Sunday and drive you to my parents' place?"

"But your condo is only a few miles away from their house. I can drive."

"I have to stop and pick up desserts. I was hoping you could pretty them up for me."

He arrived with several white bakery boxes. After Grace assembled the rugelach, brownies, mini Napoleons, and éclairs on a divided platter, he snatched one goodie and popped it in his mouth. "That looks nice. Thank you." He leaned down to kiss her cheek.

Lily eyed him as he munched. "Mommy says *no picking*."

"She's right. I'm a bad boy."

Lily giggled. "You're too big for a boy."

Grace covered the dessert tray with plastic wrap then removed a large container from the refrigerator. "Marilyn said not to bring anything, but I just can't show up empty handed, so Lily and I made a fruit salad."

They loaded the car and headed to the Charvet home. Beau turned in his seat after he parked in the driveway. "Let's go inside first, so you can meet Hurricane Zoe. I'll come back for the food."

The house was a beautiful one-story ranch from the 1980's which had been updated with plantation shutters jutting out from big glass windows. The front elevation was planted with beds of summer begonias and an arbor of hot pink bougainvillea.

Before they reached the glass-paneled front door, it was flung open by a tall slender blonde with the topaz-colored Charvet eyes. She enveloped

Grace in a tight hug. "Hi! I'm Zoe. I've heard all about you." She knelt in front of Lily. "What's your name?"

Lily smiled at this effervescent young woman. "Lily Anne Stone."

"Can I give you a hug, Lily Anne Stone?"

The little girl nodded, and the second cousins embraced. Zoe rose to her feet and wrapped her arms around Beau's waist. "I *love* getting new family." She kissed his cheek and twisted to face Grace. "Are you *really* dating my big brother?"

"Yes."

"On purpose?"

"Zoe." Beau scowled.

His baby sister gave him a sly look. "So, Bojo, when are you going to make Grace my sister-in-law and Lily my niece?"

"Whoa. Where did that come from?"

"From me. Didn't you see my lips move? You guys are perfect together, and you're not getting any younger, Bojo."

"Tone it down, Zo." Beau pressed his lips to his sister's forehead. "Come help me get something out of the car." He wrapped a strong arm around her shoulders and propelled her out the door so fast she lost her flip-flop.

"Slow down." Zoe pushed her foot back into her shoe. "You're moving like a chicken passing KFC."

Lily giggled. "Zoe's funny. She called Mr. Beau a chicken."

Grace closed the door. When it came to love, he may be just that.

"Ah, there you are, *ma petite*." Beau's father entered the foyer, tiled in large squares of creamy travertine marble which stretched in all directions. He lifted Lily to plant a kiss on her cheek. "Welcome to our home, Grace."

"It's beautiful. Thank you for the invitation."

The door opened behind them. Zoe led the way with the tray of pastries. Beau followed with the fruit salad. Marilyn came from the other side of the house and welcomed them. They walked down the marble hallway into a kitchen with light wood cabinetry and black granite countertops. Marilyn lifted a platter of grilled corn on the cob from the stove top. "Everything's ready. Let's get the food on the table."

Beau Sr. hefted a large tray of spareribs from the oven. The tangy smell of barbecue filled the air. Zoe uncovered a wooden salad bowl. Grace carried in her container of melon balls, grapes, and pineapple. Beau waited behind her with a steaming crock of baked beans in his oven-mitted hands. Lily clutched salt and pepper shakers. They trooped out to the patio where the small backyard and rectangular swimming pool were perfectly tended. It was a warm afternoon, but large ceiling fans on the lanai and water misters on each side moved and cooled the heated air.

Celebrating this Mother's Day with family made it a special event for Grace, but the conspicuous absences of Gen and her children hovered like specters on the fringe of the group. There was also the empty spot vacated by Skip.

During the meal, Grace gathered more insight into a close-knit family when Beau said he had a funny story about his little sister. "When Zoe was around three, Marilyn told Skip and me to take her to some Disney movie she wanted to see. We were teenagers and didn't want to be sitting in a theater with a bunch of little kids. It was when she was shortening a lot of her words. Remember, Dad?"

Mr. Charvet nodded. "She used to say swalk for sidewalk and broom for bedroom."

Beau smiled at his sister. "During the movie, either Skip or I would hide the popcorn from her until she yelled out: 'I want porn'."

Marilyn swatted her stepson with a napkin. "You boys were terrible. Well, if we're telling family stories, I have one from when Skip was about five. On a TV show, a man announced he was gay, and Skip asked what the word meant. I said it means he's really happy. A few days later, we had my ex-husband's boss and his wife for dinner. Mr. Brownstein had thrown his arm around Scott's shoulder, and they were laughing. Skip said in a loud voice, 'Look, Mommy, Daddy and that man are gay.'"

Lily piped up with her hand in the air. "Robert and Tariq are gay. They're really happy too."

Grace turned to face the Charvets. "Those are my neighbors and good friends. They have two daughters around Lily's age. Both Robert and Tariq have been our family since she was born."

Marilyn flashed a sad smile at Grace which seemed to convey regret for the years she could have spent with them.

Beau Sr. cleared his throat. "When I was growing up, my mother was very permissive with me and my brothers."

His son looked incredulous. "You can't mean *Grand-mère*. She didn't have a permissive bone in her body."

His father put a hand up, palm out. "Let me finish. She permitted us to operate the lawn mower, the vacuum cleaner, and the washing machine. I was the only twelve-year-old who could iron a dress shirt."

Zoe wiggled in her seat. "In second grade, I told the class my mother doesn't know who I am."

Marilyn laughed. "I remember the teacher's phone call. She wondered if I had a medical condition the school should be aware of."

Zoe turned to Grace. "When I got off the bus that day, Mom asked why I said that. I told her it was because whenever I did something wrong she would say: 'Just who do you think you are?'"

Lily patted her mother's arm. "Mommy, tell about my baby shoes."

Grace smiled at her daughter. "Lily was a year old, and I bought a red plaid dress and patent leather shoes for a Christmas portrait. I dressed her at the photographer's studio. But when he started snapping pictures, she kicked and wouldn't stop crying. When I undressed her at home, I found I had left wads of tissue paper in the toes of her shoes."

"My feet hurt," Lily said.

Grace laughed. "To this day, she won't wear any shoes which aren't comfortable from the moment she puts them on."

When the laughter died down, Lily patted Grace's arm again. "I have a story, Mommy."

With a wicked glint in her eyes, Zoe motioned her hand in an airy wave which bumped against her water goblet. She grabbed it just in time. "Let's hear it."

Lily squirmed and beamed with the attention of five adults. "I saw Mommy and Mr. Beau doing sex in the kitchen."

Silence.

Wait a minute. They never had sex in the kitchen. Well, not in her kitchen. Grace stared at Lily. "What did you see?"

"Mr. Beau kissed you on Christmas. I told Maxi. She said her daddies kiss a lot, and that's sex."

"You're right. Mr. Beau did kiss me, but that is *not* sex."

"What is sex?"

Zoe snorted.

Grace ignored her. "It's something grownups do, but little kids don't."

"Like driving a car?"

"Yes, like driving a car."

"You said I can drive when I grow up."

"That's right."

"Can I do sex too?"

Beau's father guffawed then turned it into a fake cough. "Sorry."

"We'll talk about this when we're at home." She patted her daughter's leg and put a finger to her lips.

Lily looked around the table. "Why are Pépé and Mémé crying?"

Beau Sr. and Marilyn wiped their eyes with napkins, their faces red with suppressed chortles. Zoe had her hands clamped hard over her mouth as her shoulders quivered with silent laughter. Beau was the only one who sat in serene calmness.

He shook his head at his family. "Amateurs."

Chapter 54

GRACE INVITED BEAU for dinner the following Friday night. She had chicken breasts marinating in the refrigerator and shucked fresh corn on the cob. Everything would go on the grill when Lily returned from her dance class. It was Robert's week to take the three girls. From the moment Beau walked in the door, he was distracted.

Grace kissed him. "Is everything okay at work?"

"It's fine." He opened the bar fridge and lifted out a cold beer. "I stopped at Gen's place on the way over here." After twisting off the cap, he tilted his head back for a long swig. He swallowed and swiped his hand across his lips. "Megan was there."

Grace was surprised and unsure what to say. A niggling memory of something Beau told her came to the surface. "You said they had been friends in high school. Are they still close?"

"I didn't think so. When we were alone, I asked Gen what was going on. She told me Megan went with her to the Keys last weekend. I guess she wanted to talk with another woman about her suspicions that Tom is having an affair. Believe it or not, my ex-wife advised her to keep her marriage intact, especially because of the kids." Beau's eyes shifted away. "She told Gen she regrets agreeing to end ours so quickly."

Grace studied him. Did he think that too? "You know your sister suspects you're the one who was unfaithful, not Megan."

Beau's beer bottle hit the granite countertop with a little crash. "What? When did she tell you that?"

"The day she drove me to pick up my new car. She said that, although neither you nor Megan had given a reason for the divorce, it must have been your fault because you were so generous with the settlement."

Beau's eyes turned cold and flinty. "I was generous because I wanted out as quickly as possible." He picked up the beer and drained the bottle. "I also agreed not to tell anyone in my family the real reason for the divorce."

"Why?"

"Megan insisted. She wanted to maintain her friendship with Gen and was afraid my sister wouldn't forgive her if she knew what really happened."

"So, instead Gen thinks you're the cheater."

Beau leaned his backside against the counter, closed his eyes, and dropped his chin.

Grace cocked her head and peered into his face, willing him to look at her. "It's been three years. Can't you tell Gen the truth now?"

"It's not a good time to dump that on her." His eyelids opened as if weighted. He spoke in a toneless voice. "I'll deal with this later. Right now, we need to talk about the Memorial Day holiday coming up. My parents are having a cookout. Gen and the kids will be there … as long as you and Lily aren't."

The pain of rejection spread throughout her body like splintering ice. She prayed the feeling didn't show on her face. "I see."

"I'm sorry, but my sister is being pig-headed. I thought she would have come around by now." Beau's voice rose in volume.

Grace stepped back and crossed her arms over her chest. "I don't get it. Why is she so adverse to me? I've never said or done anything to her." Her voice sounded shrill, honed by hurt.

"It's my fault. I talked about you a lot in the beginning. How beautiful you are. How smart. What a good mother you are without having any family to help you." Beau rubbed the back of his neck. "I think Gen feels she can't measure up. On top of that, her self-confidence is at an all-time low because of the situation with Tom. Then she gets the news that you're not just my girlfriend but have a family connection as well. She's definitely threatened by you and fighting back the only way she knows how. Right now there's not a damned thing I can do about it."

Past Beau's bulk and like a Magic Eye, Lily sprang into view as she cowered against the kitchen island. Neither of them heard her enter the house. Grace walked over to her daughter who hugged a pair of pink ballet slippers to her white leotard-clad chest. "Everything is okay, sweetie. Don't be scared." She kissed the top of the little girl's head.

Beau squatted in front of Lily. "I'm sorry I yelled. I'm upset about something, but I'm not mad at your mommy."

Lily smiled at him and waggled her index finger at him. "Good. 'Cause then I'd be mad at you."

Chapter 55

WITH THE NEIGHBORS, Grace and Lily attended a Memorial Day ceremony at Veteran's Park in nearby Coral Springs. Before leaving for the event, Robert explained the significance of the holiday and Grace read aloud the book, *F is for Flag*. Then they had the children place a dozen small flags in their front yards. Upon their return, they had a cookout on Tariq and Robert's patio and everyone spent the hot afternoon frolicking in the pool. The following day when Grace and Beau talked, she told him how they spent the holiday.

"Yeah, we ate out and went in the pool too." No more was said about her and Lily's exclusion from the family get-together.

Beau picked her up for their usual Saturday evening date the next weekend and they stopped at *Fat Boyz* for barbecue rib takeout dinners. He parked in the crowded lot. "I spent most of last night at Gen's house. Tom moved out."

Grace unbuckled her seatbelt. "Did he tell her he was having an affair?"

"No, but they've been fighting a lot which is not good for the kids. He said they need some time apart. Of course, Gen's sure this means he is definitely fooling around. She's pretty upset. Mom and Dad are keeping Sara and Ben for the weekend. I'm going back there tomorrow afternoon to talk with her."

An unbidden and unwelcome thought crossed Grace's mind. Will Megan also be there to comfort her old friend?

While they ate at his dining room table, he told her about Gen's emotional extreme, alternately weeping or yelling. "I thought I'd have to call a doctor to sedate her. I've never seen her like that before."

Grace understood the physical expression of a wife's heartbreak. After finding out about Michael, her anger spiked with a rage so deep and primal, she had no idea that depth of sentiment existed in her. She burned with a white-hot fury that destroyed every good feeling she once had for her husband. As a result, she acted frantic and crazy, a grief-stricken, post-partum widow. Rather than defeating her, the wrath empowered her. Had his body lain in front of her, she would have clawed his face to shreds. But after his corpse shipped from Thailand and the funeral was planned, she needed the comfort and strength of loved ones to sustain her. Thank goodness, Robert and Tariq had been there.

Her heart warmed with Beau's willingness to do the same for his sister. A devastated woman longs to confide in someone, to talk about the pain, to express every thought, no matter how trivial. The need is like a raging thirst or a gut-wrenching hunger. A therapist or acquaintance is not close enough. What she needs is someone who loves her without reservation. She listened as Beau described Gen's emotional roller coaster. By the time he had left his sister's house the previous evening, she plotted how to get confirmation of Tom's infidelity.

Beau wiped his sauce-dotted lips with a paper napkin. "Gen wanted me to lend her money to hire a private detective. She was afraid Tom would know what she had done when he checked their bank accounts."

"Did you?"

"No. I convinced her to give it a little time. Chances are she'll find out one way or another anyway."

He didn't mention Gen's new confidant, so Grace broached the subject. "Did Megan come to the house or call while you were there?"

"No, but Gen tried to reach her. She ended up leaving a voice message."

They tacitly discussed less sensitive topics after that. Grace's pale shoulders leaned forward as she nibbled on her baby back ribs. Laying down the last picked-clean bone, she reached for a wet-wipe. Before she could tear open the paper square, Beau pulled her left hand to his mouth and sucked each fingertip clean. She melted.

He planted a tender kiss in her palm. "Are you done eating?"

"I still have my corn." Grace picked up the half ear between her thumb and index finger, gazed at him, and put the cut end in her mouth. She clamped her lips around it and sucked. Her mouth opened wider as her tongue caressed the underside of the cob.

Beau's eyes widened. "What are you doing?"

She slid the cob out from between her lips, letting her teeth grate along the kernels. "I'm licking off the warm ... melted ... butter." Holding both ends of the well-pleasured cob, she took a delicate bite and chewed. All the while, she never broke eye contact with him until she finished and placed the stripped cob on her plate.

Beau stood and pulled her to her feet. She wrapped her hands around his neck. He grasped the backs of her thighs and lifted, then sat with her on his lap, face-to-face. Her sundress billowed around them. His hands scooted the hem until her bare thighs were exposed. "I really like this dress." He slipped the bodice's thin spaghetti straps down her shoulders.

"Then why are you taking it off me?" Grace's pulse quickened, and she dropped her arms.

"Because I like what's underneath even more." Beau kissed her and pulled the dress to her waist. His hands reached behind. With ease, he unsnapped the hooks of her strapless bra and dropped it on the floor. Beau stroked her bare breasts which triggered little shocks in her groin. She writhed against his erection.

"Stand up so I can take off your panties."

She murmured in sensual languor, almost unable to speak. "I'm not wearing any."

He paused then pushed the dress up to her waist. Staring at her, open across his lap, he murmured, "You're killing me."

Chapter 56

LATER IN BED, Grace lay curled against Beau's side, her head on his shoulder. She nuzzled and inhaled his unique scent. His muscled arm wrapped around her as his fingers stroked her hair.

"Grace?"

"Mmm?"

"I'm starting to fall in love with you."

"Only starting to?"

"What do you mean?"

Even though they had been together less than a year, their new world was comprised of Saturday nights to Sunday mornings at his condo, Monday to Thursday phone calls before bedtime, Friday night dinners at Grace's house, and one activity every month including Lily. They progressed from the first stage of attraction to the next stage of intimacy until the mini-breakup following their trip to the Keys. Although they resumed their committed relationship, no declarations of love had been made by either one of them until now. Grace's problem was the ambiguity in Beau's statement.

Raising herself on an elbow, she looked into his face. "Either you are or aren't in love with me. Which is it?"

His face had been relaxed, a slight smile lifting the corners of his mouth. Now he squinted, his lips pressed into a minor grimace. "What's the difference?"

"Starting to fall in love means you may not be there yet. In love means you already are. Right now, I'm definitely in love with *you*."

Beau turned to lie on his side and propped his head in his palm. "Then I would say I'm in love with you too."

Grace leaned forward and kissed him. "I'm glad to hear that."

"Do you think there's a difference between being in love and loving someone? Or are they the same thing, just different wording?"

"No, they're not the same thing. Being in love is transient, a short-term infatuation."

His mouth slackened. "I hope not. I don't want what I'm feeling for you to end."

"Your feeling will change if it becomes love."

"Again, what's the difference?"

Grace sat up and pulled the sheet to cover her chest. She anchored it under her arms and shot him a sarcastic smirk. "You're not asking the most experienced person you know about this."

"No, I'm asking the smartest person I know."

Grace took a deep breath, as if psyching herself up to lift her own weight in a clean jerk. "Okay, think about teenage lovers holding hands, talking for hours on end, hugging, kissing. That's being in love. You want to be with the other person all the time. On the other hand, adults are less intense as well as more mature ... usually. We have to deal with our day-to-day responsibilities, despite the other person often being on our minds." Beau nodded his understanding, so she continued. "Loving someone goes beyond the physical. You want them to be all they can be, despite their flaws, their insecurities, and fears. You become their personal cheerleader to motivate, encourage, and inspire them. I don't think I really understood the concept until I had Lily."

"I understand the love a parent has for a child, but what about love between a man and a woman?"

"It's the same thing; an all-out commitment on your part. You want the very best for them, you're willing to make sacrifices, you trust them completely, and give without condition."

Beau lay back on his pillow and stared at the ceiling. "Well, by that definition, Megan sure didn't love me. What about you and Michael?"

Grace bit her lip and thought about her answer. "In the beginning, I would have sworn we both loved each other. Michael was the one who urged me to get my doctorate and was my biggest supporter. For the first time in my life, I felt worthy of love and had someone I could depend on."

"Obviously, that changed."

"Yes, and soon after we were married." Grace dropped her head and stared at her hands in her lap. "He became a different person. I'm convinced Michael, the boyfriend and fiancé, was a fake who said and did all the right things to make me fall in love with him. Michael, the husband, was the real Michael Stone; the one who was a liar and a cheat."

Beau laid a comforting hand on her leg. "I guess that's why love hurts so much."

She frowned. "You're wrong. Love is the only thing that doesn't hurt; being alone in the world hurts. Having your biological father reject you hurts. Learning your husband died with his mistress hurts. Never hearing your mother say she loves you hurts. Love is the only thing that makes you forget about the pain. That's another lesson I learned from having Lily." Grace slid down until she was face-to-face with Beau. She laid a hand on his cheek. "Love is the only thing in this world that will never hurt you."

Chapter 57

WITH GRACE AND Lily's exclusion from the Memorial Day celebration, Gen had won the first battle in the War for the Charvets. The next
skirmish occurred when one Friday evening dinner with Beau didn't happen
because a call from his sister required his immediate attention.

Grace talked on the phone with him later that night. "How can a leaky
faucet take you all evening to repair?"

"Gen made supper to thank me for coming over, so I had to stay."

"I made you supper too. Did you forget?"

He responded with an assurance not to cancel on her again at the last
minute. She and Lily had finally become part of a family but, like any other
organization, there was a hierarchy. In this case, it was Gen who took priority.
After the Friday dinner no-show, Beau's sister seemed to have an uncanny
sense when he was to be with Grace and sabotaged their plans, despite Beau's
promise.

Lily came into the family room one afternoon and slumped onto her
mother's lap. "When is Mr. Beau coming to see me?"

It was the umpteenth time she had asked a variation of the question.
They had not had their Friday night dinner for the last two weeks and were
unable to schedule this month's *date* with Lily. Last week, Beau cancelled their
usual Saturday night date and was unsure about getting together this
weekend.

"He's very busy, sweetie. How about we plan to do something
together?"

That night Grace checked the internet for last minute cruises and
booked reservations on a four-day Caribbean trip. They sailed from Miami

two days later. She called Beau the night before they departed but was unable to speak with him. Instead she sent a text. *Lily and I are taking a cruise. Hope to see you after we get back on Friday.*

He responded: *See you next week. Have fun.*

Chapter 58

THE WEEKEND AFTER the cruise, Grace and Beau went out to dinner on Saturday evening. He dipped a tortilla chip into salsa. "How was the trip?"

"I didn't realize how big some of these ships are, and they're getting bigger. There was a fantastic playroom and a water area just for kids which Lily loved. I actually had a lot of free time to read."

"What about the food?"

"A bit disappointing, but we weren't there to eat. Both of us had a great time though." She straightened her leg under the table and ran her bare toes up his calf. "I hope to have another great time tonight." When he picked her up, she didn't bring her overnight bag. There were toiletries and clothes at his house which hadn't been used in weeks.

He scooted away from her inquisitive toes and stared at the tabletop. "I have to take you home when we finish eating. Dad and I are remodeling Sara's bathroom. Gen wants it finished as soon as possible. We worked on it today and got all the tiles set. I'm meeting him at the house early tomorrow morning to finish the grouting."

Grace wiggled her foot back into her sandal. "What's it going to be next weekend and the one after that?"

He appeared battle-weary, as if he had to report another loss to a commanding officer. "Work is crazy right now, and Gen wants this bathroom and a hundred other things done. I need you to cut me some slack."

Grace bit her lip and remained silent, although the words *I've given you nothing but slack for weeks* hovered on the tip of her tongue.

After an awkward minute, he sighed. "Grace, I—"

The waiter returned with a bowl of fresh guacamole. "Is there anything else I can get for you?" His eyes shifted between the two of them.

Grace drained her wine glass. "One more Sangria, please."

"Sir, would you like another Dos Equis?"

Beau shook his head. Neither of them spoke until the waiter returned with her second glass of wine. When he left, Beau leaned forward and put his elbows on the table. "I know I've been putting you off lately, but Gen needs my help right now. She wants the house fixed up, in case there's a divorce, and she has to sell. I'm just trying to be supportive until things get decided one way or the other."

With her gaze averted, Grace dipped a chip into the guacamole. "Can't you find a balance between her and me?"

He spoke at a measured pace as though an invisible stenographer transcribed every word to be read back to him later. "Gen doesn't want to be alone during the evenings and on weekends. I listen to her, help around the house, and we talk."

They sat in silence until the sound of sizzling meat and vegetables came close. Beau's fajita entree was placed on the table in front of him. He studied the food as though he was not quite sure how it ended up there.

The waiter put a second steamy pan in front of Grace. "Be careful. It's hot."

The tension-filled silence stretched between them as they ate. Grace's dinner tasted like flaming sawdust on her tongue. She swallowed with difficulty.

After several bites, she laid down her fork. "Beau, I need you to tell me where I fit into your life. Lately, I've begun to feel like an imposition."

"You know I care about you and Lily, but I can't make any promises right now. I told you that before." While he spoke his eyes never left his plate as he assembled meat and vegetables onto a tortilla.

Grace blinked back hot tears. She waited until she had her emotions under control, or so she thought. But when she spoke, her voice was thin and reedy, like a frail old woman's. "I'd been alone for four years until we met, and for the first time in a long time, I'm feeling lonely again."

His gaze darted up to hers. "Are you saying you want to date other men?"

"No. I'm just telling you how I feel." She waited for him to respond, but he said nothing. "Say something, Beau."

"I don't know when this will end, but don't worry. I'm not seeing another woman, other than my sister. When things settle down, you and I can get back to the way we were."

With more forcefulness than she intended, her words came out in a too-loud rush. "I don't want to get back to where we were. I want us to move forward."

His eyes widened at her words and vigorous tone.

The young waiter came over to their table and eyed the uneaten food in front of them. "Do you need anything?"

Beau pushed the wooden trivet and cast-iron pan toward the end of the table. "I think we're done here. You can box this. You want to take yours, Grace?"

She shook her head.

He slid her uneaten meat and vegetables toward the waiter. "Put everything together and bring the check." Beau watched the young man walked away. "Let's not talk about this here."

They left the restaurant and drove to her house in silence. Beau turned off the ignition. In the glow from the dashboard lights, his mouth was set in a hard line.

Grace waited until he twisted in his seat to face her then she spoke. "I understand you're trying to help your sister, but we're in a relationship too. You can't put me and Lily on hold until Gen no longer demands all your time and attention." She hesitated, unsure of his reaction to her next words. "Maybe we shouldn't see each other for a while."

Beau went rigid and gripped the steering wheel with bulging knuckles. "If that's what you want."

Her chin lowered in defeat. "It's not. What I want is for you to set boundaries with Gen. I don't want to be the girlfriend waiting day after day for you to find the time for me." Just like my mother did with her lovers.

His shoulders slumped and his hands dropped. "Then let's take a break for a while. If anything changes, I'll call." He looked like he was facing a firing squad. "Or you can call me, if something changes for you."

Chapter 59

THE NEXT DAY was Father's Day. For the first time in her life, Grace had a name and a face for the man biologically responsible for her existence. He had also provided the funding which allowed her to live a comfortable life and pursue a higher education, which was more than many illegitimate offspring could expect. But he remained only a sperm donor with a conscience, and for this reason, Grace struggled to call him Father. Might Mr. Mack have played a greater role in her life if he had not died when she was a small child?

She needed to tell Lily it was unlikely Beau would be the father she desired. Grace had rehearsed how to let the little girl know, in the least hurtful manner possible, but Lily preempted her plans. At breakfast that morning, Grace placed a plate of scrambled eggs on the table in front of her daughter and turned back to the stove to prepare her own.

"Today is Father's Day, Mommy."

Grace froze. "I know."

"Maxi and Erin got presents to give Robert and Tariq."

"That's nice."

"We didn't get anything for Mr. Beau or Pépé."

Although she was not ready for this conversation, Grace took a seat across from her daughter. "But neither Mr. Beau nor Pépé are our fathers."

Lily rolled her eyes. "Pépé said he's like my grandpapa. And I want Mr. Beau to be my new daddy. So, we need to get them presents. Are we gonna see them today?"

"I'm afraid not." Grace fiddled with the napkin on her placemat.

Lily's lower lip quivered. "Is Mr. Beau and Pépé mad at us?"

"No. They're just celebrating Father's Day with their own family. It's like with Robert and Tariq, who are celebrating with Maxi and Erin." Her heart broke with Lily's crumbled expression and the tears welling in her bright, blue eyes.

"I haven't seen Mr. Beau for a long, long time."

"He has some problems to work out and can't be with us right now."

One fat tear spilled over and trickled down Lily's cheek. "I miss him."

"Come and sit on my lap." With the weight of her daughter's small head resting against her shoulder, Grace said, "I know how much you want Mr. Beau to be your daddy. He cares for us very much but isn't ready to get married and have a family."

There was a catch in Lily's voice. "Is that one of his problems?"

From the mouths of babes. "He's trying to help a family that is very sad and needs him."

"I'm very sad."

Grace laid her cheek on the top of Lily's head. "Me too, but the other family needs him more."

Later in the week when Marilyn called, Grace broke the news. "I don't know if Beau has said anything to you, but we're no longer seeing each other."

"He said the two of you were taking a break."

"I guess that's one way of describing it."

"It's so upsetting. Gen and Tom. Now you and Beau." Marilyn sounded weepy. "I feel terrible that we weren't able to accept your dinner invitation. Please understand how difficult things are around here right now."

Last week in response to Lily's whining about missing Mémé and Pépé, Grace invited them for supper. Marilyn was evasive then called to apologize when they couldn't accept. Grace did not ask why they were unable to attend, even when an alternative date was proposed. Perhaps all the Charvets had broken up with her and Lily.

Grace struggled to keep thick emotion from her voice. "I'm sorry you've been put in the middle between Gen and me ... and now Beau."

Marilyn sniffled then a thread of firmness strengthened her voice. "You've nothing to be sorry about. We welcomed you into our lives, and now we're shutting the door in your face. It's just not right."

Chapter 60

THE REMAINDER OF the summer passed slower than usual. This year Grace had not signed up to teach any summer courses. She welcomed the chance to be with Lily, catch up on work and home projects, as well as having more free time to spend with Beau when his schedule allowed. Now the days rolled by with the monotony of too much time on her hands and not enough to do. She had been so focused and driven the last three years that the past weeks were, not as much a vacation, as a stretch of unwelcome inactivity. Despite, a two-week day camp Lily attended, swim lessons, ballet classes, and kindergarten clothes shopping, she and her daughter soon wearied of each other.

Grace's salvation was notification of a new course to teach which offered either a credit in English or Women's Studies. The objective was to trace the social, political, economic, and historical evolution of women in classic literature. The extra prep hours helped speed up the pace of the final summer days.

Since their last conversation in June, Grace had not heard from Beau. Marilyn informed her Gen had been doing better for the last month. She and Tom now attended marriage counseling, but he hadn't moved back home yet. Gen was still undecided whether to end the estrangement or end the marriage.

So why hadn't Beau called if the situation with Gen had changed? A plunge of despair overwhelmed Grace. Perhaps he wasn't in love with her after all. The temporary separation may have provided him an opportunity to end their relationship without confrontation.

Many of her sleepless nights involved thinking about Beau. How long would it take until she missed his memory more than him? Would Beau's loss take less time or more than Michael's, which had been was accelerated by her hurt and anger? Her cycle of disappointment in men had started with Mr. Mack's rejection. As a wife, she attained status as a woman worthy of love, but Michael's infidelity marked down her value for being not quite enough. Now here she was again, falling into second place behind Beau's sister. She was tired of fighting for love. For once, she wanted to be fought for.

Damn it. She was worth it.

Chapter 61

THE FALL SEMESTER began for the faculty with their first department meeting two weeks before classes started in August. Grace spotted Alice outside a large conference room.

She hurried over to her colleague and stared. "My God, you look wonderful."

The long, unruly dark hair Alice usually bound into a low ponytail had been cut short. Loose curls covered her head to the tops of her ears. She sported a glowing tan. "It's all due to the great outdoors. After a month in an Oxford library, I needed the space and fresh air of Alaska."

Upon completion of her project in England, Alice had flown twenty hours from London to Sitka to visit her younger sister who taught health sciences at Southeastern Alaska University.

"How's Rose doing?"

"Great. She says she'll never work at a big university again, especially one where students wear shorts year-round."

After the meeting, they headed to Alice's office. She closed the door. "Please tell me you look tired and thinner because your gorgeous man is keeping you awake all night."

"He's keeping me awake, but he's nowhere near me."

"Did you two break up?"

"I'm afraid so." Grace leaned forward in her chair. "There's a professional matter I want to run by you." She told about the discovery of her father's identity and her newfound aunt.

Alice widened her large gray eyes. "Oh, my God! That's wonderful news! I'm so happy for you."

Like a warm current, the connection of true friendship running between them said far more than Alice's words of delight. Grace reveled in the feeling for a few seconds before she spoke again. "His estate left an endowment to this university called the G.G. Educational Fund."

Alice's eyebrows squished together. "Why does that sound familiar?"

"The endowment constructed the building across the street. Remember the big sign we used to see every day?"

"Your old man is G.G.?"

"No, my aunt and I think he named it after me, Grace Georgette. What I wanted to ask you is this: do you think my position here is a result of his money? I got this job before my dissertation was approved and received tenure so quickly."

Alice stared hard at Grace. "Stop it. I can't believe you would think that. You are one of the finest scholars of American feminist literature I know. It's evidenced in your body of work. You had two job offers from other universities a lot bigger and more prestigious than this one. You turn down more workshops and lectures than most people in this department are offered. How many textbooks have you co-authored? Look at all the journal articles you've published, not to mention the committees you've been on. Your job and tenure are a result of your own excellence and hard work, not because your newly discovered father left the university an endowment when you were in grade school."

"Okay, let's say you're right. If I wanted to confirm it, how would I go about doing that? Who would I ask?"

Alice thought for a moment. "I'd say either one of the university trustees when you were hired or when you were granted tenure."

Or perhaps someone from the law firm of Sandberg Truman. A partner from their office, John Truman, currently served on the board of trustees. They still managed the endowment and, in the past, oversaw the trust which paid for her education and Juliette's living expenses.

Upon returning to her office, she called the law firm and asked to be connected with Mr. Truman's secretary. "This is Dr. Grace Black-Stone. I'd like to make an appointment."

"May I ask what this is regarding?"

"I want to discuss the estate of Dr. George Makowsky."

Five minutes later, she was on the schedule for Friday afternoon.

Chapter 62

GRACE DRESSED WITH care for her meeting with John Truman. She wore a tailored black jacket with a matching straight skirt. Despite the August heat, she put on thigh-high black stockings.

The law firm occupied all three floors of a restored Mizner-style building in downtown Boca Raton. Grace's high heels tapped a brisk rhythm across the black marble lobby lined with white columns. She headed to the mahogany reception desk where the polished brass letters of the firm's name were on the wall behind the receptionist. After getting clearance, she rode alone in an elevator to the top level. The décor was plush carpets, dark wood, and sparkling glass. Outside Mr. Truman's office, a thin woman dressed in a chic suit was seated at a U-shaped desk. She asked Grace to take a seat.

A few minutes later, the secretary gave her the go-ahead to enter through a thick wood door. A man with white hair and a matching goatee was seated at a glass desk the size of a small bed. The panorama of windows behind him displayed the downtown street below.

When Grace stepped into the room, he looked up. Mr. Truman jumped to his feet with surprising spryness. He smoothed down his tie and buttoned his suit coat. "Come in, come in."

Truman's eyes never left her face as she walked toward him. "Thank you for seeing me. I'm Grace Black-Stone."

They shook hands with the desk between them. "John Truman. It's nice to meet you. Let's move over there." He gestured to an arrangement of gray upholstered chairs around a low glass and steel table. Once seated, Mr. Truman leaned toward her. "I was told this meeting is about Dr. Makowsky. I know who you are because I handled your trust and your mother's estate."

"But I never dealt with you after her death."

A somber expression crossed the lawyer's face. "No. At the time, I transferred the probate work to a junior partner in the firm. May I ask how you know Dr. Makowsky?"

"Do you mean how I know he's my father and the provider of the trust you managed?"

Mr. Truman's eyes narrowed. "Why do you think he's your father?"

"I don't think it. I know it. When I was quite young, my mother introduced me to him. He told me his name was Mr. Mack. I remembered because I had never met any of her other male friends. In high school, I asked if my father was Mr. Mack. She confirmed he was but would tell me nothing else about him."

John Truman nodded and seemed pleased with this information.

Grace said, "Last year, I began dating a man named Beau Charvet."

Truman's eyebrows shot up when she said the name.

"A few months later, I met his stepmother, Marilyn, who thought I looked familiar. It turns out she had met my mother in the company of her brother, George. Between what she knew and I knew, the two of us concluded that her brother is my father. We confirmed our hunch with DNA testing."

"I see."

"Mr. Truman, the reason I asked to meet with you has nothing to do with my father's estate. I'm making no claim against it."

He appeared skeptical. No doubt he had dealt with many heirs, especially here in inheritance-rich Palm Beach, who swore they were not interested in their dead relatives' money. Later they battled it out in the courts for what they demanded was their share.

Grace cleared her throat. "My concern relates to my professional career at FAU and any influence the G.G. Educational Fund has had on it."

"I see you are aware of the endowment."

"I knew about the construction of a new building on the campus. However, until Marilyn told me about her brother, I had no idea of a connection between the endowment and me." This was the tricky part since the attorney was on the university board. Grace proceeded with caution. "You're in the second year of a four-year term as trustee. When I was hired, another of your firm's associates served. I believed I had succeeded professionally on my own merit, but now wonder if the endowment influenced or resulted in my employment or recent tenure approval."

He sat back with his hands clasped under his chin, elbows on the arms of the chair. He perused her for long seconds. "Tell me about your personal life."

Veering onto this tangent surprised Grace, but she answered him. "My mother died the day I graduated from the University of Florida with my bachelor's degree. I finished my master's and started on my doctorate. I met my husband in college, and we married. I was working on my dissertation when I gave birth to my daughter. She was six-weeks-old when her father was killed. I was grateful FAU hired me shortly after becoming a single parent."

"May I see a picture of your daughter?"

Grace pulled her phone out of her purse, scrolled through the Photos app, and found the folder labeled with Lily's name. She opened it to a recent picture of them on the cruise ship. Mr. Truman studied it then moved his finger across the screen to open more photos. After a minute, he handed her phone back.

The lawyer bit his lip and crossed his legs before he spoke. "First, let me reassure you that the endowment had nothing to do with your career. I was one of the trustees last year who voted approval for your tenure. It was a unanimous decision based on a number of criteria. The board considered you an asset worth keeping on the faculty."

"Did the endowment provide a chair to be filled by me?"

"There is no chair funded by the endowment. It has been primarily used for construction and programs related to the chemical sciences."

Relief and pride flooded Grace. "Thank you. I really appreciate you confirming that for me."

"You're welcome." Truman gave her a warm smile.

Now that Grace found out what she needed to know, she rose partway from her seat to end the interview and glanced at her watch to note the time. When she made the appointment, she hadn't inquired as to his hourly rate. How much would she be billed for this meeting?

The lawyer reached over and touched her arm. "Please sit. There's something else I need to tell you."

What now? A chill permeated Grace more than the frigid office temperature.

The lawyer took a deep breath and lifted his chin. He looked like he was psyching himself to deliver earth-shattering news. "I know your mother informed you of the work she did."

Grace nodded.

Truman fingered the pleat in his pants leg. "Yes, well, your mother and I had a relationship for a while. It started out as purely business, but then I fell in love with her. We talked about marriage shortly before she died."

Grace sat back in her chair, shocked. Was he one of the men who made glass promises? In Juliette's final email, she wrote about her difficulty getting a man to propose marriage. Was Mr. Truman the one to whom she referred?

His eyes grew distant. "The problem for me was that Juliette had been the mistress to other men of my acquaintance. But I had forgotten there are a lot of former mistresses who are now respectable wives in Palm Beach. I told her I needed more time." His voice grew husky. "A few weeks later, she was gone, and now I have nothing but time."

Despite the number of years since Juliette's death, Mr. Truman appeared to still mourn her passing. Perhaps his feelings for her had not been an infatuation, but a real, enduring love that outlasted separation and death.

"I'm sorry, but I didn't know. She never told me."

"Juliette was very protective of you."

Grace empathized with his grief but also wondered if he might have answers to questions she had about her mother. "Did you know that when she died I could find no record of her life?"

He stared at her. "What do you mean?"

"The only things I had were her driver's license, bank account information, and the title to the house. I found no tax records, birth certificate, or social security number. I think she kept her personal records elsewhere." She stared at him to transmit the silent message about Juliette's records being hidden away from the IRS and law enforcement.

"And you're wondering if our firm has any of that information?"

Grace shrugged. "I thought I'd ask."

Mr. Truman rose to his feet. "Give me a moment, please."

Grace's heart pounded with a mixture of terror and delight, like she had been thrown into the middle of a life-changing game of hide-and-seek without warning or preparation.

Mr. Truman walked to the door, opened it, and disappeared. He was gone only a minute then returned with a thin file folder and gestured Grace to a conference table. "When you scheduled the appointment, I requested your mother's record from our inactive storage. The Florida Bar provides guidelines as to the disposal of client files. There is no rule which requires a retention period of greater than six years after the conclusion of a legal matter."

Grace's shoulders slumped. Juliette had been dead for more than nine years.

"Bear with me," he said. "Sandberg Truman has always had a prudent policy to add a cushion of a few extra years, just in case. Our file retention is ten years and your mother's estate did not clear probate until a year after her death. For estate planning, we retain the files permanently. However, we do not maintain client-provided items, such as tax records, financial statements, or the originals of trust documents or deeds. Those are returned to the client. Original contracts, wills, and consent orders are not destroyed under any circumstances."

Disappointment overwhelmed Grace. "But I already have a copy of her will. It didn't tell me anything about her life or family."

"This file was scheduled for review by me on its tenth anniversary which would be next year. When I received it, I found something unexpected among the contents." Mr. Truman opened the folder. An envelope lay on top of her mother's Last Will and Testament and, in her mother's recognizable handwriting, was written: *Grace Georgette Black*. The lawyer handed it to her. "I think this was supposed to be given to you in the event of Juliette's death. I don't know why it wasn't. I hope it provides some answers for you."

"Thank you." Grace placed the envelope in her purse, shook Mr. Truman's hand, and said goodbye. She exited the building on shaky legs. In her car, she stared at her purse as if the letter inside pulsed with a life of its own. She started the engine and drove straight home, desperate to be alone and in private when she read what her mother had written. Inside the house, she changed into shorts and a T-shirt. With a water bottle and a box of tissues on the table beside the sofa, she opened the letter. It contained one sheet of typewritten paper creased into thirds.

December 31, 2005

Dear Grace,

In an hour, it will be a new year. If you are reading this, it's because I'm not there. By now, I hope you are successful in your career and happy with your life. I know you've always wondered about your father. Mack was separated from his wife and had no children. He was generous to me when I became pregnant.

Don't bother trying to find him. He died in 1995. He was a good man but didn't want to be my husband or a father to you. I liked Mack, but didn't want to marry him either. In exchange for supporting us, I promised to raise you to adulthood. I know I've not been a typical mother, but I've done my best.

Next year you'll be 18 years old. It's hard to believe. When I started this letter, I didn't plan on telling you more but why not since you'll soon be a legal adult. I wasn't born Juliette Black. I'm not going to tell you my real last name. There's no point. I spent most of my childhood in foster care. I won't go into my life from the time I turned 18 until I met Mack. It wasn't bad. I was just stupid but learned real quick.

I want you to know I'm proud of you and, in my own way, I love you. You're the one really good thing I've done in my life. You're smart like your father which will make your life easier than just being beautiful. I hope you one day find a man who promises to love you forever and does.

Your mother, Juliette

Chapter 63

FOR DAYS AFTERWARD, *The Letter*, as Grace called it, changed her outlook, not only on her father, but her mother as well. She always suspected Juliette had a rough childhood and learning she grew up in foster care confirmed that notion. Although her parents chose not to marry, George Makowsky did support his child, and Juliette did keep her and take care of her. With the softening of Grace's attitude towards her two flawed parents, she resolved her feelings toward Beau. Life was too short and precarious to throw away a chance for happiness. She still loved him and was willing to wait until he came to terms with his feelings, concluding that a year was a reasonable time frame.

Although anxious to share her resolution with Beau, a phone call wouldn't do. This was too important. A face-to-face meeting was needed. She debated setting up a date and time with him, but feared giving him a chance to think too hard or too long about it. An unplanned and unannounced meeting might provide a more honest gauge of his feelings, but going to his office was out of the question. Gen might be there.

Three days later, she took a chance and drove to his townhouse. The dashboard clock read seven-thirty a.m. She didn't have to be at work until nine. Several times since their breakup, she had gone out of her way to pass by his place. As she sat in her car parked at the curb, remembrances of the hours she spent there flooded her with warmth and happiness. She understood the lure of criminals to return to the scene of the crime. There was a thrill, an excitement when the location of the actual event was a few feet away. The façade of his house heightened her memories, made them more vivid, more poignant, as though all the walls were made of glass, and she could visualize herself with him in every room. Her skin tingled with how Beau's strong arms held her. The rumble of his voice sounded in her ears. She smelled his scent after they made love and lay naked in bed. The sensory overload carried her until she was compelled to drive by again.

On this particular morning, her heart beat double time in her chest. She envisioned him opening the front door, seeing her, and sweeping her into his arms even before she could deliver her message. They would both call off work, luxuriate in his bed, and he would tell her over and over how much he loved her.

With his townhouse in sight, Grace slowed her Highlander. She was surprised to see two unfamiliar cars parked out front. A spasm of elemental panic gripped her. Had he moved and no one told her? She drove to the end of the block, made a U-turn, and pulled to the curb, one house down. As she debated what to do, a woman stepped from the walkway leading to Beau's front door and headed to one of the two cars parked in the driveway.

Chapter 64

GRACE'S EYES SNAPPED shut with an avalanche of pain. When she lifted her eyelids, Megan's tall form sank into the driver's seat of a sporty car, her auburn head disappearing inside the vehicle. Seconds later, the engine roared to life, and the black Toyota raced down the street.

In the physical sense, Grace sat securely with her seatbelt across her lap and chest. Emotionally, she teetered on the edge of a crevice that dropped into a bottomless chasm. One wrong move and she'd tumble into a very dark place.

Her involuntary cry broke the silence. "No!"

She would never allow another man to make her feel that way again. Without conscious thought, Grace freed herself from the seatbelt, grabbed her purse, exited the car, and strode to the front door. Her index finger hovered an inch from the doorbell. A voice inside her head, which sounded like Juliette, told her to tell Beau he was a man who made glass promises, and she didn't want him around her or Lily ever again. She stabbed the button, once, twice, and waited with her purse clutched in her hand like a brick to be hurled at his head.

The lock snicked open and a voice dripping with infuriation said, "What did you forget?"

Her mouth dropped open when she looked into the scowling face of Tom Lundquist.

His features softened. "Grace? What are you doing here?"

"Me? What are you doing here? With ... with that woman."

Her gaze traveled from his face, whiskered with red-gold hairs, down to a rumpled T-shirt and striped pajama bottoms. His long slender feet were bare. Her mouth filled with a bitter, bile-like taste. Megan couldn't get a threesome going in the Keys with two women and one man, so she opted for two men and one woman.

Grace raised her purse and, with the same unerring accuracy she demonstrated at The Discovery Ball, she struck Tom across the face. He staggered and clutched the door frame. She whirled and had taken two steps before he grabbed her elbow in a tight grip. Lurching, she twisted around, and raised her purse aloft for another strike.

"Whoa! Hold on!" Tom shielded his face with his free arm. "Let me explain." He drew her toward the open front door.

"There's nothing to explain. You two bedswervers deserve that dirty puzzle!"

Tom pulled her across the threshold and closed the door. "What are you talking about?"

She registered her mix of a Shakespearean and Victorian curse with a slight shake of her head. All the literary research she had been doing to prepare for her new teaching assignment was affecting her speech. Just the other day she asked Lily if she had to use the privy before they left the house.

She cast a furtive glance toward the bedrooms. "I just saw Megan leave. You and Beau are disgusting. Is he still in the bedroom?"

"No, he's in Orlando." He released his grip on her arm. "Will you stay, so we can talk?"

She pursed her lips and studied the rumpled man who wore an expression of part sheepishness, part earnestness. Grace gave him a silent nod.

"You want coffee? I sure need it."

A few minutes later, they settled at the dining room table, steaming mugs in front of them. Grace eyed Gen's husband over the rim as she drank. There were purplish crescents under his eyes and his cheekbones were as sharp as shovel blades.

Tom put his cup down and wrapped both palms around the smooth ceramic. He stared into the milky depths. "I'm not sleeping with Megan, and neither is Beau."

Grace gave an audible snort of disbelief.

"Beau hasn't slept with her in over three years. I haven't slept with her in over six months." Tom proceeded to tell Grace how Megan had shown up at the dealership to buy a new car. After the transaction was completed, she invited him out for a drink. By the end of the evening, they ended up in her bed. "I'm not claiming I was drunk or seduced as an explanation for what happened. But it wasn't long before I regretted what I had done."

"Does Beau know about you two?"

The little bit of color in Tom's face drained away. "No. I don't know if he'll beat me up for hurting his sister, or sleeping with his ex-wife, or both."

"Did guilt make you end the affair?"

A slight pinkness returned to Tom's cheeks. "That … and Megan has, um … she's … adventurous in bed. When I … uh … said I was reluctant to do a couple things, she called me a creamsicle." With his pale cheeks, strawberry blond hair, and lanky frame, he did resemble the frozen treat, but, of course, Megan was not referring to his looks. "I felt like a weekend athlete who's suddenly competing at the Olympics. I don't know how Beau stayed married to her as long as he did. Maybe that's why they split up."

Grace emitted an angry condescending laugh. "They divorced because he caught her in bed with someone else." In fact, two someone elses.

Tom's eyes widened. "He did? Why didn't he say so?"

"Megan insisted he not share that information with the family, although Skip knows, and so do I. She didn't want what she did to jeopardize her friendship with Gen."

This time, it was Tom who gave a derisive snort. "Some friend."

"So, why was Megan here this morning if you broke up?"

With several fits and starts, Tom related how he ended the affair within weeks of its inception. Megan did not take it well and threatened to tell Gen. He offered to cover her new car loan if she kept quiet. "She liked the idea, and I figured I got off pretty easy."

For the last four months, Megan had been milking him for more. He also financed a tummy tuck and a weekend stay at an exclusive resort in the Keys for a wedding party.

"That's where I met her," Grace blurted out. "Beau and I went to dinner there."

"I wondered how you knew who she was. She's been hounding me for more money. When Beau said he'd be gone for a week, I asked if I could stay at his place. I haven't answered her calls or texts, so I can't figure out how she knew I was here."

"Gen probably told her."

Tom shook his head. "No way. Gen hasn't talked with Megan in years."

"That's not true. Beau saw her at your house a few months ago. After she left, Gen told him Megan was advising her on what to do about you."

Tom raked his hands through his hair, making it stand on end. "What the fuck is going on?"

"She urged Gen to keep your marriage together for the sake of the kids. Why would she do that? Don't most paramours …" There was more of her Victorian vernacular. "… want lovers to leave their wives?"

Grace and Tom shared perplexed expressions. The answer came to her seconds before him, but they both cried out the same word, at the same time. "Blackmail."

She leaned back in the chair. "How Machiavellian of her. As long as you continue to hide the affair, she has you bowing to her monetary demands. But once Gen has knowledge or evidence of the infidelity or, if you confess, the reason for the extortion disappears. Megan wouldn't want that to happen. Tom, you have to tell Gen. And you need to tell Beau too." His mouth opened and closed like a dying fish as she laid her hand on his arm. "It's the only way to stop her from bleeding you dry. She might take everything she can and tell Gen anyway."

Tom raised pain-filled, reddened eyes. "She gave me her Nordstrom bill to pay this morning." He glanced across the table to where a white envelope sat.

A momentary feeling of sympathy for Tom was replaced by the thought of how hurt Gen and Beau will be when they learn of his infidelity and Megan's treachery. In Beau's case, he would not be surprised by his ex-wife's actions, but his sister was bound to be devastated by the double betrayal.

Grace stood and picked up her purse. "It's your decision how you handle this, but I suggest you come clean as soon as possible. Have you discussed this situation with the marriage counselor you're seeing?"

Tom placed his palms on the tabletop and straightened his lanky frame as if he were an old man with arthritic knees. "No. Do you think I should?"

"Getting an outside opinion might help with your perspective and anxiety. Also, you won't be facing this alone. I know you don't want to hurt Gen and the kids, but Megan's blackmail is doing more damage every day you allow it to continue. You need to remove the leverage she has over your whole family. It may be the most difficult thing you'll ever have to do, but …" Grace stopped herself from uttering it was time for him to man up, or some other pithy saying involving genitals. "You need to show your integrity and take responsibility. Don't allow her to control the narrative because she will make you look even worse."

Tom heaved a mighty sigh. "You're right, of course. Thank you. I needed someone to say what I've known I had to do for weeks." He opened his arms and enfolded Grace in them as he laid his cheek on top of her head.

It had been months since a man embraced her. Tom had Beau's height but not his build. She adjusted the angle of her head when his shoulder blade poked her ear, but then her cheek was pressed against the boniness of his sternum. The hug was pleasant and, at the same time, uncomfortable, like wearing a pair of great-looking shoes that pinched your toes. There was a noise behind her.

"What the hell is going on?" Beau stood in the open doorway, a duffle bag in his hand, his face hard with a furious scowl.

Chapter 65

BEAU'S EYES BORED into Tom's. "This is why you wanted to stay here while I was gone?" When he lowered his gaze to Grace, with her arms still encircling Tom's waist, sadness slackened his features. "I should have known no woman could be trusted."

His duffel bag dropped onto the tile floor with a loud thunk that echoed through the townhouse. He strode forward, his chin thrust out, and his fists clenched. At the same instant, Tom and Grace dropped their arms from around each other. She stepped forward and faced Beau head on.

From behind her, Tom said, "Hold on. It's not what you think."

"Don't tell me what to think. I know what I saw." He stopped several feet short. "I've spent the last several months defending you, and all this time you've been shacking up with Grace!"

"You've got it all wrong."

Grace moved closer to Beau. "He's right. I came here this morning to talk with *you*."

Without warning, he grabbed her arm in a vise-like grip. "You're out of here." He propelled her to the open front door. She stumbled forward over the threshold. "Leave me and my family alone."

"Wait—"

Just before the door slammed shut with a bang, Beau growled, "Like mother, like daughter."

His words froze her and a stinging hurt centered in her chest. Chills ran down her as if a bucket of icy water had been dumped on her head. Like mother, like daughter. Like mother, like daughter. The refrain repeated in her head, reminiscent of a nasty schoolyard taunt. Only this time the voice had the deep, masculine timbre of the man she loved.

With heavy steps, Grace walked away from the door. A crash sounded from the townhouse followed by loud, angry male voices. She didn't stop until she was in her car. Thirty minutes later, she parked at the university and rested her forehead on the steering wheel as she marshaled her emotions before heading inside.

Her phone sounded with the clatter of typewriter keys signaling an incoming text. She pulled the device from her purse.

The message was from Beau. *Know about Tom and Megan. Sorry for what I said. What u want to talk about?*

Her fingers flew across the keys. *Doesn't matter now.*

After sending the text, she powered off her phone, grabbed her briefcase, and exited the car.

Chapter 66

MARILYN CALLED ON a Saturday morning two weeks later. "Hi, Grace. I was wondering if you and Lily were going to be home today. I'd like to visit this afternoon, if that's all right."

"Yes, of course." She almost burst into tears of happiness.

"How about one o'clock?"

"That's fine."

Lily was at her post in the dining room window when Marilyn's car pulled into the driveway. "Mémé is here. There's a man with her. He has yellow hair like us."

With a big smile, Grace opened the door. "Hi, Marilyn. Hi, Scott."

"Mémé! You came to see me!" Lily squealed and ran toward her great aunt who knelt to receive her eager hug.

Scott was tanner than when Grace had last seen him, nearly a year ago. The desert sun had lightened the ends of his hair which brushed the tops of his ears. She cocked her head at him. "Should I call you Scott or Skip?"

"Call me Skip." He skirted around his mother and hugged her. "What should I call you? Grace or Gigi?"

"Grace."

Marilyn stood with Lily's hand in hers. "This is your cousin, Skip."

He squatted on his haunches, so he was eye-to-eye with the little girl. "Hi, Lily. I'm glad to finally meet you."

She eyeballed him like a cop who doesn't believe a felon's alibi. "You don't look like Mr. Beau."

"We don't look alike because we have different mothers and fathers."

Skip put his palms on his knees to rise when Lily said, "Are you good at it?"

He smirked at Grace. "Depends on what *it* is."

"Skipping."

"Oh, that. Not anymore."

Marilyn touched Grace's arm. "I was hoping Lily and I could see a Disney movie at the theater on Hillsboro Road. It starts in thirty minutes. May I take her while you and Skip visit?"

Lily bounced in place. "Say yes, Mommy. Please."

After Grace installed Lily's booster seat in the back of Marilyn's car and they left, she closed the front door and turned to face Skip. "Would you like something to drink? Ice tea, beer, or wine?"

"I'd love a beer. I missed them while I was gone. The only ones they have in the UAE are alcohol-free."

Grace had a couple bottles of Beau's favorite still in her bar fridge. She got one for Skip and wine for herself. They sat in the family room, clinked glasses, and each downed a swig.

"Gigi, I mean, Grace, Mom wrote that you and Beau aren't dating anymore."

"No, we're not. He wasn't ready for a commitment. For Lily's sake and mine, we need someone who foresees a future with us."

"When I got home this week, I thought he looked more miserable than I had ever seen him. I would bet my closet full of designer suits that he regrets the breakup."

Beau was likely more upset with Megan and Tom than being separated from her. It seemed strange that two people could be intimate, sleep together, eat together, talk almost daily, and suddenly they don't know what is happening in each other's lives.

The subject of Tom's affair with Megan was not brought up as she and Skip talked more. Perhaps he was unaware of the drama, or that Grace had landed in the middle. She was curious about the resulting fallout from Tom's confession. Had Beau also advised his brother-in-law to confess to Gen? Was there a confrontation with Megan? Did Tom, Beau, or Gen tackle her separately, or did all three of them deal with her together?

From their brief meeting in the Keys, Grace witnessed Megan's delight in inflicting havoc and pain. A strong, united front was needed to combat such a dangerous and wicked woman. After all, the affair with Tom may have been more an act of vengefulness against Beau than a passion-filled interlude with an ex-brother-in-law.

Instead of the Tom-Gen-Beau-Megan drama, she and Skip discussed his job overseas and how she discovered her Makowsky connection. Neither of them was aware of the passing time until Marilyn and Lily returned three hours later. With the four of them together, Skip used his phone to take pictures as he and Grace posed in combinations with Lily and Marilyn.

He touched the screen. "Give me your cell number, Grace, and I'll send them to you."

After they exchanged contact information, Marilyn nudged her son. "Tell her about next month."

"Mom and I are extending an invitation to attend the dedication ceremony for the Makowsky Chemical Sciences Building. You and Lily should come as members of Uncle Mack's family."

Marilyn put an arm around Grace's waist. "George named the endowment after you. I know he would be pleased if his daughter and granddaughter were there."

"Thank you. We would be honored."

Chapter 67

THE DEDICATION FOR the Makowsky Chemical Sciences Hall was in the outdoor courtyard of the newly-constructed building. Marilyn, Skip, Grace, and Lily sat on folding chairs in the front row. Across from them on a raised dais were two lines of dignitaries, including John Truman. When the lawyer spotted Grace and Lily, he waved.

"See the man with the white hair." Grace pointed him out. "He's an old friend of your Grandma Juliette."

Lily waved back, and Mr. Truman gave her a broad smile.

The President of FAU spoke, as did the Provost, the Dean of Sciences, a chemical engineering professor, and a graduate student. They praised the new facility and how it would enhance the university's reputation as a leader in the field of chemical sciences. Following the speeches and the ribbon cutting, the Dean announced there would be tours of the building conducted by student volunteers and a reception in the lobby. A photographer from the student newspaper asked the family of Dr. Makowsky to pose with university officials.

After the photo shoot ended, an attractive young woman with black-framed glasses approached Grace. "Excuse me, Dr. Black-Stone. I'm Nina Garcia with The University Press. I would like to ask you some questions." She spoke into her cell phone then thrust it forward.

Grace stutter-stepped and came to a halt. Lily ran to catch up with Marilyn and Skip.

The student said, "Did you have any input with the decisions regarding this building, Dr. Black-Stone?"

"The only decision I made was what to wear today."

"Did your father discuss his endowment with you before his death?"

"My father passed away when I was a small child."

"Was the G.G. Educational Endowment responsible for your job at FAU?"

Grace gave the reporter a steely-eyed stare which most teachers or parents perfected with practice. "No. The endowment was earmarked for chemical science programs and the construction of this building in honor of Dr. Makowsky. There were no chairs or faculty positions funded by the endowment in any university departments. If you'll excuse me, I need to go inside with my family."

She crossed the courtyard and pulled open a glass door. When she scanned the area, her breath hitched in her throat. On the wall opposite was a poster-sized photograph of her father.

The one and only time she recalled meeting him slammed into her consciousness. His suit coat had been scratchy on her bare legs after he picked up her three-year-old self from the floor. The ceiling light had glinted off the lens of his wire-framed glasses. He had a spicy masculine scent Grace found alien.

Her reverie was broken when Lily ran up to her. A cupcake with orange frosting topped with a fondant cutout was clutched in her fist. There was a nearby display of the treats laid out to look like the periodic table.

"Look, Mommy. I'm not three. But the letters are in my name." On the white fondant square the number three was written in black royal icing. Below were the letters Li and Lithium printed at the bottom. Lily grabbed Grace's hand. "Let's find one for you."

"Wait. I want to show you something first." Grace led her daughter to the life-sized headshot on the wall and lifted her into her arms. "This is my father."

Lily stared at the image for several seconds. "He looks like a nice grandpa."

She leaned forward and kissed the glass-covered cheek. Grace put her daughter down and turned around. Marilyn stood a few feet away, her eyes shiny with unshed tears.

Skip joined them and pulled his cell phone from his pocket. "Why don't the three of you stand by Uncle Mack, and I'll take a picture?"

After several shots, a young man in a pristine lab coat announced the start of the student-guided tours. Grace wrapped Lily's cupcake in a napkin and put it in her purse since no food or drink was permitted beyond the lobby. Marilyn, Skip, Lily, and Grace attached themselves to a group led by a student named Nils.

They entered a large room dominated by a ceiling-height piece of equipment in the corner. The white metal cylinder looked like a beer-making vat with stairs to its top. Nils told the group it was a nuclear magnetic resonance spectrometer or NMR. He talked about electromagnetic radiation, isotopes, and nuclei. With his palm on the tall tank, he continued his spiel as if everyone wasn't clueless.

Lily jerked Grace's skirt. "Mommy, what's the big thing?"

Grace bent down and spoke in a soft voice. "It's an NMR."

The little girl's eyes widened and her mouth dropped open. She looked from her mother to the tall instrument. "Is that what Robert had to give Erin when she couldn't poop?"

Behind them Skip blurted out a whoop of laughter then covered it with a conspicuous cough.

Grace glared at him with a cut-it-out look which lost its impact when she smiled. She leaned down toward Lily." No. The name is really long so they called it by three letters, N ... M ... R."

They were shown seminar rooms, offices, computer centers, and various research labs. In one, Nils pointed out an argon-filled glove box. "This is used to safely handle materials in a pure and inert environment."

Lily raised her hand. "How does stuff get in there?"

"Good question. See the part that sticks out over here. It's called an antechamber. If you want to put something in the glove box you open this door, put it inside then close it up again. With the gloves, you open the door in here and bring it in."

They crossed a catwalk with Plexiglas walls which looked down into a lab where two students wore safety glasses, purple nitrile gloves, and white hard hats. Nils described the type of experimentation done in this room. "That's the end of the tour, folks. Are there any questions before we return to the lobby?"

Lily raised her hand again. "Why are they wearing hats like Mr. Beau's?"

Grace's breath caught in her throat. The unexpected mention of his name still triggered a physical response like a little dart shot into her.

Nils squatted next to Lily. "You mean the hard hats?"

She pressed her finger against the Plexiglas. "Are those thinking caps? My kindergarten teacher says to use ours in school."

Nils chuckled. "Any place something could fall from above, we have to wear them to protect our heads."

Marilyn squeezed Grace's arm. "She's so interested in everything here. Maybe Lily will be a scientist like her grandfather."

Upon their return to the lobby, John Truman approached. "This is quite an impressive facility, isn't it? Dr. Makowsky would be pleased, I think."

"It's a wonderful tribute to him."

The man bent toward Lily. "I knew your Grandmother Juliette very well. You are as pretty as she was."

The little girl with the same blue eyes as Grace's mother looked into the older man's face. "You miss her."

Truman's smile disappeared. "Very much."

"Mommy does too." She turned to Grace. "Can I have my cupcake now?"

She sat Lily on a nearby chair, spread a paper napkin on her lap, and handed her the Lithium-decorated dessert.

The lawyer watched the little girl pull off the fondant tab and lick the frosting. "If I had married Juliette, Lily would be my granddaughter today."

"Do you have any children or grandchildren, Mr. Truman?"

"Call me John. I had a son who was killed in a car accident when he was in college. I have some stepchildren from my second marriage, but we're not close."

"Lily doesn't have much contact with her paternal grandfather who lives in Virginia." Grace pointed to the photograph on the wall. "And, of course, this is the first time she's even seen *my* father."

"How would she feel about having a de facto grandparent?"

"What do you mean?"

"I know I'm not related to her by blood or marriage, but I would welcome the opportunity to have a place in her life and yours. I feel I owe it to Juliette."

He swallowed and waited for Grace's answer. John Truman's naked grief and his loneliness were still palpable after all these years. This man was her mother's lover. He may have become Grace's stepfather if Juliette had not been killed.

"Lily and I would like that."

They exchanged cell phone numbers, and he told her to call him whenever she wanted.

Chapter 68

TWO DAYS LATER a photograph and article about the Makowsky building's dedication appeared in the FAU school newspaper. An adjunct professor from the science department stopped Grace in the parking lot. "How come you didn't have the endowment pay for more full-time teaching positions?"

"I had no say where the money went."

Carolyn, her secretary, handed her the day's mail. "I saw your picture in the paper. Why wasn't the money given to *this* department?"

"Because the donor was a chemist."

She was headed home when her nemesis, Dr. William Reinhardt, entered the reception area. She nodded a courtesy greeting to him. Reinhardt flashed his trademark smirk. "I should have known you had either a rich daddy or boyfriend."

Grace halted and shot a speculative glance at the man's back as he continued toward his office. Alice was right. It was time to confront him. Her colleague sat in his office chair when she blew through the door without a heads-up knock or a request to enter.

Grace leaned over the desktop toward his surprised face. "What's your problem, Will? If you have a grievance with me, I suggest you file it with the Department Head or the Provost. Otherwise, stop the jibes. But let me give you a word of advice. If you're telling people my employment or my tenure was in any way unjustly earned, I will prepare documentation of my student and peer reviews, my publications, my committee work, and my invitations to speak at conferences compared to yours. Then I will file a countersuit of harassment. Do I make myself clear?"

The man's spine stiffened before he gave a supercilious nod.

With her head held high, she left. As she walked down the hall, Grace passed several faculty members standing just inside their open office doors. They gave her thumbs-up gestures of support. Alice was the only one who stepped out into the hallway and flipped the bird toward Reinhardt's office.

Chapter 69

THE THANKSGIVING HOLIDAY was three weeks away when Marilyn called. "I'm inviting you and Lily to dinner."

"That's very nice. Does Beau know?"

"Yes. He's fine with it." There was a moment of silence then her aunt spoke in a rush, as if her words might be cut off. "I know Bojo misses you."

Grace sidestepped Marilyn's last comment. "Will Gen and Tom be there?"

"Only Gen and the kids are coming. Beau went with them to one of their counseling sessions, and Tom confessed to an affair earlier this year. Gen was pretty devastated but having the therapist there, as well as Beau, helped her deal with the news."

Obviously, the three of them did not share the identity of *the other woman* with the rest of the family. "Are they headed for a divorce?"

"I don't know if they've contacted attorneys yet or not. Gen is being somewhat closed mouth about the situation. Based on the advice of the marriage counselor, she's taking her time making such a monumental decision."

"That's a wise thing to do. Are you sure Lily and I should attend? I'll understand if you want the holiday to be only for the Charvets considering all that has happened recently."

"Don't be silly. This is the perfect time for you and Lily to join us. It's a day of giving thanks and, despite some setbacks, we're grateful to have you two added to the family."

Grace paused. Regardless of Marilyn's assurance, she doubted all the Charvets were happy with her connection to them. But the invitation was from by *her* aunt. If any of the Charvets did not want the Stones there, then they could choose to stay home.

In a cheerful voice, she said, "So, what can I bring?"

They settled on a sweet potato casserole and pumpkin cheesecake rolls for her contribution.

After Grace ended the call, Lily came into the home office. "Who was that?"

"Mémé. We're going to her house for Thanksgiving."

"Will that girl be there?"

"Yes."

"She said you're a bad word."

"I know. Her daddy talked to her about it, and it won't happen again."

"Will Mr. Beau be there?"

"Yes." Grace maintained a neutral expression. "He's part of our new family."

Chapter 70

AT NOON ON Thanksgiving Day, they arrived at the Charvet house. Beau's car was already in the driveway. Grace pulled in behind it. She'd be able to leave first if something happened.

Gen's sporty convertible was parked with the nose almost touching the garage door. A horn beeped. Skip stopped his car next to hers. As soon as Grace unbuckled Lily's seat harness, the little girl scrambled out and ran to Skip. Crouched on his haunches in suit pants and a white dress shirt, he received Lily's ebullient hug.

"Happy Thanksgiving, Skip."

"Happy Thanksgiving to you too."

Grace met him at the rear of her Highlander. He waved in the direction of the front door. Before she could see who was there, Skip pulled her against him and planted a kiss on her mouth.

When he released her after a long hug, he grinned with a devilish glint in his eye. "I'm glad you and Lily are here today."

"Uh, we are too."

Thrown by his overt display of affection, she inhaled and straightened her camel-colored sweater dress. The black-and-tan checkered bodice clung to her breasts but the rest skimmed her slender form. She released the hatchback and reached for a box.

Skip handed her two divided reusable shopping bags, each containing bottles of wine which clinked against each other. "Let me get that. You take this."

Her cousin hefted the bulky cardboard box from her SUV's trunk. She and Lily followed him up the drive. Grace's eyes were cast downward, so she wouldn't bump into the little girl. When they neared the front door, she looked up.

Beau stood there.

He was clean-shaven and wore tan khakis with a red polo shirt. He scowled at his stepbrother.

Skip greeted Beau with a breezy, "Hey there, Bojo," and entered the house.

Beau sank down to child level and smiled. "Happy Thanksgiving, Lily."

The little girl plastered her body against Grace's leg. Her voice was soft and shy. "Hi, Mr. Beau."

Lily's behavior was so unlike the way she greeted him in the past. He rose to his feet with a confused expression.

Zoe appeared in the open doorway. "Come on in, cousins."

Lily disengaged herself from her mother. She hugged Zoe's legs and tilted her face up. "I missed *you*."

The young woman lifted the little girl into her arms and walked inside the house. "Mom, everyone's here."

Grace shot Beau a quick glance before she stepped over the threshold and entered the foyer. As she followed Zoe and Lily to the kitchen, the front door closed behind her.

Marilyn bustled around the room but stopped when they entered. She kissed Lily on the cheek. "I am so happy to see you."

"Me too, Mémé."

Marilyn gave Grace a hug. "It's wonderful to have you here again. Is that the wine Skip brought?" Grace nodded and her aunt took the bags, extending her arms. "Here, Bojo. Put these on the bar."

Grace whipped her head around. Beau stood inches behind her. He grasped the handles and walked away.

Marilyn frowned at something over Grace's other shoulder. "Skip, why are you just standing there? What's in the box?"

He shrugged. "I don't know. I'm just the guy who carried it in."

Grace said, "That's the sweet potatoes and pumpkin rolls I made. Where do you want them?"

The kitchen became a bustling place with dishes being taken from the refrigerator to the table, put in, or removed from the oven. Gen appeared midway through the preparations. She greeted Grace with a cool hello.

Marilyn touched her stepdaughter's forehead. "How do you feel?"

Gen's features tightened, and her lips pressed together. "There's too much noise in here. I'm going to lay down again. Call me when dinner is ready."

Marilyn's brow wrinkled as she watched Gen walk away. She turned to Grace who spooned homemade cranberry sauce into a cut-glass dish and said, "Migraine."

In the dining room, the seven table settings of crisp linens, crystal stemware, and gold-rimmed china sparkled in the light from a wide glass and chrome chandelier. In the corner, a child's table mimicked the adult's but with plastic plates and glasses. Beau's father decanted wine at a granite-topped bar in the corner of the room.

He smiled at Grace. "Your presence here has made my wife very happy. My son too."

Grace ignored his last comment. "We're thrilled to be invited. It's our first Thanksgiving with a family who is actually related to us."

The cork of the Shiraz popped with a loud squeak. "Then we have even more to be thankful for today."

"Have you seen Lily?"

"She's in the den."

Grace crossed the foyer, passed the living room, and walked toward the sound of a television. Beau sat on a brown leather sofa with Lily on one side and Gen's daughter, Sara, on the other. His nephew, Ben, arranged a pile of die cast cars into rows on the carpeted floor.

Beau spotted Grace in the doorway. "I've been told to keep out of the kitchen and watch the kids."

Soon dishes of sweet potato casserole, disassembled turkey, sliced ham, mashed potatoes, sausage stuffing, creamed spinach, an endive and green apple salad, candied carrots, roasted Brussel sprouts, and gravy covered the table. The buffet cabinet against the far wall was laden with Grace's pumpkin and cream cheese roll sliced into spirals, pies of pumpkin, pecan, and cherry as well as a platter of turkey-shaped sugar cookies.

"Stop, Mom," Skip called out. "One more dish and we'll have to eat in shifts."

Mr. Charvet sat at the head of the table. Skip pulled out a chair at the opposite end. Beau stood off to the side. Gen wandered into the room and laid her head against her brother's shoulder. The three little kids marched to the kiddie table where their filled plates waited. Zoe had helped them prepare their food from the array as it was carried out of the kitchen.

Marilyn was the last to arrive. She frowned at Skip. "Why are you sitting there?" He shrugged and stood up as his mother pulled out the chair next to the one her son vacated. "Grace, you sit here next to me. Zoe, sit in the middle. Gen, take the chair next to your father." She looked around. Beau and Skip stood together in the doorway. She motioned to the last two empty seats on the opposite side of the table.

Once everyone was in place, Beau's father bowed his head, his hands clasped together. "*Pour ce que nous sommes sur le point de recevoir, Seigneur, rends-nous vraiment reconnaissant.* Amen."

During the meal, whenever Grace looked at Skip, he flashed a roguish smile as if they were in on a secret prank. In contrast, Beau lifted his glass of wine to her in a silent toast. He drank and his intense regard over the gold rim of the goblet could have steamed wrinkles out of linen. Another time he raised his one eyebrow in a semaphore which sent a message she was unable to decipher, but forced her to clamp her thighs together.

Conversations swirled around the table as food was passed from person to person, and the wine was poured. It quieted a bit when the eating commenced then resumed when everyone's initial appetite had been sated. The one person who said little and picked at the food on her plate was Gen. She was in obvious distress. Her father bent his head to hers and whispered. She nodded, stood, and left the room. At the same time, Sara rose from the kiddie table.

Marilyn paused with her fork halfway to her mouth. "What do you need, honey?"

"I'm done eating. I wanna stay with Mommy." She ran out of the room before anyone could stop her.

Marilyn put her napkin on the table and started to follow. Mr. Charvet waved at her to sit. "Let them be, *ma femme.*"

A few minutes later, Ben and Lily asked for a cookie when they showed how clean their plates were. The adults leaned back in their chairs, but a short while later, the men eyed the food still on the table.

Mr. Charvet pointed to the turkey. "Pass that over here."

Skip did then he reached for the bowl of mashed potatoes. Beau speared another slice of ham from the platter. The second round of eating and drinking began.

Lily rose and stood between Grace and Marilyn. "Mommy, can Ben and I go?"

"Ask Mémé."

Ben joined them and patted his grandmother's arm. "We wanna play."

Marilyn caressed the little boy's coppery head. "You can leave the table but stay in the house."

The children raced from the room. Marilyn pointed to the buffet table. "Anyone want dessert now?"

Groans and yawns replaced replies. When no one helped themselves to more, Marilyn stacked Grace's plate on top of hers, and the cleanup began. Mr. Charvet recorked bottles of wine and took the empties away. Beau and Skip carried dirty dishes, glasses, and silverware into the kitchen. Zoe loaded the dishwasher. Grace filled the sink with hot soapy water and washed the crystal stemware and china. Skip grabbed a dishtowel to dry and handed off the pieces to Zoe who put them away. Marilyn divided leftovers into plastic bags and containers.

Mr. Charvet carried an armload of linens into the kitchen. "Do you want these in the washing machine?"

His wife pointed out of the room. "I'll want to soak them first. Come with me."

When her stint as dishwasher ended, Grace crossed the foyer to check on Lily and Ben. The television in the den broadcast the annoying sounds of a children's cartoon. Ben was on the floor, surrounded by his cars, eyes glued to the TV screen. Sara sat on the sofa with a handheld video game. Her daughter was not in the room.

"Ben, where's Lily?"

The little boy shrugged.

Grace turned toward the sofa. "Sara, have you seen Lily?"

The girl's head remained bent as her thumbs danced across the keys. "She's not in here."

"I can see that. Where did she go?"

"Dunno."

Grace put her hands on her hips and turned in a circle. Where was Lily?

Chapter 71

GRACE CHECKED THE half bath, the living room, dining room, and garage. Her fear ratcheted, and her heart beat double time. With no reservations about privacy, she entered the bedrooms and their attached baths. Gen lay curled on her side in one of the darkened rooms with her eyes closed.

Grace rushed into the kitchen where Beau, Zoe, and Marilyn were. "I can't find Lily."

Beau skirted around the center island and hurried to her side. "Where have you looked?"

Her voice squeaked with anxiety. "In every room of the house."

Mr. Charvet entered from the patio. "What's wrong?"

Beau explained, exited the kitchen, and cupped his hands around his mouth. "Lily."

Marilyn dried her hands on a dish towel. "Did you check the bedrooms, Grace?"

She nodded in jerky up-down bobs. "But I didn't open the closets or look under the beds."

"I'll do that." Marilyn left the room.

Beau's father called out Lily's name. Skip opened the front door and came inside. "What's going on?"

Zoe headed to the open patio door. "Grace can't find Lily. I'll walk around outside, you check the garage."

Beau patted Grace's back. "Why don't you wait in the living room?"

The house echoed with the sounds of Lily's name being called. Grace sat on the edge of the sofa with an elbow on each knee, her hands covering her mouth. Marilyn and Gen came from the hall which led to the bedrooms.

Beau's sister scowled. "She's not back there."

Her aunt sat beside Grace and squeezed her arm. "Don't worry. She's around here somewhere. One time, Skip fell asleep in a basket of dirty laundry. He woke up and came out of the closet when he heard the police siren." Marilyn fingered the silver cross she wore around her neck. Her lips moved in a silent prayer as she headed out of the room.

Grace died a little inside as each minute passed. Please, God, bring Lily back to me. She's my life, my heart, my reason for being. When she opened her eyes, Sara stood in the doorway of the den, glaring at her then stuck out her tongue. At the same time, Marilyn walked down the hall from the garage.

Grace jumped to her feet. "Who looked in the den?"

Her aunt stopped. "Sara said Lily left the room."

Grace rushed toward Gen's daughter who blocked the doorway. The young girl's green eyes blazed. "I told you she's not here."

Despite her haste to find Lily, Grace did not try to move Sara out of the way. The hostile child could snap back like a cornered kitten. "Let me see."

Marilyn stood behind her. "Grace, what is it?"

She pointed to Sara. "Ask her."

Marilyn tipped her head toward the girl. "Do you know where Lily is?"

Sara heaved a sigh and ran past them. Little Ben jumped to his feet to follow his sister.

Marilyn put out her hand and stopped him. "Hold on there. Where's Lily?"

Fat tears overflowed his eyes and rolled down his cheeks. He hiccupped with gulping sobs. Grace rushed in and surveyed the room side to side.

Meanwhile, Marilyn knelt in front of the little boy. "You can tell Mémé."

Grace looked behind the sofa and recliner. She opened a closet door. Coats hung from a rod and white, lidded bankers' boxes were labelled with a year and their contents in black marker. She moved the coats aside and checked the rear of the closet.

Marilyn's voice became a bit firmer. "I want you to tell me where Lily is right now."

Grace backed out of the closet as Ben pointed to the built-in cabinetry which housed the TV and DVD player. As Marilyn struggled to her feet from her kneeling position, Ben dashed around her and disappeared. Grace stared at the tall cabinet with three connected sections. The center unit bumped out beyond the two side pieces. A big screen TV sat in a wide middle opening with three wood doors below and open shelving above. Marilyn picked up the remote from the sofa and muted the sound.

Grace bent down. "Lily. Are you in there?"

No answer.

She went to her knees and opened the bottom door on the left. The interior ran from the front to the back of the cabinet, the width of the door frame. It was empty. So was the middle one. When Grace pulled on the last one, she saw nothing at first except a man's belt loosely coiled on the bottom. She bent her head and looked farther back. A child's small body was curled in a tight fetal position, her back facing Grace.

"Lily, its Mommy."

There was no sound or movement. Grace's heart stopped. Darkness colored the edge of her consciousness. She grasped the belt and flung it behind her as she thrust her head and shoulders into the small opening. With one arm extended, she grabbed a fistful of the pink cotton sweater Lily wore.

A high-pitched scream like that of a small animal under attack echoed through the enclosed space. Startled, Grace jerked and bashed her head on the wood top with a loud thud. The shrieks continued as Lily squirmed against her mother's grip.

"It's Mommy. You're okay." Grace tugged the little girl far enough toward the front for her head to clear the opening.

When Lily's arms were free, she batted at the air and sobbed. "S-s-snake!. S-s-snake!"

Grace wrapped her arms around her daughter and pulled her close. "I have you. It's okay."

With the still hysterical child on her lap, Grace rocked her and crooned the same words over and over. When Lily had stuttered the word *snake*, the scenario made sense. The little girl had been convinced or coerced to crawl inside the cabinet. Then the belt was thrown in and the door shut. The question was why.

Lily's wails brought everyone into the den. Questions were fired at Marilyn and Grace.

In answer, Marilyn pointed to the open cabinet door. "Ben told us Lily was in there. I don't know why. She's very scared."

Beau wiped his hand across his mouth and stared with worried eyes at the hysterical child. Skip stood next to Zoe as the young woman leaned against him, one hand on her cheek. Gen held a crying Ben in her arms while a tearful Sara stood in front of her. Mr. Charvet swiveled his head to study his daughter and grandchildren then frowned, as if he suspected this drama involved them.

Lily sobbed. "B-bite ... b-be quiet ... c-can't move."

Grace rubbed the child's small back in soothing circles. "You're okay. The snake is gone."

Marilyn gasped. "What snake?"

Zoe squeaked in fear and danced around as she searched the floor at her feet.

Grace nodded at the belt that lay next to the sofa. "That snake."

Mr. Charvet walked past Grace and picked up the black leather strap. "I left this on the bed. What's it doing in here?"

Gen waved a dismissive hand. "It was just a prank. Sara thought it would be fun to scare Lily."

Grace's mother-bear protectiveness raced into the red zone. "It was no prank. She was told it would bite her if she moved or made a noise."

Lily whimpered. Grace struggled to rise from the floor. She needed to get her child out of this place.

Beau stepped forward. "Let me help." He leaned close and put out his hands. "Lily, can I hold you?"

The little girl launched herself at him. He straightened and cuddled her close. She buried her face in his neck and clutched the collar of his shirt in both fists.

Grace rose off the floor and looked at the members of the Charvet family. "All my life I've wanted and wished for a family. I was so scared to be alone in the world without anyone, except Lily and my friends. But if this is the way a child is treated in your family, we were better off on our own."

Marilyn cried out. "Oh, no!"

Grace could not look at her aunt. "We're leaving."

Beau followed her out of the room. She lifted her purse off a console table in the foyer, pulled her key ring from it, and opened the front door. At her car, Beau strapped Lily into her seat.

Grace had one foot inside the vehicle when his hand touched her elbow. "Wait. I want to say how sorry I am."

Upset, she spoke in a harsh tone. "Are you sorry Lily was terrorized today? Are you sorry you accused me of sleeping with a married man? Or both?"

He didn't answer. She dropped behind the wheel and pulled shut the door. Beau watched her back down the driveway. She held her tears in check until the car stopped at the end of the block.

Chapter 72

WHEN THEY ARRIVED home, Grace sat with Lily in the family room. "Tell me what happened. How did you get into that cabinet?"

"Sara told me."

"What did she tell you?"

"Pépé had a video game in there. Like hers."

"You wanted to play with one like she had?"

"Sara said go, go." Lily motioned with a back-it-up hand gesture. "Get it."

"When you got inside, what happened?"

Lily's mouth turned down. "She threw in the snake, and it bited me."

Grace stroked her daughter's head. "You know it wasn't a real snake. It was Pépé's belt."

"It hurt. Right here." She patted her calf.

Grace rubbed Lily's leg. "I think the buckle hit you, and it felt like a bite."

"It was dark." Lily sat up with a strained expression on her small face. "Why is Sara mean?"

"I don't know."

Chapter 73

THE NEXT DAY when Grace returned from her yoga class only Robert was in the kitchen. "Tariq is covering for a doctor whose flight home was delayed. Here's your cappuccino. I didn't get the milk as frothy as he does."

"That's okay. Did Lily tell you what happened yesterday?"

His lips pressed together in a slight grimace before he spoke. "Was it just child's play gone wrong or something more?"

Grace took a careful sip of her hot drink. "It seemed more deliberate than a prank, as Gen called it. Sara brought the belt into the den for a reason."

"Why?"

"I find it hard to believe it was payback for Lily getting her in trouble at her brother's birthday party in April." Grace shifted in her chair. "I think she knew the way to hurt *me* the most was to go after Lily."

They were silent for several moments. Robert cleared his throat. "How was it seeing Beau again?"

"A bit awkward at first then uncomfortable." She sighed when he raised his eyebrows and waited. "There's still a lot of chemistry between us. It was like he couldn't help reminding me. You know, the smoldering stares, the secret smiles. After I found Lily, he carried her out to the car and said he was sorry. I asked him if he was sorry for what happened to Lily or for accusing me of sleeping with his brother-in-law."

Robert shook his head like she was the unfortunate victim of estrogen-induced stupidity. "Oh, Grace, why would you say that? He already told you he was sorry."

"I was upset and angry. I also said to everyone else that I didn't want to be in the family if this was how they treated children." Tears filled her eyes. "Have I ruined everything?"

"Not necessarily. It just means you have to do a little damage control." He handed her a paper napkin.

Grace dabbed at her cheeks. Her cell phone rang. She checked the screen. "It's my aunt. What should I do?"

Robert rolled his eyes. "Answer it."

Grace tapped her phone. "Hello, Marilyn."

"Hello, dear. How is Lily? And how are you today?" Her voice had a verbal wince to it.

"We're fine but sad because of what happened."

"I understand. We're very upset also."

"Did you find out why Sara did it?" Robert leaned sideways to listen in, so Grace hit the Speaker button.

"When she went into the bedroom during dinner, she asked her mother if the migraine was because you and Lily were there. Gen swears she didn't say yes, but Sara took it that way. She saw Beau's belt on the bed and decided to scare Lily with it, so you would go home." Her aunt's gusty sigh echoed from the phone. "After you left, Beau called for a family meeting, and we had a long talk. Will you give us another chance?"

A tremendous sense of relief washed over Grace. Her family wanted them back. "I'd like that. What I said was spoken in anger. I didn't mean it."

"I know, dear. The next Charvet family get-together at Christmas will have no drama. Trust me. By the way, I have your dishes and leftovers for you. Bojo is going into his office this afternoon and offered to drop them off. Is that okay?"

Robert straightened and nodded with vigor. He mouthed: *Yes, say yes.*

Confused at his insistence, Grace said, "Uh, that'll be fine."

"When would be a good time for him to stop by?"

"When?" Robert held up a hand with all his fingers extended. "How about five o'clock?"

When the call ended, Robert's mouth twitched with a self-satisfied grin. "This is the perfect start of your campaign."

"What campaign?"

He studied the backs of his hands on the tabletop as if the answers were written there like crib notes. "You have to convince Beau that he wants a future with you."

"Yeah? And how do I do that?"

Robert patted her leg. "Oh, honey. I'm going to excuse you on the basis that you didn't grow up with a father or brothers and were only married a couple of years. You're still riding around on training wheels when it comes to relationships with men. Now listen to me. Women think with their hearts and heads. Men think with their stomachs and private parts. That's what you need to appeal to. Logic and romance are only effective with the female, not the male of the species."

"Are you saying I should feed him then seduce him? I was already doing that. He still didn't want to make our relationship permanent."

"Yes, but there's also his sister to consider."

"Well, that's one person who will never love me, and seduction is out of the question."

"She needs to accept you on her own terms without her family demanding it. Beau will come around as soon as she does."

When Grace left Robert's house an hour later with Lily, she had a new resolve and a plan to help Beau commit to a future with her.

Chapter 74

AT FIVE O'CLOCK the doorbell rang. Lily hopped down from the kitchen barstool. "That's Mr. Beau."

"Go open the door for him."

The click of the lock and Lily's greeting sounded in the foyer. Grace dried her hands on a dishtowel then leaned on the counter. Because the day was sunny and unseasonably warm, she wore the minuscule white shorts and the gauzy top Beau had admired when they drove to the Keys. That day she had on flip flops but today she wore a pair of sandals with high-wedged soles. The shoes lengthened her legs and made the shorts appear shorter. She had applied her go-to-work makeup and curled her long tresses, so they bounced around her almost bare shoulders.

Robert had urged her to not dress like Heloise the Homemaker when Beau arrived. "You need to look sexy but casual. Remember you're appealing to both his base desires."

Beau came to a halt in the doorway when he saw her. He carried the box she had taken to Marilyn's yesterday. It was filled with containers and plates covered in foil.

She flashed a warm smile. "Thank you for *coming*." She patted an open space on the counter. "Why don't you *lay* that down right here?"

His eyes devoured her.

Lily eased into the room around him. "Look what Mr. Beau brought me." She held up a small gift bag with a folded piece of notebook paper peeking out the top. "He said to read the note first."

Beau set the box on the counter then lifted Lily and put her next to it. She handed her mother the paper and hugged the gift bag to her chest. The note was written in a childish scrawl.

Grace read it aloud. "Dear Lily, I am sorry. I feel bad. Don't be sad or mad. I want you to have this. Your cuzin. Sara."

"Can I look now, Mr. Beau?"

He bent until he was eye-to-eye with Lily. "Remember no one told Sara to write the note. We were all surprised when she wanted you to have this." He touched the bag.

Lily reached in and pulled out a rectangular object clumsily wrapped in tissue paper with a substantial amount of Scotch tape. Once the thin covering was removed, the little girl gasped. "Sara's video game. Can I play it, Mommy?"

Grace was stunned Gen's daughter had made this peacemaking gesture. "Yes, and tonight we're going to write her a thank you note."

"Okay. Down, please, Mr. Beau." He lifted her off the counter, and she ran to the family room.

Grace's gaze followed Lily as she settled on the sofa with the toy, then she turned to face Beau. His expression made her heart beat faster. He moved closer until their bodies were almost touching. His breath fanned her cheek. A pinball-like whistle sounded from the family room.

He stepped back. "Uh, something smells good in here."

"We made cookies. Would you like some to take home?"

Grace walked over to the center island where two cooling racks held the peanut butter treats. Beau didn't answer. She glanced over her shoulder at him. He was watching her back side.

"Beau?"

His gaze jerked up. "Uh, yeah. That'd be great."

Grace bent over and opened the deep drawer under her double oven to retrieve two plastic containers. Behind her, Beau made a sound between a sudden inhale and a strangled cough.

She straightened and pointed to a pot on the stove. "I also made vegetable beef soup. I'll give you some of that too."

Grace packed his cookies and soup. She handed him the food containers in a small brown bag with handles. "Here you go."

"Thanks. Uh, Grace—"

"Lily, come thank Mr. Beau for all this wonderful food he brought us." She lifted a plate of Thanksgiving leftovers from the box.

Her daughter bounced into the kitchen and wrapped her arms around Beau's legs. "Thank you for bringing Sara's game for me. And the turkey."

Grace headed to the refrigerator. "Why don't you walk Mr. Beau to the front door while I put this food away?"

Beau cast a backward glance as Lily took his hand and walked him out of the kitchen. After the front door opened and closed, Grace stood still. Round One of the Charvet Campaign completed and on to Round Two.

Chapter 75

ON SATURDAY, GRACE called Marilyn. "Thank you for the food. It was more than I expected. I won't have to cook all week."

"You're welcome. Did Lily get the letter and gift?"

"Yes. She was thrilled. Was it really Sara's idea? No one suggested it?"

"I keep gift wrapping supplies in the den. When she came out of there with the note and the bag, we were very surprised. I think Gen more than anyone else."

"Lily dictated a thank you note to Sara last night." Grace studied the sheet of paper which sat on the kitchen counter.

"That's so nice. Do you want me to give it to her?"

"I was going to mail it, but there is something else I would like you to do."

"Oh?" Her aunt drew out the word, obviously curious.

"I want to meet with Gen."

Marilyn said nothing for several moments. "I don't know if that's a good idea. She understands that everyone in the family wants you and Lily to be a part, but I'm not sure she's ready to be friends yet."

"I know that." It was unlikely that she and Gen would ever be friends. "However, I need her to accept me on her own terms and not because the rest of you insist on it. If she doesn't, I won't have a future with Beau. He'll always be torn between the two of us."

"In that case, what can I do to help?"

Grace outlined the plan she and Robert strategized. She and her aunt ironed out a few details and agreed to initiate Round Two of the campaign on the following Saturday.

Chapter 76

WHEN ROBERT PULLED his minivan into the Target parking lot the next weekend, Grace spotted Marilyn's car. "They're here."

Inside the store, they each grabbed a cart. With an affected air of casualness veneered with deliberate intent, they rolled their baskets up and down two aisles. Robert grabbed several board games off a shelf and distributed them between the two carts. "Props."

In the fourth aisle, Marilyn and Gen stood in front of a display of *Project Mc2 Core* dolls. Grace nudged Robert with her elbow.

He spoke in a louder voice than usual. "Well, at least, I can get a doll that looks like one of my daughters instead of ones that only look like Lily."

Marilyn smiled at them. Gen had a martyred not-you-again expression. Grace did her best to appear surprised.

Marilyn stepped toward them. "I guess everyone's Christmas shopping today."

Grace kept her gaze focused on her aunt. "Hi. This is my friend I told you about. Robert, this is Beau's stepmother, Marilyn Charvet." Grace kept the aunt/niece relationship out of the introduction to not alienate Gen from the start.

"It's great to meet you." Robert's genuine warmth and friendliness beamed through.

Gen remained next to her cart, eight feet away.

Grace extended her hand, palm up. "And that's Beau's sister, Gen."

Robert stretched his neck past Marilyn, as if he just noticed the other woman. "Oh, my God, what gorgeous eyes you have." He skirted around

Grace's aunt and approached Gen. "I bet when you put on eye makeup, you knock everyone dead."

He stared into her face as if mesmerized. Gen seemed unsure how to react. Her eyes slid away from him and positioned the shopping cart as a barrier between them.

Robert shook his head as if awakening from a dream. "Sorry, I get a little carried away." He held out his hand. "I'm Robert Chan. Please forgive me. It's just that you're so beautiful."

Gen put out a tentative hand, and Robert clasped it. She studied him like he was a strange creature who made her curious and wary at the same time. "Gen Lundquist."

Still with her hand in his, he leaned back and scrutinized her. "It's unreal how your natural beauty shows through despite those clothes and that hair." He touched the lank brunette strands drooping on her shoulders.

Gen flinched even though her gaze never left Robert's face.

He dropped his hand. "With a good cut and some highlights, your hair would be as fabulous as Cindy Crawford's. And, honey, did no one ever tell you yoga pants should *only* be worn to and from a yoga studio?"

It was both interesting and sad to watch Gen melt under Robert's effusive praise couched with constructive criticism. How long had it been since a man, even a gay one, told her she was beautiful?

Gen pinched the legs of her pants. "These are the only things that fit me. I haven't lost the weight I gained after my last pregnancy."

"When was that?"

Gen frowned. "More than four years ago."

Robert waved his hand at her. "Oh, you need to get rid of all your old clothes. They're out of style anyway. Throw 'em away. Give 'em away. Whatever. You need a whole new wardrobe for your curvy figure."

"Curvy?"

"Under that too-big shirt you're wearing, even I can see you have a small waist. Why aren't you showing it?" Gen looked down her body as if seeing it for the first time as Robert folded his hands in an X on his breastbone. "You know I've been working with Grace for years to perfect her style."

Gen's head jerked up, and she stared at her rival.

Robert directed her attention back to him with a wave of his hand. "Did you notice how gorgeous she was at that fundraiser in February that you all attended?"

Beau's sister gave a curt nod. Her reluctance to validate the question was apparent.

"That was all my doing. Lord knows what she would have looked like if I hadn't stepped in." He leaned closer and spoke in a conspiratorial tone. "She probably would have worn a pants suit."

Gen's eyes brightened with interest. "How much do you charge for your services?"

"I don't need the money. My partner is a doctor. I do it because it's fun. Speaking of charging, what is your credit card limit? You need to be completely outfitted from head to toe."

Gen smirked with a smug expression. "I have my husband's Amex card."

Robert clapped his hands. "Good. He'll be blown away when he sees you."

Her smile disappeared. "We're separated."

Instead of offering pity, he made a tsk sound. "When we're finished, he'll run right back."

"I don't know if I want him back."

"Fine. Then you'll be queen bee of a whole new hive. Let me check on something." Robert pulled out his phone and tapped out a number. He waited with it pressed to his ear. "Marco? It's Robert. Do you have any openings this afternoon? ... At two? Perfect. I'm bringing you a new client who is in desperate need of your magic touch ... Great. See you then." Robert had made the appointment with his friend, Marco DiMarzio of MD's Shear Magic, several days ago. The call today was confirmation that he would be there with Gen.

"W-wait." Gen's voice was a little apprehensive. "Who was that?"

"That was Marco. He only sees clients recommended by friends. I'm going to put you in his hands today."

"B-but Marilyn and I have plans."

"Mommy plans?" He glanced into her shopping cart half-filled with toys. "This is your chance to spend time and money on you, not only on your kids. How often do you do that? You have a right to make yourself happy every now and again."

Marilyn nodded. "Go, dear. You deserve it. I can finish the shopping."

"B-but—"

Robert looped his arm through hers. "Did you drive today?"

Gen shook her head.

"Perfect. If we leave now, we'll have enough time to hit a couple stores before we meet Marco. I'll drop you off at home after we finish. Grace can go with Marilyn."

"Uh, I don't know …" Gen balked, rethinking the whirlwind Robert created.

Grace needed to do something fast. She spoke in a whiny voice she never used. "Rob … ert. What about *our* shopping today? You can't just take off. We were going to have lunch."

Gen stared hard at Grace then grabbed her purse from the cart's child seat and raised her chin. "Let's go." Her head bent in a cocky tilt when she and Robert passed by. "You don't mind if I steal your friend, do you, Grace?"

When they were out of sight, Marilyn shook her head. "How did you know that was what she needed?"

"After my husband's death, I didn't care about anything except taking care of Lily and working on my dissertation. I stopped going to my yoga class, and sometimes went days without washing my hair. Robert reminded me I was now Lily's role model and the family breadwinner. He said I would never pass my orals and get a good job the way I was. We went clothes and shoe shopping, and to the hairdresser. I spent a fortune but jump-started my life."

Marilyn wiped a tear from her eye. "I wish I had been there for you. We've all been trying to help Gen, especially Bojo. But it took you to see what we missed. She needed to start feeling better about herself. When you came along, she was terrified of losing her brother and her place in the family as well."

"Well, let's hope Robert is as successful with Gen as he was with me."

Chapter 77

ROBERT CALLED GRACE at ten PM that night. "You owe me big time, my friend."

"I know. How did it go?"

"Marco and his people did an amazing job. After that, we were kicked out of the mall at closing time. Thank goodness, I had the minivan. It was filled with shoe boxes and clothes. We did stop and grab a quick bite at the food court around six." Robert paused. "I hope you don't mind, but I told Gen about Michael. She didn't know the sonofabitch had died with his mistress."

"I guess Beau never told her."

"She now views you in a whole new light. You've joined the legion of cheated-on women."

A sudden thought overwhelmed Grace with hot choking panic. "You didn't tell her about Juliette, did you?"

"Of course not. What's the next step in your campaign?"

"I'm expecting a call from either Beau or Gen to initiate Round Three."

The following afternoon, Beau called. "Hi, Grace. Are you busy?"

"I'm prepping final exams. Why?"

"I wanted to thank you."

Being deliberately obtuse, Grace replied in an offhand manner. "You're welcome. I had plenty."

"Plenty?"

"Of cookies and soup."

"Oh, yeah. The food was great. I also wanted to let you know how much I appreciate what you did for Gen. I just came from her house. I haven't seen my sister that happy in years."

"It was all Robert's doing, not mine." Grace and Marilyn had agreed to keep the campaign plans a secret. As far as any of the Charvets were concerned, the meeting and makeover were coincidental.

"Then I'll thank him."

Grace added a hint of annoyance to her voice. "Well, thanks to him going off with Gen, I wasn't able to finish *my* Christmas shopping. I'll have to go out again next weekend and hope everything on my list is still available."

Beau cleared his throat. "I thought you'd like to know since Tom moved out, he gets the kids on Fridays, and Gen gets them back after Mass on Sundays. When they met in the church parking lot this morning, Gen said Tom was blown away by how she looked."

With a false air of distraction, Grace said, "What? Oh, I guess that's good."

"Robert also told Gen how much yoga helps you relax and deal with stress. She's going to attend a class with one of her neighbors tomorrow." Beau paused then a note of suspicion overlaid his voice. "Why would Robert volunteer to do all he did for a woman he'd never met before?"

"If you knew Robert better, you'd know that's just the way he is. He was the one who helped me get back on my feet again after Michael's death. So, of course, I told him about Gen and how unhappy she was. When he met her, he jumped in with what he does best; make a woman feel good again. I was surprised Gen agreed to go."

"I guess she was ready for a change. Well, I won't keep you from your work. Uh, Grace …" Beau's voice trailed off. She waited for him to continue. "I've made a lot of mistakes when it comes to you and Gen. I know that now. Bye."

Chapter 78

MARILYN CALLED HER a week later. "I'm inviting you and Lily to our house on Christmas Day."

"We look forward to being there."

"Like I told you before, it will be a nice, normal family get-together. No drama."

"What about presents?"

"Everyone buys gifts for the children, of course. As far as the adults are concerned, we've always put names in a hat and drawn them after Thanksgiving dinner. This year we didn't do it because ... well, you know why. Anyway, everyone agreed to forget about adult presents this year. What?" Marilyn's voice grew fainter. "I'm talking with Grace about Christmas ... Okay ... Good night." The suck-smack of a kiss sounded followed by a silent pause.

When Marilyn spoke again, it was in a slightly hushed tone. "Beau is going to bed." Her voice took on a quiet but giddy excitement. "I have to tell you the change in Gen is unbelievable. When her father saw her in church last Sunday, he nearly fell over. I hadn't told him about meeting you and Robert. When he asked why, I said I wasn't sure how it went, so I didn't want to say anything."

"My Beau, I mean Bojo, called me." Grace's face flamed. "At first, he wasn't sure the makeover was purely unplanned. I did my best to convince him it was."

"The family may be skeptical, but I'll never tell them we prearranged it. Now back to Christmas."

"What food can I bring?"

"I've got it all taken care of. You don't have to do a thing."

"I feel funny coming empty-handed."

"Don't. It's a Christmas treat to have you and Lily with us."

When Marilyn said a Christmas treat, sugarplums danced in Grace's head. After the call ended, she jumped to her feet to retrieve a three-ring binder of her favorite recipes. Holiday goodies could double as gifts for her family and friends. Grace checked the pantry for ingredients on hand. Then she scoured recipes and online websites. With the cookie and candy decisions finalized, she prepared a grocery list on her phone. She had finished when it rang with an unknown Palm Beach county number.

Grace hesitated then hit the answer button on the last ring. "Hello?"

"Grace. It's Gen. Did I wake you?"

"No, I was just putting together a grocery list."

"Oh." It seemed Beau's sister was disappointed she didn't catch Grace half-asleep. "Well, I'm calling to say I appreciate you letting Robert go shopping with *me*, instead of *you*, last Saturday. We had a great time."

"I didn't *let* him do anything. He loves styling women."

"He's very good at it." Beau's sister paused for a long moment. "Robert told me about your husband and the other woman. Did you know about her before it happened?" Gen's voice lost its hard edge as a slight tremor wobbled the last few words.

"No. I found out when I was informed of their deaths."

"Why do you think your husband did it? Was it because you were pregnant and had just had a baby?"

"Honestly, Gen, he cheated on me because he wanted to. I did nothing to cause or deserve that kind of betrayal. No woman does."

"If he had lived, would you have forgiven him for the mistake?"

Grace rubbed her forehead. "I don't know what I would have done. What I do know is his infidelity wasn't a mistake. He did it intentionally. In the end, he was never given the opportunity to say he was sorry, and I was never given the chance to forgive him or not." She would not provide Gen the ammunition to say, *Grace said I should do this.*

"I just found out Tom had an affair earlier this year with a former friend of mine. I suspected something was going on. He's asked me to forgive him.

I said I would for the sake of the kids, but I don't know if I want to stay married to him."

"That's a difficult decision for you."

"Yeah, it is. In your case, you lucked out."

"I don't know that I was lucky. I was a twenty-four-year-old college student with a newborn and no husband or job."

"But you didn't have to decide whether to end your marriage or not."

Grace stopped herself from saying the only decision she had to make was whether to bury her dead husband in an expensive casket or have him cremated. "No, I didn't have to do that."

"Will you and Lily be coming to *our* house for Christmas?"

Grace smiled at the reminder of who was a true Charvet. "I've accepted Marilyn's invitation."

"Okay. I'll see you then. Bye."

Grace chewed on her lip. That may be as close as she'll ever get to a thank you and welcome to the family from Gen. But it was enough.

Chapter 79

THE NEXT MORNING Grace rolled dough into small balls then dropped them into a mini muffin pan. Lily sat at the island counter and removed foil wrappers from miniature peanut butter cups. Several disappeared into her mouth. When the hot cookies came out of the oven, Grace pushed a candy into the center of each one.

Her cell rang. "Sweetie, get my phone. My hands are messy."

Lily peered at the screen. "It says B-A-U." She pressed the answer button. "Hello? This is Lily Anne Stone ... Hi, Mr. Beau."

Grace smiled. *Be-A-U.*

"Mommy and me are making Peanut Butter Dots ... It's a cookie. You smush a Reese's in it ... Her hands have cookie on them ... Yeah ... Me too ... Bye." Lily put the phone on the counter. "That was Mr. Beau. He'll call you later."

"Okay."

"Mommy, you spelled Mr. Beau's name wrong on your phone. It should be B-O."

"His name is spelled B-E-A-U because it's French."

"They say *oui-oui* for yes." She giggled. "But it's not spelled W-E."

"You're right. It's spelled O-U-I."

"Why doesn't French spell things right?"

"In their language, it is right."

Lily sighed. "It's hard to learn spelling. My teacher said the words get bigger in first grade. That's gonna be hell." She put her arm on the counter and laid her head on it.

"Lily!"

"Well, it is."

At nine-thirty that night, Beau called Grace's phone again. "Sorry for interrupting your cookie making earlier today."

"It was no trouble, except for the spelling of your name."

There were several moments of silence from his end of the line. "You lost me."

"Lily saw your name on my phone and said Be-A-U was calling. Afterwards, she told me I spelled your name wrong."

He chuckled. "I was at Dad's house. We were talking about what to get her for Christmas. I just now tried to contact Robert, so I wouldn't bother you again, but the call went straight to his voice mail."

"He and Tariq are at a play, and his phone is probably on mute. I have the girls tonight. Lily and Maxi are already asleep in bed. The child insomniac is with me on the sofa." Erin sat up and scooted next to Grace. "Beau, I've got a better source of information than Robert. Hang on." She twisted to face the little girl. "Is there anything Lily wants for Christmas that she didn't tell Santa?"

"Hello Kitty stuff."

"She doesn't want Dora the Explorer anymore?"

Erin shook her head. "Maxi says Hello Kitty is fah gwade school."

Grace put her mouth close to the phone's speaker. "Did you hear that?"

"What's Hello Kitty?"

"It's a fictional little white cat. There's all kind of toys and clothes marketed with it."

"Thanks. I'll let the rest of the family know. Will Erin tell Lily about this?"

"You can trust Erin with any secret, unlike Lily and Maxi."

The little girl pantomimed zipping the lips. Grace hugged her close.

"Grace?" Beau's voice was low and husky. It was the way he said her name when he made love to her. He paused then spoke in a rush. "Thanks for the information. I'll see you on Christmas. Good night."

Grace put down her phone. "Do you want to know a secret, Erin?"

The little girl's eyes brightened. The plastic barrettes in her hair clicked like baby castanets when she nodded. "I love secwets."

"Men are harder to understand than a DVD manual."

Chapter 80

LILY WOKE AT six on Christmas morning. She opened her presents followed by a breakfast of pancakes and bacon. Grace cleaned up the dirty dishes and put Lily in the bathtub. She dried her daughter's hair then got her dressed. An hour later, she showered and readied herself. At noon, they arrived at the Charvet house.

Beau and Skip stood just inside the open garage door. When Grace pulled into the driveway, they hustled out, and Beau hit the exterior control mounted on the wall. The door slid down behind them. Both men strode forward, Skip in the lead. He headed toward the driver's side. Beau halted then walked around the front of the Highlander to the passenger side where Lily sat in the back seat. Skip opened Grace's car door. She exited, and he pulled her against him in a tight hug.

Upon release, he stepped back and eyed her head to toe. "You look great."

Her burgundy dress had long sleeves with cold-shoulder cutouts and a mock turtleneck. The hem stopped well short of her knees and the tops of her black high-heeled boots. The stretchy fabric clung to her body like a second skin. Her hair was pulled back off her face and hung down her back.

"Thank you. Can you help me with something?" She headed toward the rear of her vehicle.

Meanwhile, Beau had unbuckled Lily's seat belt. Grace handed Skip a cardboard box. She grabbed the handles of two Santa Claus-printed gift bags. As they rounded the vehicle, Lily scrambled out of the back seat.

Beau crouched on his haunches to face the little girl. "Merry Christmas, Lily. You look very pretty today." She was dressed in a white eyelet top with red striped leggings. The whole outfit including the underwear and socks had been under the tree.

Unlike her cool response at Thanksgiving, Lily wrapped her arms around Beau's neck. "Merry Christmas, Mr. Beau."

He smiled with his eyes closed and hugged the little girl. When he rose to a standing position, his gaze met Grace's then traveled over her body like an airport scanner. A pounding pulse began at her temples and in the tips of her breasts. The region between her thighs became heavy and swollen. They remained fixated on each other as if mesmerized by a spell too strong to break free.

Skip spoke behind her. "Should I take Lily inside while you two crawl into the backseat?"

Grace inhaled a deep breath. Lily called out from the front step. "Come on, people. It's Christmas."

The three adults reached the front door as it was thrown open by Zoe. After the young woman hugged Lily, she reached for the gift bags Grace carried. "I'll take those."

Everyone entered the foyer. Marilyn rounded the corner from the kitchen. A green apron which resembled a Christmas elf costume covered her dress. She bent and kissed Lily on the cheek then moved past her to give Grace a hug. "Merry Christmas, dear. You look wonderful." She pointed to the box Skip held. "Are those more presents for under the tree?"

Grace shook her head. "No, it's some treats we made. Lily wants to pass them out later. Where should they go?"

Her aunt smiled. "How nice of you. Skip, put it on the breakfast table for now."

Without warning, Lily plastered herself against Grace's leg.

Gen and her children came out of the den and entered the front hall.

Grace studied the woman. Despite the updates from Robert, Marilyn, and Beau, she was surprised by the makeover and drastic change that Gen was maintaining. She was dressed in black skinny jeans and a white camisole topped with a duster-length black cardigan. With heeled ankle boots, she appeared taller and slimmer. The stark black/white look was highlighted by silver hoop earrings and a chunky necklace. Her hair was no longer one straight length but layered and curled. With makeup, her new clothes and hairstyle, she was chic and projected an air of confidence.

Sara and Lily approached each other with measured steps while their mothers maintained a demilitarized zone the length of the foyer. Heads together, quiet words were exchanged between the two girls. Then they clasped hands and with little Ben skipped into the den.

Grace moved forward and before Beau's sister could react, she hugged her. "Merry Christmas, Gen." At first, the woman stiffened. Grace held on until Gen's arms encircled her in a tentative embrace. She spoke in a soft voice. "Robert's right. You are a beauty." When Grace released Gen, she didn't wait to see her reaction but turned to Marilyn. "What can I do to help?"

She followed her aunt into the kitchen. Skip stood next to the center island. He picked an olive off a condiment tray, and popped it into his mouth. His mother tossed a pair of oven mitts toward him. "Put these on and come over here."

He donned the gloves and removed a platter of prime rib from the upper oven. "Where do you want this, Mom?"

"Set it on the trivet in the middle of the table then come back for the goose."

Mr. Charvet entered the kitchen. "Merry Christmas, Grace." He kissed her cheek and whispered against it. "Thank you."

"For what?"

"You know."

With feigned innocence, Grace widened her eyes. "No, I don't."

"Then thank you for coming today."

Marilyn handed him two wine bottles from the refrigerator. "Go pour this into the glasses on the table."

The helpers carried in an orange slices and beet salad, Yorkshire pudding, sautéed mushrooms, roasted fennel, smashed new potatoes, and a stollen loaf studded with candied fruit. On the buffet was a beautiful Buche de Noel shaped and decorated like a Yule log, a layered trifle, and chocolate pecan pie.

Zoe herded the three children into the room. Like at Thanksgiving, they pointed to the serving dishes and she prepared their plates with the foods they selected. The kids took their seats. The adults milled around except for

Mr. Charvet who sat in his chair at the head of the table. Grace had maneuvered herself to stand on the same side of the room as Beau.

Marilyn entered, glanced at the adults around the room, and untied her apron. "Take a seat in front of you."

Skip hustled around the back of his stepfather and planted himself next to Grace. He grasped the middle chair and pulled it away from the table. "You can sit here next to me, cuz."

She sat in the proffered chair. Skip slid in beside her as Beau settled on her left. Marilyn was opposite her husband with Zoe and Gen on the other side. Mr. Charvet prayed in French. The meal began with plates being passed to Marilyn for slices of prime rib.

The large platter of dismantled goose was closest to Beau. "I can dish out this if anybody wants a piece."

Skip extended his plate. "I'll have some breast. I've always loved the taste of really juicy breast meat."

Beau frowned and snatched the plate away.

Skip waggled his eyebrows at Grace. "Give me a piece of thigh, too. One that I can really sink my teeth into."

Beau plopped two pieces of goose onto Skip's plate like they were rotten meat. When he extended his arm toward his stepbrother to return the dish, he brushed against Grace's breast. Both of them froze then he twitched away. A piece of goose almost slid off the plate onto the pristine tablecloth.

Several times during the meal, Grace's elbow touched his. She nudged him for the salt shaker. When he handed it to her, their fingers made contact in the transfer. She struggled to maintain a laid-back demeanor despite the frisson of excitement, the thrill of the chase, and the sexual tension that radiated through her.

Stories were bandied around the table about Christmas gifts. At first, the tales involved surprises and wishes come true. Grace glanced over her shoulder at the kiddie table. Lily looked happy as she giggled and talked with her two young cousins. Grace could barely contain her joy with the experience of a true family Christmas for the first time.

Zoe wiggled in her seat with a lopsided grin. "I remember when I was ten and opened up a present in front of everyone. It was two training bras. I wanted to die. How could you do that to me, Mom?"

Marilyn lifted her hands, palms up. "What? You were going to need them soon."

"But Skip and Bojo put them on their heads like earmuffs. It was awful."

Mr. Charvet pointed at his wife. "I remember the year you gave me the book, *What to Expect When You're Expecting.*" He turned to Grace. "It was her way of telling me she was pregnant with Zoe."

In return, Marilyn pointed her fork at her husband. "It was a wonderful gift. Then I opened yours, and it was a new steam iron."

Skip said, "You got to admit, Mom, sometimes your gifts are a little weird. I was around fourteen when you gave me a set of bed sheets and told me my nocturnal emissions were ruining yours."

"Oh, my God, Skip!" Marilyn gasped.

"You also said one day I would be thrilled to get new sheets." He swiveled his head to look at everyone at the table. "By the way, if anyone draws my name next year for the gift exchange, I love Italian linens."

Gen looked wistful for a moment. "When we still lived in Quebec, I gave *ma mère* a book for Christmas. I forget the title, but when she opened it she saw the stamp from the public library. I told her to read it fast because it was due back in a week."

The unexpected ending caused the adults to erupt into laughter. Grace had never seen Gen giggle before. The children rose from their table.

Sara tugged on her mother's sleeve. "What's so funny?"

Gen said, "We're talking about Christmas presents when we were kids."

Little Ben muscled his way forward. "Our daddy gave us new bikes this morning. I got a Yamaha. It's black and blue."

Gen scowled. "Which is what Ben's going to be. The bike looks like a motocross racer, and he's going to ride it like one."

Sara stood on her toes to draw attention. "*My* bike is for big girls. Daddy showed me. It said for eight to eleven-year-olds, and I won't be eight till next month."

Lily wedged herself into the space between Grace and Skip. Her mouth was turned down at the corners like a sad clown. Grace cast a worried glance at Sara and Ben. Had something been said at the kiddie table? "What's wrong, Lily?"

The little girl heaved a mighty sigh and motioned her mother to bend down. In a soft voice, she whispered, "Santa hasn't brought me a daddy. I asked him two times."

"I know. I'm helping him work on that."

Lily straightened. "You are?"

Skip must have overheard the conversation. "I'm trying to get you one too." Lily twisted to face him, her face lit with a wide smile. He patted the top of her head. "Give your mommy and me a little more time, okay?"

She nodded, and her blond curls bounced on her small shoulders.

Marilyn laid her napkin on the table. "Should we have dessert now or open presents?"

The three kids jumped up and down. "Presents. Presents. Presents."

All the adults took a seat in the living room. Zoe sat cross-legged on the floor by the Christmas tree. Sara perched on a footstool, and Ben sat on his mother's lap. Lily stood next to Grace's knee and fidgeted.

Zoe had gathered the children's gifts into three separate sections. "We'll do one gift at a time, starting with the youngest. Mémé and Pépé want their gift to Sara and Ben opened at the end." She handed the first one to Ben. "This is from Skip."

He tore open an Optimus Prime transformer. "Wow." He held the box in front of Gen's face. "Look what I got, Mommy."

Gen pushed the toy away from her nose. "I can see it."

Next, Zoe lifted a shoebox-sized gift onto the coffee table. "Here's one for Lily. It's from Mémé and Pépé."

With all eyes on her, she tore off the paper, opened the lid, and lifted out a pair of aqua-colored slippers. The toes were the face of a white cat with a pink sequined bow. She gasped. "Wow! I really wanted Hello Kitty."

Marilyn flashed a conspiratorial smile. "Doesn't every girl who's in kindergarten?"

As each new present was opened, the children became more excited. Ben received Star Wars Hot Wheels from Zoe, Legos from Beau, and a Disney Pixar Cars transporter from Grace and Lily.

Zoe gave Sara a year's subscription to *Girls* magazine and the current issue. The young girl then opened Skip's gift. It was Georgie, an interactive toy puppy.

"Don't worry, Gen," he said. "This one won't poop all over the house."

Beau gave his niece a Disney Descendants stationary kit and keepsake box. From Grace and Lily, she received a set of American Girls books.

In addition to the slippers, Mémé and Pépé gave Lily a watch, stuffed doll, and a nightgown. In Skip's bag was a backpack with pencils and notepads. Zoe's gift was a lunch box. All Lily's gifts were from Hello Kitty.

At last, Zoe handed over a bag and a wrapped box for Gen's children to open together. It was the latest Wii gaming system and several new games.

After hugs and kisses from Sara and Ben, Mr. Charvet shook his finger at them. "You have to promise you won't fight over this."

"We promise."

"We won't."

Gen rolled her eyes. "Yeah, right."

Beau stood up. "I need to get my gift for Lily."

He left the room. The little girl's eyes darted to Grace. Beau returned from the garage and wheeled a pink bike with training wheels into the room. A helmet, which resembled a crouching white cat, swung back and forth by its chin strap from the handlebars. Lily's mouth dropped open, but she didn't move a muscle.

Beau put the bike in front of her. "Merry Christmas, Lily." He knelt on one knee next to her. "Do you like it?"

She looked from the bike to him. Her bottom lip jutted out, and tears filled her eyes. As the first sob broke through, she lifted her arm in front of her face.

Beau leaned back and looked like the wind had been knocked out of him.

Chapter 81

AS GRACE STOOD to go to Lily, her aunt grabbed her hand and stopped her. Marilyn caught her husband's eye and nodded toward the den. Beau Sr. and Skip rose in one synchronized movement and headed that way. She waggled a finger at Zoe and pointed to the trash bag of discarded wrapping paper. Her daughter grabbed it and left the room.

"What's wrong?" Ben asked his mother.

"Why is Lily crying?" added Sara.

Gen shook her head and stood. "I don't know. Let's go into the den with Pépé. Bring one of your new toys."

Marilyn led Grace toward the kitchen. "Let Bojo handle this. He needs to learn the consequences of breaking a little girl's heart. We'll clear off the dining room table."

Several minutes later, Grace peeked into the living room on one trip with a stack of dirty dishes. Beau still knelt with one knee on the floor beside Lily. She leaned back against his bent leg. He used a napkin to dab at her cheeks while he talked. More time passed. While Zoe and Marilyn put dishes in the dishwasher and packed food away, Grace poked her head around the corner of the kitchen wall. Beau was seated in a chair with Lily on his lap. Now she talked while he listened.

At last, Lily bounced into the kitchen. "Mommy, can I pass out what we made?"

Grace opened the crisscrossed flaps of the cardboard box. Inside were stacks of tin containers. In the largest, six varieties of Christmas cookies nestled in holiday paper liners. The next biggest ones were filled with microwave peanut brittle. The smallest ones held chocolate peanut clusters and haystacks. She placed one gift tin in Lily's hands. The little girl headed to the den, and Grace followed with the rest.

Beau stood next to the bike in the living room, his hands on his hips. He still looked nonplussed, like Lily had convinced him his name was spelled wrong after all. Soon everyone gathered in the den. Lily handed the first container to Skip and the next to Mr. Charvet.

She turned for a third, halted, then held up her hand like a crossing guard. "Stop, Skip." He had removed the lid and reached inside for a cookie. Lily put her hands on her hips, like a disgusted little housewife. "You have to wait. That's the rule at snack time."

Her cousin looked like the proverbial kid caught with his hand in the cookie jar. Lily finished her distribution and nodded to begin. Beau Sr. set the smaller containers on the floor next to his recliner and opened the tin of cookies. Zoe offered to trade her chocolate haystacks for Skip's peanut clusters. Marilyn checked the contents of each before she chose a cookie to sample. Beau munched on peanut brittle. Gen did not eat anything but allowed Sara and Ben to sample from hers. During dinner, Gen had passed on all the carb foods and put only protein and vegetables on her plate.

Ben put a cookie against his mother's lips. "Try it."

Gen twisted her head away. "I'm not hungry right now. I'll have one later."

The family's compliments pleased Grace. Lily pointed to various items and explained what they were and how she helped. Soon everyone's blood sugar reached a comfortable high, and the containers closed up.

Lily stood in front of Grace. "Mommy, can I ride my new bike?"

"We'll need to leave soon to exchange presents with Maxi and Erin."

Robert and Tariq had gone to Tampa for Christmas Eve with the Mahmoud family. They returned to Boca Raton for lunch with the Chans today. She and Lily were invited to their house in the late afternoon.

Lily clasped her hands together in prayer. "Please."

"Okay, you can ride on the sidewalk for a few minutes."

Sara and Ben begged Skip to set up their Wii on the TV in the den. Gen remained seated to read the instruction manual aloud to him. Beau wheeled the bike out to the driveway as Grace fitted the helmet onto her daughter's head. Marilyn, Beau Sr., and Zoe lined the end of the drive with Grace and Beau like the Queen's entourage viewing the Horse Guards on parade.

Lily mounted the bike with ease. Shoulders back, chin up, she pedaled off. At the end of the block, she dismounted to turn the bike around. Marilyn gave her the royal wave as she rode past to the opposite corner. Zoe's cell phone rang. She dragged it out of her pocket, chattered, and walked away.

After Lily's second pass, Mr. Charvet checked his watch. "It looks like she's got the hang of it. The game's on." He hustled up the driveway and into the house.

Marilyn touched Grace's arm. "I'm going to get a box of food ready for you to take home."

That left Grace alone with Beau. She squinted sideways as the late afternoon sun shone behind him. "I'm glad you bought her a helmet."

"The clerk at the store suggested it."

Grace put her hand up to shade her eyes and looked at him. He stared at her with a flat expression. Then, without warning, Beau wrapped her in an embrace. With one arm pinned to her side and the other on her brow, she was trapped as his big body quivered.

Grace moved her free hand to his shoulder. She cupped the nape of his neck. It was heavenly to touch his skin. At last, his arms dropped, and he freed her. He turned away, and his palms rose to wipe his cheeks.

Lily came to a stop in front of them. "Did you see how good I can ride, Mommy? I can turn around now."

Grace's gaze never wavered from Beau. "Very good. Let's see you do it again." Lily took off. "Talk to me, Beau."

He cleared his throat. "I'm sorry for hurting you and Lily. I didn't mean to."

"I know. You were scared to risk your heart again."

"The biggest mistake I've ever made was letting you go. I've ruined both our lives and Lily's too."

"No, you didn't. I've learned that lives are very resilient. It's not easy, but mistakes can be corrected. As the saying goes, that's why there are erasers on pencils."

Lily stopped in front of the driveway again. "Mr. Beau, I know how to do it now. Can you take the training wheels off? Please."

"Show us again. Then your mom and I'll decide."

Lily rode off into the sunset. Beau's gaze was warmer and brighter than the aura of the lowering sun which shone around him. The love in his eyes hit Grace like a thunderbolt. His heartfelt stare didn't lead to a kiss, but it made her want one. He shot a significant glance over his shoulder as Lily pedaled away.

"Beau, we need to talk but not here."

"When and where?"

"How about you come to my house tomorrow?" Grace did a quick schedule calculation. "Around two o'clock?"

"Sounds like a good time for us to talk." His eyes darkened. The meaning behind his intense expression made Grace's toes curl.

The little girl slowed her speed as she drew near. "You're not watching, Mr. Beau."

He swiveled his head toward her. "Head to the other corner. I'm still thinking."

She lifted off the seat, stood upright on the pedals, and raced away as the bike wobbled back and forth on the training wheels.

Grace nodded. "Okay, tomorrow it is."

"We have a lot to discuss."

His velvety voice sent shivers through her body. Grace straightened her spine and gave him a steady stare even though her legs felt like they were melting into her boots. "We'll have a good long talk."

"I agree. It'll be good ... and long."

Lily stopped beside them. She straddled the bike. Her face was pink and a little sweaty. She laid her forearms across the handlebars and panted. "I'm done ... riding ... my bike today. When ... can you ... take ... the wheels off?"

Grace unfastened the helmet's chinstrap. "Mr. Beau is coming to our house tomorrow afternoon. He'll take them off then, and we'll teach you to ride without them. Why don't you go into the house and ask Mémé for something cold to drink?"

"Soda?" Lily perked up and climbed off the bike.

"All right."

The little girl ran into the garage and opened the door. "Mémé, Mommy says I can have soda. You got Pepsi?"

Beau watched Lily disappear into the house. When he faced Grace again, his eyes sparkled, and he seemed to vibrate with suppressed energy. "I'm going to enjoy watching you run in circles while Lily learns to ride on two wheels."

"Me? I'm not the one who bought her a bike."

"Tell you what. We'll take turns." Beau wheeled the bike towards Grace's car.

"Deal. You go first while I pray she's a fast learner."

Chapter 82

GRACE AND LILY headed next door at five-thirty after piling the presents and containers of food into a four-wheeled cart used for trips to the green market or when Grace gardened. After gifts were exchanged with the neighbors, they ate a light supper of international leftovers from the Mahmoud, Chan, and Charvet holiday meals.

The girls sat on the living room floor around the Christmas tree to play with their toys while their parents retreated to the family room. Grace took a seat in a recliner while the two men moved to the sofa.

Robert poured wine into three glasses and passed them around. "So, how did it go?"

Grace sipped the Chardonnay then held her glass on the arm of the chair. "Very well. Gen looks fabulous, by the way."

"What did she wear?" Robert's eyes glowed when she described how Beau's sister dressed. "What happened when you saw her?"

Grace told how the two little girls made peace. "I decided if the kids could do it, Gen and I should. I walked up, put my arms around her, and said she looked beautiful. I didn't let go until she hugged me back."

"What about Beau?"

"Skip helped me there. He did little things to make Beau jealous, but I didn't play along. Instead I touched Beau whenever I could."

"Did it bother him?"

"I don't know, but it certainly had an effect on me. We ate then the kids opened their presents. Lily was thrilled. Everyone bought her Hello Kitty."

Robert looked confused. "*I* didn't know about that."

"Beau called me one night when I had the girls to ask what Lily wanted for Christmas. Erin was still awake and told us about Hello Kitty."

Tariq's large brown eyes opened wide. "She never mentioned it to us."

"Hel-lo." Robert patted his partner's knee. "Did you forget our steel trap of a daughter? I swear that child cannot sleep at night because of all the secrets she's holding inside. I haven't decided if I should steer her toward a career as a psychiatrist or a spy. I'm not sure which one is more dangerous."

"Things were going well until Beau gave Lily a bike. She cried. Gen's kids had told about the new bikes their daddy gave them for Christmas. I suspect Lily was upset when she received a bike from a man who isn't her father. Anyway, Marilyn had everyone leave the two of them alone to talk." Grace tried to sound casual. "Later, Beau and I decided we also need to talk. He's coming here tomorrow afternoon. First, he's going to teach Lily how to ride her bike without the training wheels."

Tariq had a broad smile on his face. Robert looked dubious.

Grace licked her bottom lip. "Can she come over here for about an hour, so we can talk in private?"

Robert pursed his lips and shook his head. "No, she better spend the night. You're going to need more than an hour *to talk*."

Chapter 83

THE NEXT MORNING Grace poured maple syrup over French toast on Lily's plate. "We need to pack your overnight bag. You're going to sleep at Maxi and Erin's house tonight."

Lily wiped away her milk moustache with the back of her hand. "Why?"

"Use your napkin. Mr. Beau and I are going to talk after he teaches you how to ride your bike. It might be late by the time we're done."

"You gonna talk to him about marrying us?"

Grace choked on her coffee and coughed several times to clear her throat.

Lily swirled a piece of French toast in syrup. "I told him he could."

"Could what?"

"Marry us."

"When did you do that?"

"After I cried. I told him only daddies give bikes to little girls."

"What did he say?"

"He'd like to be my daddy. I said he'd have to marry us." Lily held her fork in the nonchalant manner of a Hollywood starlet with a lit cigarette. "But we won't let him if he makes us sad. He promised not to."

Grace was numbed with shock. At the same time, she almost burst into hysterical laughter.

Lily patted her arm. "It's okay if you don't want to marry Mr. Beau. I told him I'd find us a new daddy then."

At two in the afternoon, Lily called out from the dining room window. "He's here."

Grace came from her bathroom. She pulled her long ponytail through the snapback of a baseball cap. When Beau knocked, Grace opened the door. He wore body-hugging jeans, a T-shirt, and sneakers.

Lily bounced out to greet him. "Hi, Mr. Beau. Are you going to take off my training wheels now?"

He lifted the two adjustable wrenches in his hand. "The first thing we're going to do is raise them up an inch."

"But I want 'em off."

He glanced at Grace. "When my dad taught us, we went to a park with a grassy hill and coasted down it several times before he took off the training wheels." He viewed Lily's shirt and shorts. "She needs to be covered up in case she falls on the asphalt. Gloves would help too."

"I'll find something. C'mon, Lily, let's get you changed."

They met Beau outside fifteen minutes later. Lily had on jeans, a sweatshirt, her Hello Kitty helmet, and gloves with various colored fingers. Grace sat on an iron bench in the shade of a live oak tree to watch.

Beau gave instructions and showed Lily how to get started with one pedal up and forward. Suddenly she took off. He grabbed the back of the seat in time to steady her. They circled the cul-de-sac with only slight wobbles. After she demonstrated her proficiency in riding, she stopped the bike, and put her feet on the ground. The cat helmet bobbed as she talked to him. He stood with his hands on his hips and chewed his lip. Grace walked down the drive and into the street.

"Please, Mr. Beau," the little girl begged. "I want to ride on two wheels."

He looked like he'd rather gnaw off his arm than see her get hurt. When Grace approached, he heaved a sigh of relief. "What do you think?"

"Why don't we practice in the backyard? It's pretty flat, and if she falls, it'll be on grass."

He removed the training wheels, and they headed to the backyard. The surface was not as smooth as Grace thought it would be. On one rough, bouncy circuit, Lily caught her front wheel on a pop-up sprinkler head. The bike came to an abrupt halt. She was flung forward. Beau caught the bike, but Lily tumbled sideways to the ground. After that, they returned to the street. Beau ran hunched over, his hand on the little girl's shoulder.

After circling the perimeter of the cul-de-sac several times, he grimaced. "Hold on, Lily."

She stopped the bike, and he arched his low back, wincing.

Grace came forward. "Let me take over."

"I just need a break and a cold drink." He walked stiff-legged up the drive and into the house.

When he was out of sight, Grace ran alongside the bike as her daughter circled the street. Without warning, Lily turned into the driveway, rode around the island then back onto the asphalt. Soon she was outpacing her mother who raced to catch her.

"Give it up," Beau called out. "She's got it."

Grace walked over to stand beside him. She grabbed the bottle of water from his hand and swigged the remainder. Lily rode with confidence in a big circle. The neighbors' garage door rolled open. Maxi came down the driveway on her two-wheeler, followed by Erin on a Big Wheel. Soon the three girls rode in formation.

Robert walked over and greeted Grace and Beau. He watched the wheeled pack circle in front of them. "Are you guys stalling or *really* into kids on bikes?"

No one answered.

"All right then," he said. "I'm going to get Lily's overnight bag from her bedroom. I'll be right back." His flip flops slapped their way up the drive.

Beau twisted to watch Robert walk away. "Her overnight bag?"

"You said our talk would be good and long."

He smirked and stared straight ahead. "You said that. I just confirmed I could handle it."

A thrumming began in her groin. Robert returned and commandeered the wheeled troops up his driveway.

Grace touched Beau's elbow. "Let's go inside."

"Mr. Beau." Lily ran toward them, without the catted helmet. She flung her arms around his long legs and tilted her head back. "Thank you for teaching me."

He squatted down, and she wrapped her arms around his neck. When he kissed her cheek, Lily slid a glance up to Grace. Her daughter's eyes narrowed as if to say: *The rest is up to you.*

Chapter 84

INSIDE THE HOUSE, Grace poured them each a glass of iced tea, and they moved to the family room. She took a seat at one end of the sofa and sipped her drink. "I really enjoyed celebrating Christmas yesterday at your parents' house."

"Everyone was happy you were there."

Grace arched her eyebrows. "Everyone?"

Beau nodded. "Yes, even Gen. Things are going so much better for her now."

"She looked great."

"She's talking about going back to school, finishing her teaching degree, and getting a job after Ben starts kindergarten."

"How are things with her and Tom?"

"It was tough for Gen to find out her husband had an affair with her friend. Kind of a double whammy."

"And for you, too."

He leaned forward and studied the tips of his shoes, lips compressed. "Knowing Megan like I do, I guess I wasn't surprised. But it was still a shock that she did it with Tom. Now I regret not telling my family about the reason for our divorce. It allowed Megan to weasel her way back in and break my sister's heart this time."

"You couldn't know she would do that. Decent people can't comprehend that kind of base behavior. Gen called me to talk about Michael and what I did. She told me Tom had an affair with a former friend of hers. I take it she hasn't forgiven Megan?"

Beau sat upright and turned to face Grace. "Are you kidding? It's all we could do to stop her from hiring a hit man."

"Does Megan know that Tom confessed the affair to both you and Gen?"

Beau flashed a crooked smile. "Does she ever."

Grace cocked her head, narrowed her eyes, and waited.

"One smart thing Tom did was not pay off her entire car loan. He was making monthly payments and stopped after that day at my condo, but he didn't tell her. When she received a notice that the payment wasn't made, Tom gave an excuse about sending the check in late. He waited until the second payment was missed then called the repo company and had her car picked up. He left her a message to call him at a certain time. When she did, he put Gen on the line. I don't know what was said, but I was told Megan won't be bothering any of us ever again."

Grace took a sip of her iced tea. "I guess that's a fitting punishment since the purchase of the car instigated the whole affair."

"She was also fired from her job."

"What?" Grace jostled her glass and drops of liquid splashed onto her jeans. "She was fired because she blackmailed Tom?"

"She was fired for revealing sensitive bid information."

"To whom?"

"To me. Dad advised me to follow up on her offer to steer some Department of Transportation contracts to Charvet Crane. He said I shouldn't allow our divorce to affect business opportunities. I didn't ask her for specifics about the other bidders, but she sent me a text with the low and high offers already submitted and told me to come in somewhere between them. In the end, I decided it just wasn't worth it and never bid. When I found out about the affair, I contacted her boss and showed him the text. She was fired the same day her car was repossessed."

A mean feeling blossomed in Grace's chest. Megan was not as invulnerable as she projected. Grace and Beau sat in companionable silence for a little while longer, as if buoyed by the shameful satisfaction that a scheming woman had finally suffered consequences for her actions.

At last, Grace set down her glass. "I guess it's time we talked about us. May I go first?"

Beau nodded and extended his hand in invitation.

"When I agreed to Alice's urging and Lily's demands, I didn't expect to fall in love with the first man I'd date. But I did. Despite our breakup, I still love you." Beau smiled, and she continued with what she had rehearsed. "The words *I love you* were the last ones Michael said to me. I believe he meant it, but he never wanted to talk about feelings, especially when he hurt mine. As a result of my childhood and marriage, I haven't had much experience in sharing my thoughts and emotions with a man. But with you, I don't have to hide my weaknesses and fears. I trust you not to use them against me. It may not be tattooed on your chest, but I believe you would never do wrong to me or Lily."

Beau shifted in the chair with a pained expression.

Grace hurried on. "When our relationship started, I was most concerned with making sure Lily and I didn't get hurt. That's unrealistic. Relationships of all kinds can hurt, but they can also give you great joy. For the last five months, Lily and I just haven't been happy without you. Our lives aren't complete if you're not in them."

She heaved a deep breath and waited for Beau's response. When he said nothing, she clasped her hands tight in her lap. Had she blown this reconciliation?

A moment later, Beau rose to his feet and stood in front of her. He grasped each side of his T-shirt's neck opening and lifted. His head disappeared then his abs became visible. Finally, he was bare-chested and Grace noted that his torso looked different.

Additional words had been added to each tattoo on his chest, and a new line was inked in the center between his nipples. She stood and stepped closer.

Aimer toutes les femmes de Charvet Fiez-vous en peu hommes
Fait de mal à personne

As her fingers skimmed the words, she murmured, "Love all women ... Charvet?"

"Love all Charvet women."

She smiled up at him. "Trust few ..."

"Men."

"Do wrong to none?"

"The French translation is: *do wrong to no person.*"

"Did the added ink hurt?"

Beau grimaced. "Like hell." He pointed to the bony part in the middle where the *do wrong to none* line was added. "Especially here. But I did it, so you'll always know I love you."

Grace smiled at him. "Say it again."

His eyes stared into hers and darkened with intensity. "I love you, Grace. I've never felt this way before. It scared the hell out of me. I also want you and Lily back in *my* life. I've been miserable without the two of you."

She moved her hand to his heart and covered the *do wrong to no person* tattoo. "I need a promise from you first."

His expression was serious. "What is it?"

"Any relationship can lose its thrill, its passion, and we've both been hurt by infidelity. Promise me that if you want out, you'll tell me. Don't cheat first. We can either work on what we have or call it quits. Michael wasn't unfaithful because he didn't love me. He had an affair because he didn't respect me."

Her dead husband always desired a woman who showered him with seduction. He craved flirtations and adoration. For Michael, a wife and family were requirements to further his career more than desired relationships. If their marriage had lasted longer, Grace was confident he would have become a serial cheater. His death caused a single catastrophic heartbreak instead of the small cuts of repeated suffering. In the end, his life insurance provided her with a mortgage-free home and a college fund for Lily. It was unlikely she would have received either in a divorce settlement.

Beau covered her hand with his. "I promise. We'll talk first. Like you, I didn't deserve to be cheated on either."

"I promise I won't repeat your heartbreak."

Grace laid her head on the chest of this muscled, rough-looking construction guy. His lips brushed against her forehead. An arcing current raced down her entire body. She caught her breath. His arms came around her and held tight.

She squeezed him against her. "I love you so much."

"I love *you*, Grace. Thank you for giving me another chance."

Beau put his hands on her face. With tenderness, he drew her mouth to his. The sweetness and love contained in his kiss filled her with joy. His tongue traced the softness of her lips, teased the seam, and begged for entrance. She opened and soon became lost in the sensual glide of his tongue.

She murmured against his mouth. "Let's go take a shower."

Beau lifted his head and gave her a devastating smile. "Good idea."

Grace took his hand and led him to the master bathroom. She flipped on the light in the separate space where the toilet sat. The rest of the oversized bathroom was in semi-darkness. She twisted the shower faucet and lit candles on the double vanity. The kerplunk of clothes dropping onto the tile floor sounded behind her. She looked over her shoulder. Beau was gloriously nude.

"Raise your arms." His breath tickled her ear.

He ran his hand from her waist, up her torso, and along her arms as he lifted her shirt. When her bra was removed, he pulled her back against him with one hard-muscled arm around her waist. His large frame outlined her smaller one as they stared into their mirrored reflections.

"You are so beautiful," he whispered.

Grace tilted her head back to rest on his chest. His tanned hands covered her milky-white breasts as his thumbs rubbed her with gentle strokes. She writhed against him, shameless in her desire.

He whispered, "Take off your pants."

His words penetrated the sensual fog that enveloped her. She unzipped her jeans and skimmed them down her legs. Then she hooked her fingers in the elastic of her panties and pushed them to her ankles, lifting her feet free. Beau entered the walk-in shower.

When he extended his hand to her, she asked, "Is the water okay?"

As the water sluiced over him, he pulled her toward him. "Everything is perfect."

Chapter 85

AFTER DRYING OFF, Beau wrapped a bath towel around his midsection and eyed his shorts and jeans lying in a heap. "I guess I'll put those clothes back on. I didn't bring more."

Grace tied the belt of her silk kimono and scooped everything up as she padded out of the bathroom. "Keep the towel on or not. I'll throw your things in the washer. Are you hungry? I've got plenty of Christmas leftovers."

"Sounds great."

She laid out a buffet of yesterday's food. They each filled a plate and ate in the breakfast room. After several bites, Grace laid down her fork. "Lily told me some of what you two talked about yesterday."

"Which part?"

"About her bike should be a gift from a daddy."

"Yeah, she pretty much laid it all out for me. If I don't marry you two, she's going to find someone else, and I have no doubt she will."

Grace ran her fork through a scoop of mashed potatoes on her plate, making furrows like planted rows of seeds. "Beau, you know how I feel, and Lily wants you for her father. I know that's a lot of pressure on a man who isn't prepared for a ready-made family. A few days before I went to your condo, I received a letter my mother wrote to me in the event of her death."

Beau's head tipped to one side in a sympathetic, engaging manner, as if he were ready to offer condolences. "Who gave it to you?"

"A lawyer named John Truman. He's a university trustee and his firm handled my mother's estate as well as the trust fund my father provided for my upbringing and education. I made an appointment to see him because I wanted to know if the G.G. Educational Endowment was responsible for my job."

"Like it was for mine?"

"What do you mean?"

"The one at the university. Marilyn insisted dad's company and mine be hired as subcontractors for the construction of the Makowsky Building. After all, the funding came from a family member. BC Construction erected the exterior walls, and I did the crane work. So, was the endowment also responsible for your position?"

"Mr. Truman said it wasn't." Despite the trustee's assurance, niggling doubts assailed her. Had her biological connection to a mega-donor given her an advantage over other comparable candidates? "But, during the meeting, I learned he and my mother had been intimate."

Beau's eyes widened. "He was one of her sugar ... I mean, one of her boy ... uh, one of her—"

Grace smiled at Beau's flushed cheeks. "Mr. Truman said they were in love and had discussed marriage, but he stalled in making a commitment because of my mother's past associations. He's been grieving her death ever since. It's kind of sad, really. He's all alone. Had they gotten married, I would be his stepdaughter and Lily would be his step-granddaughter."

"You would have ended up with a father after all."

Grace shrugged one shoulder, pushing away the thought that she was destined to never have one in her life. She prayed that didn't also happen to Lily. "In the letter, my mother confirmed that Mr. Mack was my father. Juliette wrote that he didn't want to be her husband or my father. Although she claimed she didn't want to marry him either, I don't know if I believe that or not. Anyway, the best part is she finally said she loved me."

Beau reached over and laid his big hand on her arm. "I'm a good example of how hard it is for some people to say the words. I'm glad you finally know how she felt. Did she tell you anything about herself or her background?"

"It's just as I thought. She was raised in foster care until aging out. From my DNA testing, I found there are some cousins who aren't related to the Makowskys. I'll try to make contact with them and see what I can find out about the maternal side of my family. Anyway, with what Mr. Truman said about him and my mother, as well as the information in her letter, I was forced to think about us. That's why I went to your condo that day. I wanted to tell you I was willing to wait for you to decide if you wanted a future with Lily and me." She gave him a lopsided smile. "But we won't wait forever. You can't put Lily on hold too long without her driving *me* crazy."

Beau chuckled. "So, how long were you going to give me?"

"A year."

"A year, huh?"

"That seems reasonable, don't you think?"

He frowned with masculine concentration. "No. I can't agree to that."

Grace stared at him. Had she misread his declaration of love? Was the mutual agreement to resume their relationship just a stalling maneuver on his part, like Mr. Truman had done with Juliette?

Beau laid his knife and fork next to his plate, slid his chair back, and dropped to one knee. The towel gaped open. He adjusted it and wheeled Grace's chair away from the table, the rubber casters squeaking on the tile floor. He spun her to face him and took her hand. "Grace, love of my life, I can't wait a year. Will you and Lily marry me as soon as possible?"

Tears filled her eyes. "Of course, I will. But you'll have to ask Lily yourself."

"It won't be as easy getting a yes out of her. She's a tough negotiator." Beau looked down at his towel. "Obviously I don't have a ring on me. But the three of us will go shopping for one, if that's okay with you."

"That's perfect." She leaned forward, placed her hands on his beard-roughened cheeks and sealed the deal with a kiss.

Chapter 86

ON A SATURDAY afternoon in May, Grace and Tariq stood just inside the open patio doors of John Truman's home. It was a glorious sunny day. Balmy breezes skimmed across the Intracoastal Waterway. Beyond the expanse of a stone veranda and across the green lawn, the inlet water sparkled in the diamond-dusted sunlight. Rows of white folding chairs filled with guests in their lightweight finery dotted the lawn under an arbor of palm trees. A pristine aisle runner led to a pergola decorated with swags of tulle and potted snowy gardenias. Music played from speakers inside a nearby tent.

Alice, in a lemony strapless gown, moved from the patio where she waited with Robert and the children. She stepped onto the runner and strolled past seated family members, friends, coworkers, and acquaintances. When she reached where Beau and Skip waited, she took her position to the left of the aisle.

Robert nudged Maxi and Sara forward. Beau's niece was dressed in palest lavender while Robert's daughter wore a soft blue dress. With precision, both girls dropped one white rose petal for every step they took. At their destination, Alice held out a hand and positioned them in front of her.

Erin and Ben followed. He wore tan slacks and a white shirt, the same as all the males in the wedding party. Erin was dressed in minty-green. Her hair had been cut short and looked adorable with soft ringlets. She smiled and waved to people she recognized. Ben was wide-eyed and held onto Erin like a lifeline as she led him down the aisle. Maxi scowled. With urgent jabs, she pointed to the basket looped over Erin's arm. The little girl looked into the woven carrier still full of petals and stopped dead. Ben was jerked to a halt. Erin pulled her arm free of Ben's grasp. She turned around as her bottom lip quivered, and ran back to her father. Guests put out their arms to stop her, but she evaded their barriers. Meanwhile, Ben stood alone on the white runner. He spotted his parents and ran to them, his blue eyes filling with tears.

Lily wiggled free of Robert and hurried to intercept her friend. She hugged Erin. With their arms around each other, the preschooler wailed. "I fahgot my flowahs."

Robert rushed forward with a tissue. "It's okay, honey. You can start again."

Lily released Erin and patted her chest. "You'll be better this time."

Robert thumbed off a last tear and nudged her up the aisle. Unlike Maxi and Sara's measured procession, Erin grabbed handfuls of petals and threw them to the ground. She halted where Ben was cuddled on Gen's lap and motioned him to join her. He shook his head with vehemence and buried his face in his mother's bosom.

Erin frowned and gave him a dismissive wave as she continued up the aisle alone. She halted in front of Beau and smiled up at him. Alice waved her over. Erin looked into her basket, flipped it over, and upended the remaining petals on Beau's feet, like a garbage collector depositing a trash can's contents into the back of his truck. Beau threw back his head and laughed.

Guests smiled and talked among themselves. Tariq rolled his eyes at Grace. Lily, in her pink dress and shoes, lifted her mini-spray of flowers waist high and led Robert to the runner. Despite his longer legs, the little girl hustled him down the aisle like they were late for an important meeting.

The music changed, and guests rose to their feet. Tariq offered his arm. As Grace walked toward Beau, her long, ivory chiffon dress floated against her legs. Sunlight warmed her shoulders and neck, bared by her upswept hair, spaghetti straps, and low backline.

Her soon-to-be-husband stood wide-legged at the end of the aisle with his hands clasped together in front of him, tall and handsome. He wore tan linen pants and a white dress shirt, similar to the ones from their date to Little Palm Island in the Keys. When she stood in front of Beau, the ardor in his amber eyes and his tender smile filled Grace's heart to overflowing.

He took her hand in his, raised it to his mouth, and kissed the back. *"Ma dame, mon amour."*

They turned to face Art, the wedding official, who waited at the top of the pergola steps. In a sonorous voice at odds with his small stature, he intoned into a wireless microphone. "We are gathered here today to celebrate one of life's greatest moments, the making of a new family. We will witness the joining of Beau, Grace, and Lily in a marriage of love and joy. If there is anyone present with just cause why these three hearts should not be united, speak now."

Lily spun around and glared at the assembled guests. Satisfied that no one would dissent, she twisted to face the officiant. "You can go on now, Mr. Art."

Grace took her daughter's hand. She hiked up her dress and climbed the two steps to the floor of the pergola as Beau held her elbow. Alice and Skip followed. Bodies shuffled and chairs creaked as the wedding guests took their seats. Tariq and Robert along with the flower girls sat in the first row.

Art waited until everyone was in place. "We are gathered here because something extraordinary happened. Maybe it was caused by the fall of a metal beam. Maybe it was destiny. But Beau and Grace met, fell in love, and are finalizing their commitment today."

Grace looked up at her husband-to-be. He gazed back with an expression of awe and unexpected delight.

Art continued. "Romance is exciting but as fragile as glass. True love is forever and strong as steel. It's never being too old to hold hands. It's standing together to face both the good and the bad. It's expressing your appreciation and showing your gratitude. It's not only marrying the right person but the right partner. The bride and groom have chosen to write their own vows for today. Beau, you may go first."

Lily and Grace handed their bouquets to Alice then turned to face him while Art held the microphone in the space between them.

Beau wiped his palm across his upper lip, pulled a piece of paper from his pocket, and took a deep breath. "When I found out I had to write my wedding vows, I panicked. I'm not much of a writer, but Lily offered to help. All these promises I make today come from my heart." He paused. "I promise to stay with you the rest of our lives. I'll do my best to make sure you're happy and safe. The two of you will always come first." Beau read the next words to himself and snuffled with laughter. "I promise to give you lots of kisses and hold you tight when you're scared. I promise not to make you sad by working too much."

Lily whispered, "I wrote that."

Beau folded the paper and put it in his pocket. His expression turned serious. Grace stood immobile in the thrall of his fierce gaze. "I promise to be everything you need or want. I'll take care of you and Lily. I love you both with all my heart. I am yours forever." Grace sniffed back tears as Beau squatted in front of Lily and took her small hand in his. "Thank you for sharing your mommy with me. I wasn't there when you took your first step or said your first word, but I'll be there to listen to you and love you from now on. I'm honored you chose me for your new daddy."

Lily threw her arms around Beau's neck. They hugged and whispered to each other. At last, Beau rose to his feet again. Grace smiled at the two people who meant the world to her as an audible sob rang out from the front row. She glanced over her shoulder. Tariq had a comforting arm around Robert who wiped trails of tears from his cheeks.

The wedding officiant raised the microphone in front of her. "It's your turn, Grace."

She shifted her gaze to the man who just told her and everyone present that he loved her. "My mother advised me to find a man who would love me forever. Lily helped me find him in you. In addition to loving me forever, I know you will love Lily like she is your own."

Beau nodded. "I already do."

Grace placed a hand over her heart. "Every day you demonstrate your honor and integrity in how you treat me and the people I love. You respect us. You embrace our differences. You do your best to help when there is a need. I promise to love you fully, fearlessly, and without reservation. I need you beside me as my friend, lover, and soul mate. My heart is yours, today and always."

The only thing which kept Grace and Beau apart was Art's arm and the microphone between them. He pulled it away and put it to his mouth. "Please take each other's hands. Do you, Grace, take Beau to be your husband? Do you promise to love, honor, cherish, and protect him, forsaking all others?"

"I do."

"Beau, do you take Grace to be your wife? Do you promise to love, honor, cherish, and protect her, forsaking all others?"

"You bet I do."

"The rings?"

Skip stepped forward with a platinum diamond wedding band in the palm of his hand. Beau picked it up and slipped it onto Grace's finger. Alice reached over Lily with a simple, white gold band. Grace had a little difficulty getting it past Beau's knuckle, but then it dropped into place.

"Both of you repeat after me … This ring is a symbol … of our unbroken circle of love … A love freely given … May this ring … always remind you … of the vows we have taken … and my love for you." Grace and Beau turned their heads toward Art. "By the power vested in me, I now pronounce you husband and wife. You may—"

Beau wrapped his strong arms around Grace as his lips covered hers. Applause and cheers erupted from the guests. After the kiss ended, he whispered in her ear. "*Aimer toutes les femmes de Charvet.*"

Lily squeezed between them with her hands together like a diver off a platform. When she cleared their bodies, she spread her arms wide. "We got married!"

The End

LOOK FOR JANET'S NEXT BOOK IN SPRING 2021, THE
FIRST IN HER LOVE ON A LEASH SERIES

Love to the Rescue: A Dachshund Love Story

www.ingramcontent.com/pod-product-compliance
Lightning Source LLC
Chambersburg PA
CBHW021946170626
46808CB00001B/43